FATAL MISCALCULATION

Asan dodged to one side in a feint to distract the guards and gathered himself to seizert, but even as he vanished into that momentary lurch of displacement he heard the sound of a strifer being fired from Martok's direction.

Asan felt the thin strifer beam spit him as cleanly and precisely as a jen-knife, high in the back under his shoulder blade and out his chest. He spun and tumbled in his mind, yet his body was nowhere, lost in the displacement between time curves. His body shouldn't be hurt, not here, and yet it was. He was falling, falling hard, his rings lost in the chaos so that he was blind as well. Pain flooded him in a great cold wave.

Martok had won, he thought dimly. Aural had won.

It seemed a wretched way to die, gunned down in the back in the grim, damp coldness that would become his grave. Wretched for a former vat boy. Wretched for a Tlar leiil.

He blacked out.

FATAL MISCALCULATION

Asan dodged to one side in a feint to distract the guards and gathered himself to seizert, but even as he vanished into that momentary lurch of displacement he h—— sound of a strifer being fired from Martok's

Asan felt the thin strifer beam spit him a—— precisely as a jen-knife, high in the back und—— der blade and out his chest. He spun and tu——— mind, yet his body was nowhere, lost in the displaceme—— between time curves. His body shouldn't be hurt, n—— here, and yet it was. He was falling, falling hard, his rings lost in the chaos so that he was blind as well. Pain flooded him in a great cold wave.

Martok had won, he thought dimly. Aural had won.

It seemed a wretched way to die, gunned down in the back in the grim, damp coldness that would become his grave. Wretched for a former vat boy. Wretched for a Tlar leiil.

He blacked out.

Ace Books by Jay D. Blakeney

THE OMICRI MATRIX
THE GODA WAR
THE CHILDREN OF ANTHI
REQUIEM FOR ANTHI

REQUIEM FOR ANTHI

JAY D. BLAKENEY

ACE BOOKS, NEW YORK

This book is an Ace original edition,
and has never been previously published.

REQUIEM FOR ANTHI

An Ace Book/published by arrangement with
the author

PRINTING HISTORY
Ace edition/February 1990

ISBN: 0-441-71401-3

Ace Books are published by The Berkley Publishing Group,
200 Madison Avenue, New York, New York 10016.
The name ''ACE'' and ''A'' logo are trademarks
belonging to Charter Communications, Inc.

PRINTED IN THE UNITED STATES OF AMERICA

10 9 8 7 6 5 4 3 2 1

Sits he on never so high a throne, a man still sits on his bottom.

—MONTAIGNE

Chapter 1

It was Kathra, the eve of season's end. The night of blood rained down upon Altian. Purple-white lightning forked the sky, blasting light through the palace windows. Thunder rolled like boulders crashing together. The protective bubble that had curved for centuries over the inner city lay cracked open like the splintered halves of a nhulk egg. Quakes and tremors shook the floor and walls. Death cries wailed into the air, lost in the violence of the storm. And on the roof, dark things clawed to get inside.

Zaula awakened with a sharp cry and sat up among her cushions. Breathing hard, she clutched her swollen womb. She could hear the fetus screaming inside her, its agony twisted even more by the violence of the night. She flinched, her ears deafened by thunder. Overhead, the terrible clattering came from falling ice needles, not the demons of Merdar trying to get inside. She had been dreaming again. The storm raging outside had not yet destroyed the palace. She was still safe.

Her ragged breathing gradually steadied. She sighed, wiping a film of cold sweat from her face. Incense still burned from a tiny *havsk* near her sleeping cushions. The acrid scent comforted her. Finally she lay down again.

But she could not go back to sleep.

By Anthi's mercy she had not died at the moment of Hihuan's death. His ring-bonding with her had been so new, so barely formed, so *hated*, it had not killed her. Unlike most wives who counted it an honor to die thus with their mates, she was glad to have escaped. For she still loved Fflir, in spite of the forced bonding with Hihuan before he left for battle and in spite of Hihuan's child growing within her.

By day, with the distractions of maintaining official mourning for her dead leiil when in truth her heart sang with freedom, she

1

could push her fears to the back of her mind. There were meetings with obsequious ministers and officials, delegates from the great houses who surrounded her like vitches with dripping jaws. Everyone was eager to seize power in the present chaos.

But at night, when her nightmares raged and there was only her own breathing to listen to over the screams of the baby, she could not escape the terror within her heart. Were this child not the growing seed of a Tlar leiil and therefore a sacrilege to kill it, she would have the little thing torn from her as an act of mercy. For what kind of creature could form and grow properly without the rings of its father to guide it into full life? Her own rings, damaged as they were by Hihuan's cruelty and death, were not sufficient alone to support the fetus. She had hoped for Fflir's swift return because the fetus might have accepted the nurture of a substitute father's rings, but Fflir had become a traitor fawning upon the usurper Asan.

She wept, hating Fflir for his betrayal yet longing for his return.

As soon as she delivered the child, she would no longer be Tsla leiis. She could not return to her own house, for her kinship had been relinquished to take on the high titles of her marriage. Without Fflir to take her away, she would be forced to remain in the palace without rank, a ghost in the shadows, ignored and ill-fed. She would not even have the right to govern her child's upbringing.

She buried her face against the soft cushions, her tears seeping into the fabric. The fetus twisted inside her womb as a dagger might. She gasped, choking back a scream.

She would not die. She would not give Hihuan's ghost that satisfaction. She would live, and this child would live. And she must find a way to keep her place.

Tomorrow, season would end. And the end of season meant Asan's long-dreaded arrival.

Ever since the Battle of the Leiils upon the windswept Ddreui plains, the inhabitants of Altian had crouched in fear, waiting for the legendary Asan to sweep down upon them. Chancellor Aabrm had fled at the first news, taking with him jewels, two transports, and a wealth of food. A few other cowards followed his example, but most waited as Zaula waited. If she fled, she acknowledged Asan's right to usurp her child. Those who remained about her, however, might choose to support Hihuan's heir, or they might bow in oath-sworn allegiance to Leiil Asan and hope for a better position in the reorganization of power.

Asan, that ghost of the past, that legend which walked again, that destroyer of Anthi, was not likely to show her mercy. If she did not bear a child of the right sex, none of the great Tlar houses would support her against him.

She must know!

She swept her hand out over a light cube. Darkness remained around her. With a grimace she chastised herself for forgetting that Anthi was no longer with them. All the luxuries of unlimited heat and light had vanished. She struggled to light the coals in the brazier beside her bed, and when a feeble flame ignited, she struck a summons with her ruby-encrusted mallet.

A guard answered the call promptly, saluting with a crash of gauntleted fist upon battle shielding. "My leiis?"

"Prepare my litter. And a cadre to accompany me."

The masked face stared at her. "N-now, my leiis? Thou are going outside? But the hour is not safe."

"And what safety lies in the day? Obey my order, or summon another to your post."

He stiffened at the affront to his honor. "I serve thee in all things, noble leiis. Thy litter will be prepared. Or thy transport."

"And what need have I of armored transport waking the entire city when stealth is of greater importance?" she said. "Go at once, and see that the rest of the palace is not awakened."

"By thy will."

He strode out, and she rose clumsily from her bed to dress in warm leggings, a long crimson gown trimmed in borlorl fur, a protective leadweave cloak, and an unmarked mask. After some thought, she slipped a pouch of dried meat pellets into her pocket and armed herself with a jen-knife. Closing her eyes, she drew several deep breaths for courage.

Outside, beyond the protective walls of the Court of Women, cold air whipped her. A jen cadre stood at attention beside her litter. Overhead, lightning clawed the sky. She flinched as she picked her way through puddles of melted ice needles and climbed into the litter. Her body was large and awkward. By the time she settled herself behind the privacy of the curtains, she was panting heavily.

The child turned inside her, and she curved an arm around

the swell of her abdomen as though to reassure it. Her rings could have sent it direct communication, but she made no attempt to awaken that agonizing pain. She longed for the soothing *sonthi* ministrations of a priest. But Picyt was dead, and the House of Kkanthor dissolved. Vengeful Bban'n hunted down priests and spitted them mercilessly for food.

The pon commanding her personal cadre stuck his head through the curtains to see if she was ready. "Is my leiis determined on this venture? It is not wise—"

"It pleases me to set forth now."

Without further argument, the pon called his men to position, and the bearers picked up the litter with a sway that made her queasy. She reclined against her cushions, her fists clenched on costly fabrics and her face set behind her mask.

The bronze gates of the palace opened, and she was carried out into the broad avenue. Proud villas stood dark and silent on either side. Their insides had been gutted by fire and pillaging.

Despite the lateness of the hour, the city did not sleep. Furtive shadows darted from street to street, drawing back from the path of the guarded litter. Death struck in narrow alleys. Chinks of metal scraping stone and the quick rustle of cloth betrayed scavaging through debris piles or the patting search of bodies. Because there was no one to burn the bones of the dead, vitches gnawed on carcasses, too hungry to run as the litter passed by.

Peering out through the curtain slits, Zaula saw distant flickers of firelight where Henan'n and Bban'n huddled together for protection.

It was a night where to be alone was to die, for since the eye of Anthi had shut no one was safe—not Henan slaves turned out from the warm villas by hysterical masters, not the fleeing families of the Tlar'jen which stood in the Outerlands under the usurper's command, not the Bban merchants and laborers, not the thieves, looters, food stealers, or priest hunters, and not the Tsla leiis herself in spite of her guard. Tension stretched around her, tightening upon the weak shield of her mental rings.

She could have sent for a seer. Yes, and then the whole palace would have known of her uncertainty and fear. The whole palace would have also known the verdict immediately. To have that knowledge first might prove to be her only advantage.

The Street of the Salvi'dara-dla wound through the back quarters of Vector Nine, a mean, stinking way where tethered chakas bleated at their passage. Snarling vitches rushed from a dark doorway, diving for the bearers' legs. It was their practice to slash knee ligaments with their fangs so that their victims could not run. But the bearers wore armor, and Zaula heard a curse, a savage squeal, and the deadly crackle of a fire-rod. Scents of burning fur and flesh filled the air, and Zaula raised a perfume cone to her nostrils.

Long minutes later the litter was set down. A masked face peered in at her. "We have arrived, my leiis."

"Are you sure of the house? Is it marked clearly?"

"Yes, noble leiis."

She drew in a deep breath and touched the hilt of her jen-knife for reassurance. Making sure her mask was well secured, she descended from the litter.

Flanked by her guard, she stood in the stinking street while the pon knocked on a door with the hilt of his knife. The knocking echoed off the earthen walls. Far to the north, lightning still flashed, but the storm had passed over the city. Zaula shivered in the cold, nauseated by the smell of something rotting.

A hissing from the shadows made one guard spin, but the thing scuttled away. Zaula let out her breath with a ragged sigh and touched her stomach as the child shifted inside her.

What if the seer no longer inhabited this foul den? Both she and her baby could be endangered by this night's business, for the growing seed of a Tlar leiil was not to be exposed to travel of any kind.

The pon knocked again, harder this time. Down the street, a shutter opened, then banged shut again. Something rustled behind the door.

"Begone!" snarled a voice roughened with age. "I have no food and nothing to burn for a fire. Begone, Lli-scum! Or know the power of the four moons!"

One of the litter bearers made a furtive sign with his fingers, but the guards twitched in anger.

The pon rapped again on the door. "Open by the command of the Tlsa leiis."

The reply was an insult upon his ancestry.

Drawing his fire-rod, the pon blasted the corroded bolt and kicked open the smoking door. Someone inside wailed with despair. He ducked through the low doorway and descended the steps into the house, his black cloak billowing behind him. Zaula felt a rush of warm air escaping out into the street. There came sounds of a brief scuffle and another wail abruptly cut off.

"Noble dame," called the pon, slightly breathless. "All is now safe."

The guards swept Zaula inside the dreadful place, where all was darkness and stench. She blinked, her eyes gradually adjusting to the vague scarlet glow from a Lli idol. The mingled aromas of spice, potion, cheap incense, and *yde* choked her.

"Light," ordered the pon. "And build a fire. Quickly, old woman!"

"If you have come here for refuge, you'll get none," said the old crone. "Already the Bban'n have caught your scent and come hunting—"

"Merdarai!" The pon whirled to the door with his men, fire-rods drawn. "Make haste, noble dame."

Zaula shivered, drawing her cloak tightly about her. The thought of being trapped here by Bban savages frightened her.

"Have you lost your powers, Uxa Vaani?" she asked. "Are you no longer a seer who can recognize one who has come to you before?"

"Dame Zaula! Ahh . . ." At once the seer scuttled through the cramped darkness, rattling and puffing as she lit a meager fire and from it set a torch glowing.

Her dwelling was but a single room which sprang into being from the darkness. There were a cot hidden behind a tattered chaka hide, a battered metal table, and a single metal stool. Zaula sank onto this and held out her chilled hands to the fire. Shelves filled the walls, supporting countless bottles and jars and small bundles of herbs. Chaka dung fueled the fire. Its acrid stench made Zaula cough. She would leave here stinking like a Bban nomad.

"If thou had but warned me, good leiis—"

"Hush," said Zaula nervously. "There is not much time. I want you to look upon my womb with truth and tell me . . ." She bit her lip and glanced over her shoulder. "Pon Oomx, take the men outside."

"I dare not leave the Tsla leiis unguarded—"

"Go!"

They swung open the door, letting in a draft of icy air that nearly blew out the fire, and filed out.

"Now," said Zaula. "Hurry. I must know the sex of my unborn child."

Vaani's fingers spread open in surprise. "But surely thou can—"

"Just do it! Hurry, old woman. You will be well paid."

Zaula drew out the pouch of meat pellets and laid it on the table. Vaani's nostrils twitched, and she sucked on her blackened teeth in appreciation.

"The leiis is generous."

Zaula kept her hand on the pouch. Her eyes burned at the old woman who was wasting time. "Hurry, or I shall give you nothing. Do you think the Bban savages will pay you more to detain me here?"

Vaani tapped her wrist in amusement, her silver Henan eyes glowing. "The Bban'n will let me live through the night."

"And I shall give you something to eat," snapped Zaula. "Which is more important?"

"A full stomach is primary," said Vaani, and placed her withered hand upon Zaula's stomach.

Despite all her intentions, Zaula flinched at the questing brush of the old woman's rings against her own. She drew hers aside, shutting her eyes on the pain, to expose the baby. How long did it take? Surely a moment only. Yet Vaani's hand seemed to stay clamped upon her for an eternity. Her mind—twisted, foreign, and tinged blue with doses of *yde*—probed with a liberty that infuriated Zaula. Yet she endured it because the more knowledge of the child Vaani gained for her, the stronger chance of survival she would have.

"Well?" she demanded.

Vaani lifted her head. Her silver eyes were unfocused and dull. Then she blinked and drew a sharp breath.

"Old woman! Tell me—"

"The child in thy womb is female, noble dame."

Female! Zaula drew back, slumping in her chair. After all these bleak months living in fear and apprehension, to know the truth at last stunned her.

"You're sure? Absolutely sure?"

"I have looked with truth," said Vaani, affronted. "What I have said is so. I honor thee in thy good fortune, noble dame."

Zaula smiled, only now beginning to believe it. Relief flooded her. Asan had the right to slay a son of the fallen tyrant, but daughters carried the blood. In her womb, Hihuan's line continued. Zaula's hand slid protectively over her stomach. The great houses would support her cause, not Asan's.

Vaani had the food pouch and was peering into it. Zaula rose to her feet, wishing she had brought even more wealth to distribute.

"My thanks, seer—"

A commotion outside made her turn. Shouts and the whine of a fire-rod panicked her.

"Bban'n? I must flee this place."

"Wait, good leiis." The old woman's dirty hand closed over Zaula's wrist with surprising strength. "Do not go out into the battle."

"But I dare not be trapped here. Loose me!"

When Vaani did not release her, Zaula drew her jen-knife. At once Vaani stepped back.

Outside, someone screamed in death. Zaula jumped, uncertain what she should do. As she hesitated, the sounds of fighting ceased. Zaula drew an unsteady breath. Her jen cadre was more than a match for the rabble. She need not be afraid.

The door opened, and a cloaked figure descended the rickety steps with a faint clatter of battle shielding.

Zaula hurried toward him. "Pon Oomx, I am ready to depart at once. . . ."

Her voice trailed off as she realized it was not her pon who towered over her, but a stranger. His mask bore the proud tracings of the House of Mura-an, and his battle shielding gleamed gold in the flare of torchlight. The cloak sweeping off his shoulders was black embroidered with purple and gold threads at the borders.

"Greetings, Noble Unar," said Vaani with a triumphant cackle. "I told you she could be brought here."

"Yes." He stared at Zaula from behind his mask, filling the sordid room with his height, blocking her from the steps out.

"My men?" asked Zaula, dry-mouthed.

He swept out a hand, palm down. "Thou has new servants, noble leiis. And a new jen cadre. Allow us to serve thy will."

"My will is that you get out of the way. Let me pass!"

"Ah, have care, noble leiis," he said smoothly, still blocking her path. "The night is full of many dangers."

Panic cut off her air. She shrank back, trying not to show her desperation. "You dare much, you and your house."

"My house intends to rule on behalf of Hihuan's revered daughter."

Zaula gasped. "How did you know? So soon, when even I—"

Vaani's cackle shamed her. "Noble dame, just because thy mental powers have been shattered does not mean the rest of us are helpless. Thou has come to me before. It was a simple thing to persuade thee to come again."

"Tonight was my own idea," began Zaula hotly.

"A suggestion skilfully placed to coincide with thy own apprehensions and curiosity," said Unar. "Well done, Vaani. We shall reward you amply. Come, noble leiis. There is someone at my citadel who wants very much to meet thee."

Zaula drew herself erect. "It pleases me to return to the palace. If you wish to rule Ruantl, you must vie with the other houses in the honored way."

"Oh, noble dame, do not be so naive! Now that I have thy honored person in my keeping, I do not intend to let thee go. And if thou wishes thy daughter to grow up with the joy of her mother's company, thou will accept the assistance of Mura-an."

"The House of Mura-an is the most powerful, now that Kkanthor is no more," she said slowly. "If I accept your assistance, what need is there to bear me away from Altian? Why am I not permitted to return to the palace? It is there that Asan must be faced."

"Thou are not the person to stand against him," said Unar coldly. "Hihuan's child must be in a place of safety away from Altian. Now come, good leiis. The night grows short."

Despair filled Zaula. She would never be free. Hihuan was dead, but she remained a game piece to be moved here and there by those stronger than herself.

"Why should I trust you, Noble Unar?" she demanded.

"Would thou prefer the Spandeen as thy protectorate?" he mocked. "Or even the infamous Soot'dla?"

"Those traitors!" Zaula stiffened. "It is just that you do not respect tradition, noble. You do not come asking—"

He laughed. "No! Good leiis, thou will find I do nothing in

the traditional way. I'm not asking thee; I'm taking thee. Now come.''

Seizing her arm without heed for royal protocol, he wrested the jen-knife from her hand and dragged her outside into the icy air.

"May Lli cross thy shadow, good leiis," said Vaani with a cackle, and slammed shut her door.

Zaula looked right and left, hoping some of her men had survived. But not even her litter remained in sight. Soldiers bearing the insignia of Mura-an stood watchfully in the shadows. Unar hustled Zaula along so quickly she had to struggle to keep up with his long strides. She felt pain in her abdomen and clutched herself.

"Slow down. I beg you, slow down, or there will be no child at all.''

With a muffled oath, he slackened his pace, but his grip tightened on her arm. "It is not far to my transport. Hurry.''

"I cannot. Please. . . .''

But he hurried her on, giving her no more than that brief respite. The footsteps of his cadre echoed behind them. Ahead, shadows lurked and furtive little vermin, gleiglits probably, scrabbled along the stinking gutter. Zaula stumbled, panting now and dizzy.

"Please. . . .''

He scooped her up into his arms and carried her the rest of the way down a twisting alley barely wide enough for two men to walk abreast. At the end of the alley a small transport waited, steps down, guards on alert. Zaula saw the feral glow of Bban eyes watching from the surrounding darkness. She pressed a hand against her mouth to muffle a scream. If the savages should attack now . . .

But Unar carried her into the transport and seated her. His hand lingered a moment on her shoulder, and she stiffened with a new fear. As long as she carried, she was inviolate. But after the birth, what would become of her? What might Unar require of her in exchange for his protection?

She shrank lower in her seat as Unar moved away to strap himself in. His cadre came aboard, clanking of battle shielding and arms, their voices low and muffled behind their masks. The hatch was secured. A building whine warned her of liftoff.

Her hands clenched on her seat. She tried to relax, but her tension only mounted. The child within her cried out as they left the ground, and Zaula bit back a moan. Shivering, feeling the fever returning, she wondered if either she or her precious daughter would survive this night.

Chapter 2

Boredom . . .

Asan yawned behind his mask as his two cintans argued over the best way to march to Altian without running into a Bban ambush. He sat on a tall chair carved from precious orad wood. He could sense the age of its molecules as his gloved hands curved around the arms. Supposedly it had been brought to Ruantl with the first two colonists. He shifted restlessly on the hard seat, and the voices faltered.

"My leiil wishes to speak?"

Asan flipped his palm down in a swift negative and motioned for them to continue. He yawned again, wishing he had taken a porter out over the low ridges below the Tchsco Mountains. The black desert of the Outerlands was boring too, nothing but an endless expanse of barren dunes and rock. But at least it would have been more interesting than yet another war council.

There had been plenty of strategy meetings during the days of season, in which everyone had been cooped up in the mountain stronghold. Only the occasional Bban raids had provided any excitement at all.

And when the officers were not discussing advance tactics and siege methods, a whole contingent of self-appointed chancellors tried to give him advice on setting up a new government.

He had never thought life at the top would be tedious detail and decision making. Where were the Sybaritic apartments, dancing girls, lavish parties, attentive slaves, and good times?

He had climbed his way up from being a vat boy in a GSI laboratory complex to a blackmarketeer to the ruler of Ruantl, and what did he have to show for it? Approximately 5.9 sextillion tons of planet composed of sand, rock, gold, platinum, blue silver, lead, corybdium, zinc, iron, nickel, copper, zinium, and pressurized carbon nodules. Rubies, sapphires, and highly diverse rezonide crystals were as common as pebbles. To the west beyond the Ddreui plains lay mercury pools. And most of the planet was uncharted.

Frowning, he ran a fingertip around the rim of his goblet. It was made of gold and blue silver alloy and studded with sapphires that winked in the light of the torches. Even the belowcaste Henan slaves wore more wealth in the form of jewelry than most executives of the Galactic Space Institute owned in protected vaults. Asan thought he was probably the wealthiest man in the universe. But what good was it on a planet where children threw fist-sized rubies into lakes to tease wild borlorls and gold was as common as dirt? If he couldn't find a way to distribute these minerals off-planet, then it was all useless to him.

Right now he would have given half of all he owned for a serviceable spaceship, or even a long-range communicator.

"And does my leiil agree?"

Asan glanced up with a blink. He hadn't heard a word. But he had grown adept at handling moments like this. He moved his fingers in a quick signal to Pon Fflir at his side.

As heads turned to watch Fflir leave, Asan stood up. He walked over to the board where tiny sections of Altian were marked in colors to indicate the interests of the various major houses.

Ggolen had stuck a bronze flag into the red sector of the Soot'dla. Asan frowned, one finger tapping the base of his mask. He had met once with Dame Agate. She was a shriveled up old crone who had tried to look upon him with truth and gotten her own rings scorched. Because she was on his side, she expected him to roll over with gratitude and accept her advice. But power was too new to him for him to be willing to share it with anyone.

He looked for Llor's cluster of flags and found them surrounding the city. Asan grimaced. That was just like Llor, so eager to cover all bets he never won any of them. How he had managed to become a cintan of the Tlar'jen was a mystery.

"I see no purpose in surrounding the city."

Ggolen and Llor exchanged glances. Ggolen puffed out his chest, and Llor hastened around the end of the mapboard to join Asan.

"Great leiil, please consider once again my reasons. The—"

"No," said Asan, sweeping out his hand. "Altian is in chaos. There is no force there keeping order. Why not just move in?"

Masked faces looked at one another in consternation. Murmurs broke out among the soldiers crowding the cavern where council was being held.

"Without the Goddess Anthi we dare not," whispered Ggolen. "We have advised thee several times before, noble leiil. Such a plan is too rash."

"Let us go in slowly, a vector at a time. With Dame Agate's support—"

"Which house has the greatest knowledge of technology?"

This time even Ggolen stepped back. "Kkanthor, great leiil. But surely it is not thy plan to allow them to re-form."

"Demos," muttered Asan to himself. "No, besides Kkanthor. Who has technicians? Anyone?"

"Mura-an claims knowledge—"

"But it has never been proven, Ggolen!" exclaimed Llor. "Great leiil, I beg thee not to turn to them. They are a devious house and power mad. They cannot be trusted."

"No, and they have ties to Kkanthor," said Ggolen.

For once the two men agreed on something. Asan tried to hold down impatience.

"I don't intend to trust them," he said. "But if they have technicians, then I want an alliance."

"Great leiil! It cannot be done without losing the Soot'dla and they—"

"I know," said Asan with a sigh. "They have food."

"Indeed, great leiil," said Yvn from the crowd, "it is not something to dismiss. The fields of the Soot'dla feed Ruantl. It is unwise to lose their support."

"We won't lose it," said Asan.

The confidence in his voice made them glance at each other. Asan gazed across the crowd. Somewhere among the cloaks and masks was a Soot'dla spy. Asan smiled to himself. Dame Agate thought she had him in a corner. It was time to let her know otherwise.

"Without the guidance of Anthi, growing food won't be as easy for the Soot'dla as it has been," he said, and listened as gasps of horror spread through the men.

Yvn raised his hands. "Then we are truly doomed."

"No," said Asan sharply. "Anthi will return."

"When? She has spoken to thee again, great leiil? Praise to Anthi!"

Asan stood silent, scornful of their eagerness. They were superstitious idiots. They could not even understand that Anthi was just a life-support computer, not a goddess. He had no intention of telling them that all he had to do was switch her back on.

"It is not our place to question the ways of Anthi," said Ggolen at last, and the questions ceased.

"No, it is not," said Asan. "Anthi will return when it is time, not before. We'll take the most direct route across the Outerlands, flank our formation with the transports, and retake Altian central. The outer sectors are—"

"Forgive me, leiil. Does thou mean vectors?"

"No, I do not! Vector is a mathematical term indicating direction. Sector means an area."

An abashed silence fell. Then Ggolen bowed.

"We beg thy pardon for our ignorance, great one. We have tried to keep the words of the ancient days true."

Asan cleared his throat, a little ashamed of his irritation. "Very well. As I was saying, the outlying areas of Altian are unimportant. And we will contact the matriarch of the Mura-an for alliance negotiations. Also, as soon as that is accomplished I want to see representatives of the Spandeen."

"Those tricksters!" said Ggolen in displeasure, ignoring the growl from Llor who was of that ancestry.

"I am not asking for your approval, cintan," snapped Asan.

The Spandeen were merchants who traveled farther than anyone else. They would be able to tell him about the southern continent.

Ggolen stepped back with a gesture of apology. Llor tried to smooth ruffled tempers by tapping the mapboard.

"Forgive my failure to understand, great leiil, but why use the transports in the way thou has ordered? Surely it would be better to send them ahead."

"Why? They are armored. They might as well be used as protection against Bban attacks."

"But how?"

Asan sighed. "Rig delayed bombs and drop them out the rear exhaust ports. That ought to discourage the Bban'jen."

"Indeed." Llor sounded awed. "What a tremendous innovation—"

"It's a stopgap junk tactic used by fighters who've run out of real ammunition," said Asan impatiently. "Those transports have mounts for heavy guns. Too bad no one can remember how to make replacements."

"We beg thy forgiveness, great leiil, for our failure to maintain technology—"

"Yes," snapped Asan, and stepped off the central platform. He didn't want to listen to excuses. "Prepare the jen. We depart at dawn."

They snapped to attention and saluted. "By the will of Asan!"

He strode out through the men who moved aside quickly for him. It was a relief to be done with the meeting at last. No more war councils for a while, he promised himself.

Fflir waited for him outside in the dusty expanse of the transport pad carved out of the mountainside. The visible sun was already low. He'd missed most of the afternoon. But at least his porter was ready. Beside it stood five others and a cadre of guards to protect him. Asan cocked his head at these.

"Do not protest, great leiil," said Fflir with a laugh muffled by his mask. The sunlight shone on the thin bronze insets marking his rank, house, and allegiance. A cold wind whipped out his cloak. "We must go with thee. There have been eight Bban'n killed around the perimeters since the last dawn. They know we are about to leave. Season is over. There is no surprise to it."

Asan tapped his fingers ruefully on his wrist and was about to answer when a distant vibration brought his head around. He listened, spreading out his rings.

"Leiil? What it is?"

Asan snapped his rings down tightly. "Metal craft approaching 280 kps."

"Forgive me, leiil. I did not understand thy words."

With a blink Asan realized he had spoken in Standard. Excitement flared through him, and he whipped out his fire-rod as he ran to his porter and fitted his knees and heels to the controls. It roared to life beneath him and he lifted while Fflir and the guards were still running for theirs.

A gong sounded across the pad, and the maintenance crew who had been playing the Bban game of kri-gri sprang to their feet. A man ran toward Asan, waving his arms.

"Warning! Warning! A craft approaches—"

His words were drowned out by the scream of a ship flashing

overhead, a long needle of silver reflecting the sun before it vanished behind the mountains.

"It went into the lower ridges!" shouted Fflir. "Great Anthi, what was it?"

"A ship!" Asan threw back his head and laughed. "A real, honest-to-God ship. Come on!"

"Wait, leiil!" Fflir's porter swung in front of Asan's. He held out a hand. "Whose is it? Where does it come from?"

"Who in Merdar cares? It's a space-lander, and I want it."

Tlar'n were pouring out of the stronghold, staring at the sky and gesturing. Asan lifted his porter at maximum pulse and flew into the valley below the stronghold with Fflir and the cadre flanking him.

By the time they topped a low ridge and found the ship resting crookedly at the end of a long, smoking groove, Asan's excitement had cooled to caution. His gloved fingers lifted and the cadre hovered on either side of him. Asan's eyes narrowed.

"GSI configuration," he said angrily. "They must have finally heard Saunders' distress beacon."

"Please explain, leiil."

"GSI stands for the Galactic Space Institute. They rule many, many systems. They are my enemy."

The cadre stiffened as one man, and Fflir said, "Then they are our enemy as well."

"Good. It was a poor landing. Either they were in trouble, or their pilot is a fool. But it looks intact. I want it to stay that way, Fflir. No Bban'n are to get near it."

"We shall guard it to the blood, noble leiil." Fflir spoke briefly into his wrist communicator to summon more men.

Below, the vessel's hatch opened.

"Let us attack, leiil!"

"No." Asan grabbed Fflir's wrist. "They know we're here."

"But they have not yet come out. Have they rings to sense us?"

"No. But they have machines that can scan us just as well."

"A small matter. We'll blank ourselves out."

"No. They'll still read the porters. We must attack on foot in the Bban way."

"There are eight inside the transport, Pon Fflir," said one of the men.

"And six of us." Fflir glanced at Asan. "Is it sufficient?"

"Tlar'n against humans? Yes."

Asan landed his porter behind the ridge with a soft whine of air. His boots sank into the corrosive sand, and he crouched low, moving along the ridge just below the crest. Fflir followed at his heels.

The cadre split into two pairs and ranged out in opposite directions, running fast and silently over the sand. Asan paused to make sure of his position. On the other side of the ridge he could hear voices and the scrape of movement. His fingers worked rapidly, and Fflir tapped his arm in acknowledgment.

With his fire-rod in one hand and his jen-knife in the other, Asan sprang up into the air and flipped himself over the crest of the ridge in a tucked roll that landed him halfway down the other side on his feet. He fired before the humans could react. One man in the hated green GSI uniform dived to one side and scrambled for cover beneath the ramp. He fired a strifer, and Fflir fell with a cry.

Asan knew the next shot would be for him. Gathering himself, he seizerted a split second before the man fired and reappeared next to the ship.

"*Choi-hana!*" He used the Bban cry, and with a grunt the human rolled over and fired at him.

Asan snapped out his rings to a small point, deflecting the spit of death. The human screamed, and Asan struck swiftly with his jen-knife, stabbing through his arm to pin him to the ground. He kicked the strifer out of reach and ducked out from under the ramp in time to see his cadre finish off the remaining humans.

Asan raised his fist in victory, and they returned the salute.

"Noble leiil . . ."

That choking gasp came from Fflir. Asan ran to kneel at his side. Fflir was fumbling to draw his jen-knife.

"Steady my hand, leiil, that I may spread my blood honorably—"

"Hush, fool," said Asan gruffly, wresting the knife away. He tapped Fflir's mask in reassurance, then pressed a hand to Fflir's side where blood flowed through the rip in his tunic. "You won't die from this. Their weapons don't eat away your flesh like our fire-rods do."

"Ah . . ." Fflir sank back limply.

"Help him." Asan beckoned to two of the guards. "You and

you, see to our prisoner. I want him kept alive for interrogation.''

''By the will of Asan.''

Asan focused his rings into a protective shield and cautiously moved up the ramp. The ship was a corvette with most of its size taken up by powerful engines. Its configuration class was used by the military arm of the GSI for courier runs and fleet convoy scouts. Eight crewers were probably the maximum number it had room for, but he hadn't lived this long by making stupid assumptions.

Half crouched, he moved silently into the belly of the ship. Giving his eyes a chance to adjust to the shadows, he smelled the scents of recycled air, metal, and zine. His lips curved at old memories of when he was a human too. Pausing by a ladder, he rested his hand upon a rung. Even through his gauntlets he could tell the difference between how humans stressed their metals and how the Tlar'n fashioned theirs. He climbed up the ladder slowly, his senses focused.

No mind touched his rings. But not all GSI crewers were human.

His head and shoulders emerged into a tight turnaround, with the bridge ladder on his left and crew quarters on his right. He checked out the living quarters, then continued up to bridge level.

Instrumentation panels blinked on standby. Harness webbing lay tossed across seats as though the crew had been too excited to stow them according to regulations.

He paused there, just drinking in the sight. Until how, he hadn't realized how much he missed this. He tucked away his fire-rod and pulled off his mask and gauntlets. A whisper of tanked air touched his face from the ventilators. He ran his fingers along the navigation station.

''Blaise Omari was one of the best,'' he whispered, remembering those two years of service on the SIS *Forerunner* and its subsequent crash here in his effort to escape detention.

A steady blip on the sensor screen told him this crew had indeed been homing in on one of Saunders' distress beacons. Asan frowned and switched it off. Then he sat down in the captain's chair. It didn't fit his tall body. The contours were all wrong.

He rose to his feet in annoyance and called up the last log

entry. The words came out of the speaker in curt Standard: "Acknowledging instructions per beacon one. Log buoy launched to mother ship. McKey called in the split time for his ship. We are to separate formation three miles into atmosphere. He will acknowledge rendezvous with beacon two . . ."

Asan switched off the log. He didn't like the sound of any of that. The GSI hadn't just sent in an explorer; they were coming in with force. Damn Saunders and her regulations; why couldn't she have left things alone?

But just the same, he now had a ship of his own. His gaze swept around the bridge again with satisfaction. This would suit his purposes perfectly. All he had to do was figure out a way to warn off the GSI.

Asan snorted at himself. He might as well try to tow away the black hole of this binary system. Now that the GSI had finally ventured into the Uncharted Zone, they would chart farther. And once they found a promising world, they never released their grip.

His hand clenched. Ruantl was his. And he would keep it, even if he had to take on the whole Institute.

Chapter 3

It was one thing to sit and gloat over his prize. It was another to let the ship be corroded by the sand. Being grounded here for several hours would damage the hull beyond recovery.

Asan frowned as he paced the confines of the bridge. He could not fit the ship in the transport pad. They'd explored most of the caverns during season, but none were large enough for a hangar.

Flipping open a locker bin, he found ration packets and grinned. He broke one open and munched on the contents. Once he had hated fiber bars and Q-cals. Right now, they tasted just like home.

He returned to the communications bank. There were two people in mind who could help him with his distribution problem. Either would be eager to strike up a partnership, especially for a healthy percentage of the profits, and both could supply him with the mining equipment he would need.

Martok had the widest range of contacts. Asan uneasily remembered the old days. BLZ-80-4163, Tobei, and Blaise Omari . . . all those identities of Asan's past had worked for Martok. In some ways Martok knew too much about him; the crime lord also thought that he owned him. But Asan belonged to himself. Perhaps he'd better go with Lin Ranje and the pirates of Scorpio constellation.

Rubbing his jaw, Asan decided to move the ship off-planet. Her crew had been cocky enough to leave the safeguard locks turned off before they exited the ship, so it would be easy for him to take her up. But if he did, he'd better not encounter her sister ships.

Leaning over, he activated distance scanners and set them for the planet surface. A blip showed almost at once on the edge of sensor range. He matched coordinates and marked the second distress beacon approximately thirty-seven kilometers northwest of Altian. His frown deepened. Saunders had never been there. Before she died, she wouldn't have had a chance to set a beacon there. But Aural could have done it.

Once the leiis of the man who had possessed the body he now inhabited, Aural had been resurrected at the cost of Saunders' life. Aural was his enemy. She hated him for switching off Anthi. She despised him for freeing the Bban tribes from Tlar domination. She had killed Giaa, the Henan girl he loved, and she had done her best to betray and kill him. She wanted Ruantl for herself. But if she thought she could manipulate the GSI, she would soon find out just how big a mistake that could be.

As he directed the scanners toward space to search for the second ship, a beep from communications startled him from his chair. Swallowing, he frowned at the blinking panel for a long moment. But the chance had to be taken. He didn't want a follow-up team getting in his way.

His fingertip flicked on the receiver, and a message crackled across the speakers. He'd forgotten how slowly humans spoke.

"*Spitfire*, come in. Daro, are you there? *Dorian Grey* calling *Spitfire*."

Asan drew in a deep breath and raised the pitch of his voice by a half octave, slowing his words as much as he could. "This is *Spitfire*. What's up?"

"I was going to ask you the same question," said the exasperated voice. "Who is that? Harley?"

"Uh . . . right. Repeat message, *Dorian Grey*. The black hole is causing all kinds of static interference down here."

"Get Captain Daro on, won't you? We're moving out of frequency range in eighty-six seconds."

"Not here," said Asan, wishing he'd never answered at all.

". . . copy? Repeat that."

Asan reminded himself again to slow his words down. It made his throat hurt. "Daro is not here. He's outside, taking a walk."

"Are you trying to be funny, Harley?"

Merdar take you, thought Asan. "Uh, no, sir. We just landed and—"

"Never mind. I'm sending down the rendezvous coordinates for you and *Vicemiam*. Stick to schedule."

"Copy," said Asan, sweeping his hand across the controls. "Standing by to receive."

As soon as the coordinates came in over rapid computer chatter, he shut off the communicator and sat back in relief. The air vents blew across his perspiring face. As a Bban would say, he was wasting water.

He sat forward again to punch in a cross-channel access to the astrogation screen, then compared the readout to what he dug out of the log. The coordinating ship, *Dorian Grey*, was exiting this system to survey the vicinity. Good. That got them out of his way for a while.

The human he'd kept alive for interrogation had worn captain's stripes. Perhaps it was time to have a talk with Captain Daro. The ship could stay here safely until he rounded up some technicians to help lift her off-world.

He heard the scrape of a footstep down in the ladder well and turned his head. It was about time his jen cadre rejoined him with reinforcements.

"How many men did you bring?" he called, standing up to flip one last switch. "I think at least two cadres should be staked out on either side of—"

He blinked at the masked figure who climbed up into the bridge behind him.

"Fflir? That was a fast recovery—"

He broke off, throwing himself to one side as Fflir drew a fire-rod. The blast missed him by less than a hand-span, searing a hole in his cloak as he sprawled across the polished deck. Pain throbbed in one shoulder from slamming into a chair base, but he was already rolling frantically to put himself behind the navigations console. Another shot went wide, and panel circuitry exploded in a snap of fire.

"Fool!"

Infuriated more by the damage being done to the ship than by Fflir's betrayal, Asan did not bother to even draw his own weapon. His rings snapped out in one savage blow, and his opponent crumpled. The scent of Bban musk filled the air.

Straightening, Asan moved cautiously to the dead man's side. He could see now that the markings depicting Fflir's rank and house were nothing but crudely painted lines designed to fool him at a distance. With his boot toe Asan flipped the mask away. It spun across the deck with a clatter. He stared grimly down at a Bban face. The scarlet eyes were open and glazed with death.

The bony plates of cheek and jaw gleamed white in the bridge lighting.

Asan scowled, turning away to finger the smoking hole in his cloak. He should have been more alert.

He fitted his mask into place and was pulling on his gauntlets when he heard another sound below. Asan froze, but only for a split second. Then he drew his fire-rod and knife with a silent snarl. On quick, quiet feet, he moved to the ladder. Where there was one Bban, there would be more. He would pick them off as they tried to climb up here.

The first came up, dressed in jen uniform like Fflir's impersonator. Asan fired, and the man tumbled down with a scream.

"Choi'hana, chielt-kai!" shouted Asan. "I spit upon the honor of Bban cowards!"

That was all it took to incite them past caution. Another sprang up the ladder at him and another. Both died, but a third behind them threw a mental attack at Asan, who reeled back. Steadying himself, he fired, but he was too late to stop the Bban from gaining the bridge and diving to one side. It was enough distraction to allow a fourth to hurl his jen-knife at Asan, who could not dodge in time.

The metal bit deep into his shoulder, knocking him back into the weaponry station. Dazed, feeling the hot spurt of blood, he dared not divert his mental shielding into the enormous amount of energy required to close the wound. The Bban attack was still hammering at his mind. One individual could not be that powerful. Several minds must be augmenting the attack.

"Choi'heirat! Za! Za!"

The shouting grew louder as two more Bban'n came climbing onto the bridge. Gasping with pain, Asan lifted himself on one elbow to gun them down, but a swiftly hurled jen-knife clipped his wrist. His fire-rod clattered to the deck. Growling, Asan hurled his own knife and saw it catch one of his attackers in the throat.

"Chi'gra!" ordered the tallest Bban. A scarlet band of pon rank gleamed at the throat of his uniform. "Let him live."

Two sprang at Asan, who still lay sprawled on the deck, and held their weapons on him. The mental attack eased up, but not enough for him to call for help. Anger mixed with desperation filled him. His own men should have been here by now.

"Do not move, Tlar," growled one of the Bban'n. A powerful hand gripped Asan's arm. "If you seizert, you'll take me with you to the land of Merdar."

Asan swallowed hard behind his mask. Perhaps they did not yet know who they had captured.

The officer moved to the ladder. "Luun," he called. "Inform the elders that we have succeeded in taking Leiil Asan."

So much for that hope, thought Asan. The loss of blood was making him dizzy. He let his head fall back. Now that adrenaline wasn't holding him together, shock set in. The knife in his shoulder felt as huge as an axe. He grasped it and pulled it out. Half of his chest seemed to go with it.

One of the Bban'n stamped on his forearm and kicked the bloody knife out of reach. The air reeked with the stench of musk, blood, and burned flesh.

"Let us leave this machine, Saar," said Asan's guard.

The ex-pon came over to stare down at Asan. "Not yet. Bind that wound. He is not to spread his blood upon the sands."

Obediently they hacked a strip off Asan's cloak and bandaged his shoulder. The handling was rough enough to send him skating to the edge of unconsciousness, but he held on.

When they propped him up and installed him in a chair at the helm, he waited a moment to gather his breath, then lifted an unsteady hand to tug off his mask. Cool air touched his clammy face.

"Regard his cowardice," said one of the guards. "As soon as blood is spilled, he offers his mask in surrender."

Asan laughed scornfully and tucked the mask behind him. "I haven't surrendered; I've just run temporarily out of weapons."

The ex-pon flicked an impatient gesture at his men. "This machine is shielded, Tlar?"

"Yes," said Asan, and closed his eyes.

His other senses remained alert, however. And it was as though the removal of his mask reassured them that he would not try to escape, for they relaxed around him.

Satisfied, Asan opened his eyes and stared at the former officer. "What is your name, pon?"

"Saar, great one!" said the pon, stiffening to attention. Then he growled and broke his stance as though in shame at the lapse.

Asan smiled. "You were in the jen a long time, eh, Saar?"

"All of us," said one of the others angrily. "We served with honor. We served Tlar-dung to the blood."

Their feral eyes glowed. He smelled a fresh release of musk and cautioned himself. He must not prod them too far.

"And you still wear your uniforms?"

"Only to trick you," said Saar. "When we saw the landing of this machine we knew you would come forth from the Teeth of the Sleeping Giant. Our hordes are there now. Yes, great one. You look displeased. Did you not expect us to attack?"

"You're fools," said Asan sharply. "You can't take the stronghold."

"But we shall. And then the Jewels of M'thra, the ammunition stores, the transports of the Tlar'jen, and the food caverns will all be ours." Saar barked in harsh amusement. "Even this great machine is ours now."

"*Chi'ka!*" snapped Asan. "This ship is mine!"

They all barked as Saar tapped his fingers upon his wrist in scorn. "Then why do you sit bleeding and weaponless?"

Asan held back his anger. The man had a point. But he wasn't surrendering this ship.

In the distance he heard a series of booms as though explosives had been set off. He sat erect with a wince, and at once a gloved hand gripped his shoulder.

"Make no move."

Asan's mind leapt out, only to be blocked in its questing by the Bban force ranged against him.

"It is the battle, leiil. One you will not see."

Asan frowned. The vibratory patterns of the explosives were unfamiliar to him. They must be Bban weapons. But what kind? Was this an unexpected Bban development, or had the Bban'jen received help from Aural? It sounded as though they were able to blow a hole into the Tchsco Mountains. If so, Anthi was in danger.

His fists clenched, but there was nothing else he could do. The Bban'n thought Anthi had been destroyed, so the computer wouldn't be a primary target, but she could be inadvertently damaged if the lower chambers were breeched.

Loosing a sigh, he slumped across the console. The first glimmers of a plan occurred to him.

"If desired, we can drug you for the pain," said Saar as one of the guards tipped Asan back into the uncomfortable seat.

He did not have to feign a groan. "No. Nothing. I would like to see the battle."

Saar snorted. "Fool. You do not leave this machine until the elders are ready."

"You are the fool. We can watch it on the viewscreen. Push those two green buttons on that panel over there, and the scanners will pick up everything."

"A trick—"

"Pan'at cha," said Asan in contempt, and all three Bban'n reached for the knives at their belts. "What trick is it? I am touching nothing. I cannot operate an alien machine such as this. It requires several men all working together. Surely you saw us take them."

"We saw," said Saar, but his voice remained suspicious. "Little men with striped eyes. *N'kai.*"

"They are called humans," said Asan. "They are small, yes, but very clever. They know how to make machines even more wondrous than this."

"It is the Tlar'n who worship machines! Not Bban'n!"

"But even the Bban'n see the use of some machines," said Asan softly. "This ship has scanners that can show us the battle. All you have to do is turn them on."

They glanced at each other, clicking behind their masks in curiosity.

"Why should you wish us to see the battle?"

Asan held back a smile. "Because I wish you to see Bban blood spread upon the sands. You will fail."

"Ny!" said Saar, and strode over to the sensors. "These?"

"Yes. Push them together."

The viewscreen winked to life with a crackle of static that made all three Bban'n jump. The snowy interference cleared almost immediately to show the panorama of desert.

"That is the area surrounding the ship," said Asan. He closed his eyes and breathed deeply a moment. "To see the battle you must direct the sensors toward the mountains."

"How is this done?"

"The controls to your right. No, lower. Yes. Those. You calculate the angle and . . . May I?"

He reached forward for the auxiliary panel on the helm console before him, his fingers brushing sensor controls even as one of the guards whipped a fire-rod on him.

"Take care, Tlar-dung!"

Asan moved his hands away. "Look at the screen."

Unwillingly they turned. The viewscreen waved badly out of focus, but it showed the mountains in black silhouette against the amethyst sky. Brilliant bursts of fire shot rubble into the air. The Bban'n cheered, releasing so much musk Asan nearly choked.

"We are destroying them! *Cha'hoi*, brothers! *Cha'hoi!*"

"I think I can clear that picture," said Asan after a moment. "If I am permitted to try?"

"Yes," said Saar, caught up in watching. But his fire-rod remained aimed at Asan.

Hiding a grin, Asan improved the magnification. But at the same time he let his left hand drift over a linkup to pull in all functions except communications and life support to his console. The lower hatch closed, and the engines began warming with a subliminal whine.

Saar turned at once. "What is that? What have you done?"

Asan looked directly at him. "If you want to watch the whole battle for the next several hours, then power has to be on. We can't drain the short-term batteries."

Saar cocked his head to one side, and his hand twitched uncertainly on his weapon. But another explosion caught his attention, and Asan eased out a breath of relief. He sagged back in the seat, wincing and lifting a hand to his throbbing shoulder. He was still cold and shaky. But three against one wasn't too bad, provided his luck held.

The pressure on his mind was giving him a headache. He shut his eyes and began doing calculations. When the chance came he was going to have to shoot out of here by the seat of his pants. If he were too far off, he could launch himself past the safety margin of orbital approach and end up in the pull of that damned black hole. At least this ship was a corvette, known for maneuverability and quickness. He'd always wanted to have a try at one.

He opened one eye and thought about his chances of reaching one of the weapons lockers where strifers would be stored. No good.

"There! You see!" shouted a guard. "It is working perfectly. A three-pronged attack, just as the elders planned."

Saar glanced at Asan. "Lli sees Tlar shame this day. Did you really expect us to save our strike until the Tlar'jen were on the march?"

Asan frowned, wishing he wore his mask. Saar barked and reached into his pocket.

"A wager, Vliin. Two food pouches to—"

It was time. Asan slammed his hands down on the controls, and the *Spitfire* lifted in a quick spin. The jolt of takeoff threw the three Bban'n to the deck, and Asan gave them no time to recover as he canted the ship to a forty-five-degree angle and sent it screaming into the sky. They tore through atmosphere, and shuddering g-lurch held them pinned in place.

Asan grimaced against the agony in his shoulder and blinked off dancing little black spots. He fumbled for web harness and strapped himself in. During that moment of inattention, Saar climbed to his knees and lifted the fire-rod, but Asan tilted the ship in the opposite direction, knocking the pon flat again.

"If you kill me now, you will all die!" he warned them.

The sound barrier bucked the ship, and they lifted with a new ease that set his boards blinking above nominals. His hands flew over the controls, setting in course coordinates without benefit of the astrogation computer. It was foolhardy, but he had no time to be sure.

The viewscreen blanked, then the auto-set recovered and Asan had a glimpse of Ruantl curving small and dark beneath a wisp of atmosphere as they reached space. The mental attack ceased with the distance, and Asan sighed in relief.

"*By'hia,*" said Saar, kneeling shakily there before the screen. He had lost his mask and his weapon, but at the moment he looked as though he did not care. He lifted a hand to mouth and forehead. "*Lea'dl,* have mercy upon us."

A shrill keening came from one of the guards. Saar stepped over the body of the other and struck him. "*Chi'ka,* fool!"

But the noise grew louder. The guard staggered up, his mask gone, his yellow eyes glowing in terror. "*Ny! Ny!* We are in the hand of demons." Spreading out his arms, he rushed at Asan, who tensed.

"Saar, stop him!"

The fire-rod spat blue death, and the guard crumpled just short of the console. Asan and Saar stared at each other. Then Saar thrust his fire-rod through his belt.

"For this moment, I am in thy hands, leiil," he said. For the first time his voice held respectful inflections.

Asan showed him one palm, then returned his attention to his instrumentation, slowing the craft's velocity by careful degrees. And now he did take the time to double-check himself with the computer. He found himself off by a dangerous margin, made corrections, and eased the ship down into a low, stable orbit.

When he switched to automatics and sagged back in his seat, Saar rose to his feet and came forward.

"The legends say thou are a god. I do not believe in legends since I have been released from the oppression of Anthi. Now, I believe again. What is the will of Asan?"

It was tempting to yank the *Spitfire* from orbit and send her out into deep space. But just as he had fought to keep this little ship, so would he fight to keep Ruantl. He couldn't leave yet.

"I am going to park the ship here in orbit while I return to the surface."

"Is there no fear in thee? To return is to become a Bban prisoner again. Why? Thou are a god with the ways of Beyond in thy keeping."

"You have a lot of confidence in the Bban'jen."

"It will win."

"Look, Saar," said Asan, switching tactics. "Your elders refuse to trust me, but I am the one who released your people from Anthi's oppression. I'm not interested in waging war with the Bban'n. Instead I want to organize this planet into utilizing its natural resources to the fullest. And I need Bban metallurgists and miners."

Saar growled. "I am a warrior, not a smith!"

"The *n'kai* who came in this ship, why do you think they came here?" asked Asan.

"It is not of reason. A *n'ka* surrendered his life to be the catalyst of thy resurrection. Perhaps these are also—"

"No! They are not. They will make Tlar domination under Leiil Hihuan seem as nothing if they conquer Ruantl. They possess all the ways of Beyond. They have a whole fleet of ships such as these. And ships that are even larger. They are our enemy. We must fight them together if we are to preserve our world for ourselves."

Saar turned away, his jaw clicking. "This is talk for the elders."

"Then help me make them understand that we must ally ourselves together. Will you do that, Saar?"

"What trick is this? Thou wish to go to the elders?"

"Yes. And it is no trick."

Saar drew his jen-knife and held it at Asan's throat. For a moment Asan did not even breathe. The sharp blade of green corybdium pressed against his jugular. Saar's ugly face moved only inches from Asan's. The stench of his musk hung between them.

"Thou are full of tricks. Thou has killed all my men, and dishonored me. Thou has taken me off the sand of my fathers into the realm of the gods. I look into thy Tlar eyes, and all I see is deception."

"I could kill you with a glance, Saar."

The pressure on his throat increased just enough to break the skin. Blood tricked down into Asan's collar, and for a moment the sting of the minor cut overcame the deeper ache in his shoulder. Then Saar moved away.

"Kill me, great one. I am dishonored. I am nothing."

"I am going to seizert off this ship back to the planet's surface," said Asan, choosing his words carefully. "I can return to the Tchsco stronghold to fight beside my men. But I would rather appear in the dara of your elders. I wish to speak with Uxe Ookri and Uxe Ggil. Will you be dishonored if you bring me there? I cannot find it without a sharing of your mind."

Saar glanced sharply at him. "Share with me? A Tlar share minds with Bban? *Lea'dl*, what lie is this?"

"No lie, Saar. Just true Tlar honor. Bban'n and Tlar'n must join together. Unless we do, we are all doomed. I need your help. Will you give it?"

Saar drew himself to attention. "I will take thee to the elders. I will serve their decision. And if they say to kill thee, leiil, then I will do so. I do not help thee because thou has asked. And I shall never trust thee."

"That is your choice," said Asan. "You'll regret it."

Chapter 4

Torchlight flamed into the night sky, throwing the rocky foothills below the Tchsco Mountains into stark images of stone and shadow. The air was still as though the desert held its breath. Asan's cloak hung limply from his shoulders as he trudged behind Saar. He panted inside his mask, hot from his exertions of crossing the Outerlands and climbing up into the foothills. Now and then, however, as they paused for Saar to take his bearings, the cold temperature of the night sank through Asan's bones and he would shiver. His legs felt leaden and awkward. He knew it was the loss of blood that made him weak although he had closed the wound before they seizerted from the ship. Stumbling just before he crested a ridge, he bent his knees to keep his balance and slid perhaps two body lengths in the soft black sand.

He stayed put for a moment even after he stopped sliding, drawing in deep breaths of the dusty air. It was cold enough to sting his nostrils, and he sifted through the night scents of Bban musk, distant fire smoke, and animal spoor.

At the crest of the ridge, Saar stopped and glanced back. His tall spare frame was silhouetted against the ruddy glow tinting the night sky. "Tlar?"

His growl was pitched low for Asan's ears only. Asan sighed. An hour ago he'd still been addressed as leiil. The closer they came to the Bban dara, the less respectful Saar became.

Saar released his musk in a nauseating cloud and took big, sliding strides down the ridge to Asan's side. Dislodged, fist-sized stones rolled past Asan. He reached out and caught one, then tossed it away. His mind felt clouded with uncertain images of a past that were not his. How many centuries ago had this body lifted its face to another night sky, one crowded with stars,

32

and breathed in a softer, sweet-scented breeze while the soldiers sang of victory?

They were close enough now for him to hear the exultant chants of the Bban'jen. The weird ragged noise surged up and down the scale.

He had no friends; early in his life he had learned to make none, for friends died and friends became enemies. And yet, each time he looked up at the mighty peaks of Tchsco standing dark against the night sky, a terrible cry rose in his heart.

What of Fflir? he wondered. Fflir had been the first Tlar to swear allegiance to him. Fflir had ignored the lapses committed so often at first when Asan was trying to adjust to this new body and its unfamiliar abilities. Fflir drilled him in seizerting and other battle techniques. Fflir saved him from boring meetings.

And what of Ggolen and Llor and Yvn? What of Hoyee, the ancient Henan slave who woke him in the mornings? What of the arms master, the technicians, and the acrobats? What of the human prisoner Daro, whom he needed?

His fist clenched until its gauntlet stretched tightly across the back of his hand. Damn these Bban fools!

"Tlar?"

Saar tapped him on the shoulder and jumped back as Asan sprang to his feet. They faced each other in the shadows of the night, tensed and hostile in spite of their truce.

"I slipped," said Asan after a moment, relaxing. "That's all."

Saar turned up his palm. "The wastes are our place. *An.* We are very close. Hear them?"

"I hear."

"It is the song of victory. Bban'n are free. At last they have conquered the hated ones."

Asan frowned inside his mask, wondering if Saar knew the true reason for such hatred, the reason that stretched all the way back through time to the Duoden Conflict and even further than it.

"Revenge is wasteful."

Saar barked in Bban laughter. "Thou are angry, Tlar leiil. It is hard to lose."

"We have all lost!" snapped Asan. "How many men died today without purpose?"

"To spread Tlar blood upon the sands is always to the purpose. For too long we have lived degraded under Tlar rule. Now we are free!''

"You fool, have you forgotten the humans already? They will make all of us slaves if we don't band together and forget this stupid feud.''

Saar reached for his jen-knife, his musk filling the air. But although Asan tensed, Saar did not draw his weapon.

"Again you speak matters for the elders' ears. *An.*''

"Someday, Saar, you will have to learn how to think for yourself," said Asan bitterly. "Whether the Tlar'n control your mind or your elders, you still aren't free—''

"*Chielt,*" said Saar in scorn, and strode away.

They crested that ridge and another, then suddenly they were surrounded by a dozen or more Bban sentries, running up to them in silence. Javelins rattled in their hands. Saar flung up an arm and spoke one word sharply. The sentries fell back into a circle around them. Red eyes and yellow glowed at Asan from the shadows. He could feel the hot desire to spill his blood.

Beside him Saar drew a breath of pride. Asan could almost guess the words he would speak.

Swiftly Asan flung open his cloak so that the dim light from the sickle-shaped moons overhead glinted off the bronze insignia upon his chest. He drew his jen-knife and focused his rings into a shield about himself that shimmered a faint blue.

"I am Asan," he said in commanding tone. "I will speak with your elders.''

They fell back, clicking to each other. Saar hissed in fury.

"Thou robs me of pride, Tlar," he growled. "Thou—''

"I rob you only of falsehood," said Asan. "You are not bringing me here as a prisoner. I come of my own desire. Let's go.''

This time he was the one who strode forward. The sentries melted aside to let him pass, then followed as Saar fell in at Asan's heels.

If he had to enter the enemy dara as leader of a defeated army, Asan supposed this was the most impressive way to do it. Head high, cloak flowing back from his shoulders, he strode down a beaten track into a valley ablaze with torchlight. He held his jen-knife over his heart to make it clear he came of his own volition and not as a prisoner. And as he passed through the tall metal stakes bearing severed heads of the tattered Slitk monks who had come during season for asylum and proclaimed him a god in a ceremony so acutely embarrassing Fflir had teased him for days afterward, Asan pretended he saw none of the spoils of war.

He stepped onto leather mats covering the trail, occasionally kicking aside a mask or gauntlet or untidy stack of fire-rods that had spilled from the large piles of loot on either side. There were more metal stakes and more heads. He kept his mask facing forward, but his eyes flicked from side to side in sick recognition. No one had been spared.

He gripped his jen-knife so hard his knuckles ached from the strain. His eyes burned hot with the urge to blast these Bban curs from existence.

Go back to the ship, he thought. *Two sweeps on maximum bomb spread and that will be the end of these savages.*

It would also be the end of him. The other human ships would be alerted and come after him. Then only the GSI would own this planet, his planet.

He wasn't going to let it happen.

Ahead, the Bban'jen stood like a wall before him, their backs turned to him, swaying together as they chanted their victory to the new moons of Lli. The sentries shrilled in unison, and the chanting faltered as the horde turned slowly, a few at a time, then more, to watch him come.

They were dressed in all their finery—wide leather trousers and jerkins overlaid with lead mail so supple it shimmered silver in the torchlight. Their hideous faces were swathed in protective leadweave cloth so that only their eyes glowed at him. Most wore long, barbed swords studded with hilt jewels and jen-knives thrust through their wide belts. Some held ruby-encrusted goblets; others swayed as though they had already sampled too much of the drink being poured from swollen chaka skins.

The women were resplendent too. Beneath leadweave cloaks and embroidered gauntlets shone gowns of transparent pria cloth laced with gold and silver threads. Exotic scents crossed the air, mingling with the smokiness of burning herendi dung and huge spits of sizzling zantza haunches.

Asan was conscious of overwhelming thirst and hunger, then in anger he forced those needs back.

Undaunted by the sudden silence, he passed through their midst. Insolently they parted for him, some of them not moving

from his path until they were only inches apart. Bloody jen-
knives were drawn. He could hear their growling. It would take
only an instant of drunken boldness for them to forget the gesture of truce he came under. Then he would be one more head
upon the stakes, providing target practice for children armed
with dung.

The leather mats upon the ground became handwoven carpets
of scarlet and blue patterns. His boots left dust marks upon
them. He came to a large circular tent in the center of the dara,
one with sides of transparent leadweave.

On either side of the entrance poles, large *havsks* held fat
cones of burning incense that sent green smoke into the air.
Asan could see dancers in filmy garments and silver bells upon
their ankles and wrists twirling inside the tent. Henan girls veiled
with shining hair to their knees served platters of food. Bailanke
and flute music whispered together in strange melody patterns.

As Asan stopped at the entrance and stood staring inside,
however, the music and dancing stopped. For a moment the only
sound was the roaring crackle of the fires and the thudding of
his own heartbeat. It was stifling behind his mask. Sweat stung
his eyes, and as he blinked the world seemed to shimmer blackly
around him. His mind went blank as he felt the pressure of other
minds against his rings. Suddenly he wanted to get out, crack
orbit, and leave this radiated dustball behind. Even all the wealth
in the universe wasn't worth some things.

But the Tlar pride in his body refused to budge. He stood
there motionless until one of the elders rose to his feet and came
to the entrance of the tent.

Asan recognized him as Ggil, and an old pain flickered in his
heart. Giaa's father. Asan thought of silver eyes and shining hair
and the warmth of her love. Then he closed the thoughts away.
Giaa was dead; her own father had used her as a pawn, and
Aural had killed her.

In that moment as the two men stared at each other, Asan
was glad he wore a mask. Silence stretched taut between them,
then Ggil clicked his jaw.

"The mighty Asan," he said, his voice a soft rasp. "Come
to surrender?"

Asan stiffened at the thinly veiled amusement. "No. I have
come to bargain."

Bban laughter barked all around him. Ggil gestured, and Asan entered the tent. Saar came in one step behind him. Bban minds pressed against Asan's protective rings. He glared at all of them, and pressed back.

Another elder, cruelly scarred across one eye, gestured rapidly at Ggil before barking loudly and rocking himself back and forth. Asan looked at him.

"I am glad you are so amused, Uxe Ookri," he said coldly. "Only the Bban'n are foolish enough to laugh on the eve of their own enslavement."

That brought them all to their feet, jen-knives whipping out.

Ggil lifted his head. "Brave words, Tlar. Brave words to hide the shame of your defeat. Your men are dead, and you stand in the tent of victory. We have saved a stake, a tall bronze stake, in a place of honor for your head."

Asan raised one brow inside his mask. So the gesture of truce was to be ignored. Tired of it anyway, for holding his knife over his heart was making his wound ache, he sighed and removed his mask. It was the gesture of surrender, but he didn't care.

He tossed the mask onto the ground along with his cloak and gauntlets. He sheathed his jen-knife. Crossing the tent, he took a jewel-encrusted ewer from the unresisting hands of a female and poured himself a tall goblet of sour Bban ale. Gulping half of it down and gasping as it jolted the breath from his lungs and started a fire burning in his stomach, he seated himself on a chair of metal and leather and stretched out his long legs.

He faced the expressions of fury around him with a smile. "No lies," he said. "Alien invaders have arrived. Didn't you see their ship pass overhead this afternoon shortly before your attack? They will enslave all of you or kill you, and then you will wish to the farthest reaches of your pitiable Bban souls that you had your Tlar masters back."

"*Pan'at cha!*" snarled Ggil, and slapped the goblet from Asan's hand.

It rolled across the carpeted ground, and the ale left a stain upon the bright patterns.

Ggil struck at him with a knife, but Asan's rings knocked the weapon from Ggil's hand. It clattered upon the goblet, and there was a heartbeat of silence within the tent.

Asan sat there, facing the elder, his long body tensed in the chair. His eyes burned with anger barely held in check. Then he forced his hands to uncurl from the arms of the chair.

"You seem to forget, Ggil, that I am not like the other Tlar'n. I command the same powers with or without Anthi."

A low, resentful mutter went around the tent.

"There are no invaders," snapped Ookri. "You lie. We would have known if any—"

"It is not a lie," said Saar suddenly, causing them to glance at him in surprise. Pulling off his mask and tucking it nervously under his arm in jen fashion, he faced them. "Small men with striped eyes in great metal ships from the sky. I saw this thing. By the four moons of Lli, I swear it."

"Chielt," Ookri snarled at him. "You come trotting into the dara at his heels like the pon dung you used to be and echo all his lies. He has twisted your mind, and you do not know it."

Saar stiffened, his hand flying to the hilt of his knife. "I saw it! I went to the realms of the gods in it. If you doubt my words, Uxe Ookri, send warriors to the hills where a scar is burned into the sand. Have them bring back the corpses of small men with striped eyes."

"We have seen the place. There are no bodies," said Ggil.

Asan glanced up. It was too late to tell Saar the bodies would have been charred to ashes in the backlash of takeoff.

"I took one human as prisoner," said Asan carefully, aware even as he spoke that the question was futile. The Bban horde kept no prisoners in battle; his would not still be alive. "Did you find him when you took the stronghold?"

"Enough of this game," said Ookri. "Summon the warriors. They fought well today. It is their right to take his head and eat the flesh from his bones."

"No!" said Saar. He stepped between the elders and Asan. "My life is his. He killed all my men and spared me. He has spoken only the truth to you. Together we rode the skies in the ship of the invaders. Together we shared minds to seizert back to the sands. He knows what these humans are. He knows what they can do. He understands how their machines work. And they have such machines! All kinds, to serve them. How can we, with our swords and our bombs and our chaka herds, fight machines?"

"If you had fought with your brethren today instead of cowering behind Tlar skirts," growled Ookri, "you would know how."

"Even the Tlar'n do not have machines such as these. The

Tlar'n cannot go beyond the world and return. Even when Anthi ruled us all, they could not do so much.''

Ookri raised his hand. ''You speak blasphemy—''

''I speak by custom! It is my right as a blood warrior sworn under Lli. I brought the Tlar leiil to camp under truce. You cannot take his head unless he is a prisoner, and he is not! Defy the Tlar'n, Uxe Ookri, but you cannot defy the law of the tribes!''

''See the Tlar smile?'' said Ookri, releasing his musk. It smelled sour and thin, the stale musk of an old man. His one eye glared balefully. ''He manipulates Saar's mind. It is another trick.''

''The law remains the law,'' said Ggil wearily. ''We shall not take his head yet.''

Asan eased out the breath he'd been holding. ''One small step toward becoming civilized,'' he said. ''Holding to law in the face of temptation.''

Then because it was a pompous thing to have said, he grimaced and shook his head.

Jen-knives whipped out.

''No tricks!'' snapped Ggil suspiciously. ''You will remain in the camp while we debate.''

Asan sighed. ''Debate all you like. In the meantime the humans have probably made contact with Aural. Once they team up, we can forget about any chance we have. I need your help. This isn't a matter of Tlar and Bban hostilities. We don't want the humans here. Because there won't be a future for any of us if they—''

''The Tlar future has already ended,'' said Ggil coldly. ''Take him away.''

Asan whirled, ready to snap out his rings, but the three guards who entered the tent held fire-rods aimed at him. The fight went out of him, and for a moment he knew that old, dry-mouthed fear. He'd died from a fire-rod wound once; he didn't want to do so again.

Ookri tilted up his scarred face. ''I smell Tlar fear. Ah, how sweet the scent. *Choi'heirat, eh, dar kai?*''

Asan's fists clenched. He was through with these short-brains. As soon as GSI strafings took the edge off them and cut their numbers in half, they would come crawling back to their old Tlar masters. Meanwhile, he wasn't going to sit cross-legged in a nomad tent and wait to be executed.

Aware that the guards would be expecting him to try something, he relaxed his muscles and bent to pick up his mask and cloak. There. He caught the imperceptible slackening in the two nearest guards. They expected nothing from him until he had his protective clothing on.

With one flip of his wrist he sent his mask spinning at the throat of a guard. His other hand flung the cloak over the head of the next. His rings snapped hard at the third. Asan gathered himself to seizert, but an immense blow to the back of his head scattered his inner control.

His head felt as though someone had turned it into a copper gong and struck it. For one instant he thought he would be sick. Then his knees buckled, and he was falling, toppling over and going down slowly as though in freefall. But the ground with its crimson and blue carpet rose to meet him. It hurt, hitting the ground.

And as though the world speeded up again around him, pain split his skull, a scarlet tide of pain that blinded him and made all the broken fragments of his rings shatter more.

The last thing he heard was the shrill barking of Ookri's laughter.

Chapter 5

In the Mura-an citadel northwest of Altian, Aural seated herself beside the fool's bed of purple cushions. She stared at the toe of her embroidered slipper in an effort to keep her temper. She was not quite sure why she had bothered to come here. The fool had served her purpose in delivering a living child. There was no need now to pretend to give her consequence.

"I want to see my child," Zaula was saying. Her voice was tired and petulant. Her face was drawn and sallow, with dark smudges beneath her eyes. "I have the right. To hold her, to nurse her, to—"

"—enfold her in your rings?" asked Aural cuttingly.

Zaula's dark eyes widened with hurt. Her small plump hand clenched upon the rich coverlet. She swallowed several times before she spoke again:

"I must thank you, Dame Aural. Without your help the child would have died."

"Yes, I know."

Aural rose to her feet and crossed the narrow, plainly furnished room. Her pleated robes rustled about her legs as she moved. The smallness of the room fretted her, as did the incense burning to hide the birth smells still lingering on the air.

She should leave. There was nothing more to say to the fool.

Her eyes narrowed as she swung about to stare at Zaula's tired face. The small, voluptuous body, once so swollen and awkward, now was shrunken beneath the coverlet. Zaula was no one, of no importance in any sense, a widow without rank and without house.

But she had born a child, and Aural could not.

I shall make Cirthe mine, Aural thought. *You, little fool, do not even have sufficient command of your rings to communicate*

41

*with her. But already I see into her mind and know her as you
never shall.*

"There should be music in celebration," said Zaula fretfully.
"I should be holding her in my arms, the two of us lying in state
to receive the first homage of the houses. I have heard no salutes
fired, no cheering, nothing but this awful silence. The matriarch's women have not come to me to give me their kisses or
to bathe me in scented water or to present me with embroidered
robes. There should be a feast given and a naming—"

"Her name is Cirthe," snapped Aural, impatient with these
unimportant matters.

Zaula gasped. "You have touched her mind? Already? Without . . . That was my right, Dame Aural. I am her—"

"You cannot look upon her with truth. Why should we wait
for you to humiliate yourself? Cirthe has been taken from your
care. Do not start more of your sniveling. You knew from the
first it would be like this. As for feasting and celebrations, do
not be naive. We are scratching for survival, even with the wealth
of Mura-an about us. And the Tlar'jen in the Outerlands have
been destroyed."

"Unar has fought the usurper? But—"

"Fool!" Aural laughed scornfully. "Unar could not defeat
Asan. No, no, my innocent, the Bban horde has risen. And the
savages are victorious."

Zaula gestured, her hands shaking. "They will come here
next."

Aural's smile widened. She hoped the Bban'jen came quickly.
It would be amusing to pit those savages against the fierce little
humans.

She glanced at Zaula. "Are you afraid?"

"Aren't you? No, you are not. What will become of—"

"If you are quiet, keep your place, and cause no trouble, you
will be ignored. Do not ask questions, do not seek to impose
rank on others, and do not go near Cirthe."

"But—"

Aural raised a hand to silence her. "You are nothing! As long
as you remember that, you will have shelter and food."

Tears silvered Zaula's dark eyes. She pressed her clenched fist
upon her stomach. "Throughout season I carried that little circle
of life within my womb, her rings entwined through mine. Now
we are broken apart as cruelly as though I had born her in the

midst of our enemies. Is your womb so barren, Dame Aural, that you have forgotten what it means to bear life?''

Aural stepped back, a breath hissing through her teeth. Rage filled her.

"You'll regret your insolence!" she cried, and struck Zaula with her rings, leaving the fool crumpled and unconscious upon her cushions.

Gathering her pleated robes in her hands, Aural strode from the chamber, only to whirl upon the guard who had been waiting for her outside.

"Bar this door!" she said. "Let there be a guard at all times. No one is to enter. And she is not to come out. Let only food be brought to her. And very little of that."

The guard saluted stiffly, too well trained to ask questions. "By thy will."

"Yes," said Aural, seething. "By my will."

Leaving the guard behind her, she hurried along the corridor with its arched ceiling of stone and did not pause until she turned a corner out of sight. Then she reached out and caught a stone buttress, jerking herself to a halt. Her anger was a haze in her mind, burning through her until she longed to lash out again and again in destruction. She should have killed the fool. Stupid, arrogant *piedwah*—her insolence would not be tolerated again.

Awkward memories, long suppressed, rose into Aural's mind. She remembered the days of heartbreak when she still walked at Asan's side yet could not match her rings to his in order to create a child. She tried every physician, every healer. She even cast the forbidden stones at the Temple of Lli, risking her life on the chance of awakening ancient dangerous forces.

There had been a faction of political lobbyists who urged Asan to put her aside for a more fertile bondmate. Those had been days when she could not sleep for fear that she would awaken to exile, yet Asan had not put her aside. She'd been grateful then, so grateful she'd sobbed into Asan's palm.

If only that Asan still lived. Aural's fists curled tightly. The human essence that inhabited his body husk was a weak fool. Why hadn't Asan fought to live? Why had he let the centuries of sleep stretch out until it was too late to come back to life? If Asan, the true Asan, had not died, there would have been no need to have taken *yde* to remain strong. There would have been no need to fight these wretched fools in order to bend them to her will. There would have been no disconnection of Anthi and no Bban uprising.

But regrets served no purpose. She walked alone; she would rule alone until Rim and Vauzier could be resurrected to join her.

At least now she had a child and a planet of her very own. Cirthe had been shaped and guided by Aural's own rings in the last days before birth. It had been Aural's bonds she had broken as she entered the physical world. It had been Aural who had felt the pain of that separation. It had been Aural who first gazed down into those small blue eyes and looked upon Cirthe with truth. Cirthe was unique. Her mental patterns were complex and powerful. She fed hungrily upon Aural's mind, tapping knowledge as other infants suckled for food.

As for Ruantl . . . this miserable rock was all that remained of the once mighty Tlartantlan empire. The people here were a pitiable remnant of what had been a once-proud race. But she would rebuild the empire. The brief linkage with the human Saunders' mind had told her about the worlds inhabited beyond Ruantl's system. She would take those worlds and rule them eventually. The first step required bringing more humans here; thus, she had activated the distress beacons.

Now the humans had come, and she was ready to deal with them.

Glancing over her shoulder, Aural slipped a small vial of blue powder from her sleeve. She sprinkled some of it onto her tongue and pressed it against the roof of her mouth, closing her eyes against the bitter taste that gradually melted into a haze of comfort. Her rings steadied and grew powerful beneath the influence of *yde*. She was Aural, true leiis, Enchantress of the Winds and Keeper of the Blood. The ancient titles sang in her bones.

Swallowing the powder, she opened her eyes. She blinked slowly, bringing the world back into focus. Her sight was heightened on all levels, augmented by the drug. She could see molecular patterns, energy waves, and thought streams.

She smiled and closed her eyes, forming her rings into order. She quested the heavens for the ships and found one that contained no life. Puzzled, she found the second ship. Eight minds were there, some of them crudely receptive, some of them as blank and impenetrable as a force shield.

For a moment she considered seizerting there, but the distance daunted her. She could see and hear them; she watched them at work, sitting chained like slaves to consoles of equipment. They spoke to each other. Their voices were serious, high-pitched, and slow. She concentrated on their speech patterns, but those were difficult to understand. Monitoring their thoughts, chaotic and not ordered by rings, was not much easier. Frustration filled her.

She projected an image of herself into their midst. Several shouted. One jumped up from his chair, gesturing. His hand signals made no sense. He looked like an idiot. She frowned, displeased to find him in charge.

Then a second man, one seated apart from the others, unfastened the restraints around his body and rose to his feet. He was the calmest of the group. He spoke to the others, his voice sharp but controlled, and they quieted. He stared at Aural with a frown.

He was a short creature, matched in height to most of his crew, yet the top of his head did not come to her shoulder. His hair was the color of vegin wood—dark brown tinted with red—and cropped short to his head. His face was haired below his nose and across his jaw. His eyes were small and repulsively colored. She had never seen eyes that were dots of green in the center surrounded by the white of blindness. He could not have complete vision with such eyes. She wondered how he managed to do his work. Yet all the others had similar eyes and they seemed as unimpaired as he.

She let her image shimmer closer to him. His strange eyes grew wider, but he did not move. They faced each other.

Human, she said. *Hear me.*

She spoke to his mind. He winced and lifted a hand to his temple. Then he turned away from her and spoke sharply to one of his crew.

Human. She probed deeper into his mind, cutting across resistance barriers and drawing his chaotic thoughts into a small ring.

Must identify alien life form. Projection. Hologram? No, unlikely. Mental. Demos, my head aches. No telepathic hijinks with me. No! What the devil was Saunders doing all the way out here? I'll have her busted down to the bottom. Knew her brother. Just as stubborn. Does this alien know her? Why haven't they put out a communication buoy? Or at least fired warnings? Not even a fleet. Must be wide open. But who is she? Beautiful. A giantess. More than beautiful. Get out of my head, damn you!

I am Aural, she said, steadying him. She forced his thoughts into order, seeking the ability within him to answer her. *Communicate your name.*

McKey. Angus. Captain Angus McKey of the SIS Dorian Grey. *Number 444—*

Enough. Why have you come here? To conquer us? We are an independent people. This world is our own.

We come in peace, said McKey. *We—*

Don't lie! I look upon you with truth. You have orders to investigate this world and if it is promising you will claim it for your masters.

Our sensors have told us—

I am not interested in your machines. Let us bargain together. I shall give you the mineral wealth of this world in exchange for your ships and crews to man them.

I am not authorized to make deals. That is for my superior officers—

Relay to them.

McKey hesitated, then he said, *We are here in search of a downed ship. The* Forerunner. *Have you encountered either her or her crew? Captain Asos Lute? Navigator Rhyi Saunders? A criminal drone masquerading as Helmsman Blaise Omari? Hassid? Any of these?*

Your questions are unimportant at this time.

Have you knowledge of these people?

Aural frowned. She disliked his insistence. For a moment she withdrew from his mind. He swayed, his face paling to a queer gray color.

Yes, she replied at last. *I have knowledge.*

Where?

First our bargain, Captain McKey. There is war and unrest among my people. Assist me, and I shall assist you.

Her strength was exhausted. She withdrew her image from the ship and snapped back within the shaky circle of her own rings. Her eyes fluttered open, but it was a moment before she could see. Her breath rattled in her throat. She reached out and touched the comforting solidity of stone, cold and gritty beneath her fingertips. Her knees gave way beneath her, and she sank down in a heap, fumbling in her sleeve for the vial of *yde.*

She licked up the last of the bitter-tasting powder in desperation, then closed her eyes as it took hold of her and renewed her strength. She should not use *yde* so often. Her addiction might get out of hand. But this time her recklessness was justified. As soon as she had rested she would contact the humans again for their answer.

She rose to her feet and smoothed her pleated skirts. It was time to put the second part of her plan into motion.

The soft patter of slippered feet warned her a split second before a voice as tart as aged honey said,

"Plotting alone in the coldest corner of this old pile. Is there an aesthetic pleasure in it? Does shivering inspire you? But I am being disrespectful once again. How tiresome of me."

Aural paused a moment, seeking to control her anger, and did not turn to face Dame Pasau until her expression was smoothed into nothing that would betray her. She had not missed the deliberate usage of the familiar "you." Dame Pasau, like far too many others, refused to completely believe that Aural had returned from the mists of legend to supremacy as Tsla leiis of this miserable world.

"I have been to visit Dame Zaula," Aural said as though her rings were serene and her fists were not clenched inside her wide sleeves.

The impudent expression vanished from Dame Pasau's face. Suddenly she looked exasperated and old, her fawn-tinted skin withered at the mouth and eyes, the elaborate tattoo covering her forehead faded of its once-brilliant color. She had been born in the House of Spandeen and was still inclined to their love of excessive display. Her gown was all of gold, stiff and shimmering, with exquisite beadwork across the wide skirts and a pleated ruff standing up behind her head. She looked as though she were dressed for a visit of state, and for an instant Aural thought she was on her way to visit Zaula in the manner of custom.

"Poor idiot," said Dame Pasau. "Does Zaula understand that there will be no visits, no feasts, no homage? She has never been an intelligent person. Her marriage to Leiil Hihuan was an unrivaled feat of political maneuvering on the part of her father and matriarch. But she must forget all that now. I hope you have not raised hopes in her head by going to her?"

Aural narrowed her eyes. "She is the fool, not I."

"She should have died. It was a difficult birth. My head still echoes with all the screaming last night. But then she should have died when Hihuan did. Now she will meddle. She will drive Unar mad, or else bewitch him. He never could resist a pretty little body.''

"She won't meddle.''

Something flickered in Dame Pasau's eyes. "A riddle, is it? What have you done, locked her away? A waste of guards, especially now when Unar needs all the manpower he can find. The Soot'dla have arrived.''

Aural blinked, startled by that last, unexpected statement. "What?''

"Ah, so there *are* things you don't monitor.''

Aural frowned, angry at herself for showing surprise and angry at Dame Pasau for provoking it. "They have come quickly.''

"Of course. It is an emergency. The Bban horde must be stopped from committing any more atrocities. Come,'' said Dame Pasau, actually taking Aural's sleeve. "Don't look at me as though you mean to strike me dead for my impertinence. I'm too old to care, and there's more at stake here than your notions of self-consequence.'' She paused and cocked her head. "Or don't you want to be present when I receive Dame Agate, the traitoress?''

Aural stared down at her, and after a second her anger began to fade. Reluctantly she returned the matriarch's smile, recognizing for the first time that perhaps she had a better puppet here than Unar would ever be. Better, because Dame Pasau would assume she was an ally and would never know the extent to which she was being used in a far larger, far more serious contest.

Aural gestured graciously. "Lead, noble dame.''

The reception hall of the citadel was long and narrow with a tall vaulted ceiling that made it impossible to heat or light adequately. Fires had been lit in braziers set all along the room, but they were a poor, smelly comfort. Aural's eyes stung from the smoke. She retreated, deciding not to go in. These petty political meetings bored her.

But as she backed up, she collided with a muscular chest. Her smallest rings flickered against Unar's, and sparks struck in a friction that made her shiver with excitement. She turned quickly to face him, smiling into his eyes.

He smiled back, his handsome face relaxing from its stern lines. His gaze roamed, savoring the beauty of her lithe body. Pleased, she tilted back her head, basking in his worship. Unar was a straightforward man, ambitious and sufficiently short on conscience. He was very easy to lead.

"My Unar," she murmured, her voice husky. Her rings enticed his to level one, darting, teasing to level two. She heard the breath tangle in his throat. "Battle armor. Guards around you. Rationed fuel flaming in every hearth. Is all this display just to impress the Soot'dla?"

His eyes were beginning to glaze. She watched the struggle in his face as he sought to control himself away from her seduction.

"There—there is no time for anything less," he said thickly, averting his gaze from hers. "A regency must be declared. The houses must unite now before the Bban horde strikes again. Then we'll show those curs how the true Tlar'jen fight!"

"You sound as though you have been practicing those ringing phrases in your chamber."

He frowned. "Now that Asan the usurper is dead—"

"Not dead!" she said swiftly. "I feel his life. How he has escaped yet again, I don't understand, but—"

Unar gripped her arm hard, making her wince. "You told me you did not rebond after your resurrections."

"We did not! Don't doubt my word." Angrily she pulled free. "If he died now I would be safe, but I would still know it. There are times, Unar, when your jealousy is tiresome."

He started to answer, but in the reception hall a gong sounded. His eyes flickered past her.

"It is time," he said, pushing her aside. "Go and bring the child. They will insist on seeing her."

Furious, she lifted a hand. "I am no nursemaid, to run and fetch! I am—"

"Bring her," he said, and entered the reception hall with his guards behind him.

She clenched her fist, tempted for a moment to strike him dead. Her long hair, burnished ruddy gold in the flare of torchlight, swirled and lifted about her with a crackle of static electricity. She could destroy this place, hurl it to rubble with not one stone left lying atop another. She could leave these tiny men who dared call themselves descendents of the mighty Tlartantlans to perish out in the cold desert of a barren world. She could expel her breath and lash the winds to a fury unmatched by the black devis of Kathra season.

Her rings spread, dark with anger, and a low rumble shook the citadel beneath her feet. The walls trembled. Dust rained down from the ceiling, and a crack split the mosaic pattern of celadon and amber tiles set into the jate-stone floor.

"Thus . . ." she breathed, laughing to herself, and spread her fingers.

The tremor stopped, and the silence within the reception hall broke into a confused babble of voices. Dame Pasau called out, demanding a return of order. A pair of guards ran past Aural, their footfalls heavy, their shielding rattling beneath their cloaks.

Dame Agate—the tall, emaciated matriarch of the infamous Soot'dla—appeared in the doorway to face Aural. Behind her, there were still requests for order and no cessation of the noise.

Aural stared at Dame Agate, hating her on sight. Agate had the haughty curves in nose and cheekbone of the oldest blood-lines. Her hair was scraped back tightly from her face and kept hidden beneath a cowled hood of leadweave. She wore tattered work clothes of leadweave and leather, nomad clothes, Bban clothes. Aural's nostrils wrinkled back from the scents of sweat, dung smoke, and animals.

Agate's gaze caught the movement of swift revulsion. Her eyes glittered.

"Thy powers have not been forgotten by all, noble leiis," she said. Her voice was raspy and low. She turned her head so that Aural glimpsed the house mark burned into her right cheek. "I have met thy ring-mate on the plains of Ddreui—"

Aural swept her palm down. "That union is dissolved. We walk no more together."

Dame Agate shrugged as though the denial was unimportant. Her eyes grew distant with visions. "The mighty Asan. Tall, handsome, powerful. Straight from the legends of my girlhood, unchanged and no disappointment. Now, I meet Aural. Another legend come to life. Will all the Jewels of M'thra rise?"

"Of course. We are the true race. We have been sealed away too long."

"Is Asan dead?"

Aural half turned away. "Your questions are impertinent, old one."

"He must reactivate Anthi."

Agate's choice of words made Aural glance back. She frowned at the old woman, who spread her fingers wide.

"I am not superstitious, like the Bban tribes, nor am I lazy, like my fellow Tlar'n. We need Anthi to work again. The food will not grow properly—"

"Food." Aural lost interest.

"Has thou lost the need to eat? Has thou lost the need for warmth? Are thou so strong thou needs no planetary defenses to protect thee from those who have come in spaceships?"

"What do you know of those?" demanded Aural sharply.

Dame Agate smiled and turned over her hand. Her palm was crossed with thin scars. "My rings of sight are strong, noble leiis. I require no *yde* to help me see what is happening around me."

Aural drew in her breath with a hiss, unable in that moment of fury to speak.

"The houses must unite around the infant. We must bargain a truce with the Bban tribes in order to face whatever has come to our world." Dame Agate paused, a frown creasing her face. "The last time a ship came to Ruantl, Asan was the result. And thyself."

"And the destruction of Altian."

"Complex patterns," said Dame Agate, turning her head as someone shouted within the reception hall. Then she stared right at Aural. "Our world is our own, noble leiis. Do not give it away."

To be read as easily as though she were a Henan slave . . . Furious and somewhat alarmed, Aural gathered her cloak around her and seizerted to the central chamber of the citadel. The safest, most defensible area, normally it held a generator to power the stronghold, but none of the equipment worked without Anthi. It had been converted into a nursery, with two attendants stationed there at all times to regulate the fires burning in the braziers and to care for Cirthe's needs.

The attendants were gone. She knew that even as she materialized in the oval room hung with tapestries and carpeted with white borlorl fur. Her feet sank into the thick fur, and she almost stumbled as she ran to the tiny bed carved from rose quartz. Lined with the softest, costliest fabrics in the Mura-an treasury, it too was empty.

Cirthe was gone.

"No!" shouted Aural.

Panic snapped her rings apart. She stood there blind and shaking, unable to think. Unar could have sent a servant to fetch the child. Just because Aural planned to spirit Cirthe away did not mean that another had done so first.

Drawing in a deep breath, she focused herself, forcing calm to her rings as she re-formed them one by one. She quested first through the reception hall, delicately, well aware of the agile minds gathered there who could sense her intrusion. No, Cirthe was not there.

Again a sense of panic destroyed her concentration. She cursed and continued her search, level by level, desperation making her faster and less cautious.

Cirthe!

It was as though the infant had ceased to exist. There was not even a ghost ripple of Cirthe's patterns fading among the overlapping structures of time and essence. Where could she be? More importantly, who had taken her? Who was strong enough to conceal Cirthe's unique patterns?

The answer whispered through her mind, a vision of the Soot'dla scar entwining with her thoughts. She clenched her fists inside her wide sleeves. While Dame Agate had delayed her with conversation and insolence, Cirthe had been abducted.

Aural's lip curled. She would teach the old woman to meddle.

Gathering herself, she seizerted into the reception hall with a flash of blue fire. Startled, several warriors stumbled back from her, their hands reaching for weapons they had removed before entering the citadel's inner walls.

On the dais at one end of the hall, Unar shot to his feet in spite of the hand Dame Pasau clamped on his forearm.

"*Lea'dl*, noble leiis! What is this—"

"Treachery!" said Aural, her voice ringing out. She swung, pointing at Dame Agate, who sat encircled by her warriors, hands folded, eyes glittering. "She has taken—"

A tremendous clap of sound, like thunder only sharper, cut her off. The walls shook, and several people cried out in alarm. The noise grew louder, rumbling overhead as though the heavens themselves were falling upon the citadel. Torches snuffed out with loud pops.

Suddenly Aural couldn't breathe. She gasped, struggling with lungs that were paralyzed. Around her men began choking, their hands at their throats, shaking themselves from side to side.

Aural staggered toward the dais. The world wavered and darkened around her. She had to seizert out of here.

But there wasn't time. She was losing control. Her rings were fuzzy shadows swirling away from her. She stumbled into someone. A hand clutched her arm. She blinked and focused. It was Unar. His face was contorted and a queer shade of brown. He tried to speak. It came out as a gargled sound.

The humans! she thought. The treacherous fools would pay for this.

Her body arched back in a last convulsive effort to breathe. Then she was falling, unable to hear anything more, and conscious only of a fading sense of rage that death should be so swift.

Chapter 6

Old dreams chased Asan. Dreams of drone labor in the steaming slop pits on Dix IV. Dreams of being hunted down by city patrollers, of not being able to run fast enough, of being held back and trapped, helpless and quaking, a shard of stolen metal clutched ready in his hand, the tremor of his heartbeat thudding out of control. . . .

Asan sat up with a choked cry. "No, you *flins*! You won't take me!"

"Noble leiil."

A strong hand gripped Asan's shoulder, shaking him. Asan blinked, coming abruptly out of the dream. He frowned at Saar's ugly face inches from his own. Saar's scarlet eyes burned into his.

"Noble leiil?"

"Yes." Asan lifted an unsteady hand. "I'm all right. It was just a dream. A . . ."

His voice trailed off and he stared past Saar, only now taking in the stone walls around them. There was very little illumination coming from a smelly torch burning just outside the barred opening in the cell door, and in the gloom he saw a metal cot identical to the one he was lying on and a short metal stool. The air was cold and held a suggestion of damp.

He frowned. This wasn't the Bban dara.

He swung his legs off the cot.

"Easy, noble leiil," said Saar, trying to stop him. "Not yet. Rest a moment."

Asan shrugged off Saar's hand, yet he remained sitting there without attempting to stand. His fingers curled around the edge of the cot. He had a sense of disorientation, of having missed an essential block of time. His mind quested back, seeking it,

54

and found nothing but darkness and a confused impression of travel.

He swallowed, conscious of intense thirst.

"Where have they taken us, Saar?"

Saar growled and pushed himself upright to his feet. His pon uniform was dirty and torn. His boots were split at the soles. A half-healed scar marked his cheek in an angry pucker.

He spat, his body tense and half seen in the gloom. "*Ah'hi*, noble leiil. We are in the citadel of the Mura-an. Sold as spoils of war to Tlar-dung. My blood is a pool of shame."

"Sold?" Asan's head came up in surprise. "Why?"

"Thy words were true. The humans have come in war. Tlar'n and Bban'n have made truce—"

"Good!" Asan stood up, but the room spun around him. Dizzily he sank back down and put a hand to his head. "What did Ookri hit me with?"

"A gong mallet. Thou has walked close to the shadow land for many days."

Asan grimaced. "I'm not in Merdarai yet. Have they given you a water pail?"

"Water? A Bban warrior is not worth water. But if thou are in thirst, I can call the guard."

"In a moment."

With more caution this time Asan got to his feet and walked to the door. He was so weak his knees wavered, and his muscles were stiff and awkward. His stomach was a knot of hunger, and a small but persistent ache remained in the back of his skull. Bit by bit, however, he felt some of his strength returning.

He reached out and touched the scarred iron door with a wary fingertip. The energy charge crackled, and he jerked his hand back, his finger tingling from the shock.

"A weak field. We could get through it."

"Thou are not strong enough yet to seizert. And where would we go?"

Asan glanced at Saar sharply. "You would follow me?"

"Thou are leiil. I serve thee."

Saar saluted stiffly, and Asan returned it.

"You have my thanks, Saar."

Saar growled, turning away as though in embarrassment. "I have learned the meaning of a true leiil. The elders sold this warrior, who had served them with honor to the blood. They are no different from the Tlar-dung they sought to destroy." Saar glanced back at Asan, his scarlet eyes troubled. "I beg thy pardon, noble leiil. My words are clumsy. Tlar-dung are those such as the tyrant Hihuan and his—"

"I understand." Asan grasped his forearm for a moment. "I give the care of my blood to your loyalty, Pon Saar. Now let's see about getting out of here."

"Again I ask thee. Where will we go?"

"To my ship. The *Spitfire*."

"Thou has not that much strength. It is hard to seizert so far. Let us wait until they have brought food."

"Good point." Grinning, Asan returned to his cot and sat down. "How long?"

"Soon." Saar stationed himself at the door. "Rest again, noble leiil. I shall give thee warning."

Asan stretched himself out, pillowing his head on his interlaced hands. Tlar'n and Bban'n finally believed the humans were a threat. Whatever the humans had done to teach them that lesson, Asan knew more men had been lost. And right now, with the shaky, almost nonexistent technology here, he was not only outnumbered, he was outgunned. He couldn't take on the GSI and win.

So he'd better figure out a way to get help. And the only help he knew about was Martok.

Asan frowned uneasily. His former boss couldn't be trusted either, and Martok sure wouldn't appreciate an appeal for help from one Blaise Omari, not after Omari skipped on an important delivery.

But of course Martok wouldn't know who he was. Asan had the perfect cover, an impenetrable new identity. And Martok would be eager to barter illegal weapons for an exclusive mining agreement.

Asan sighed. Now all he had to do was break out of here, get his ship, and somehow slip out of the system undetected by the humans. Simple, right?

No way.

Security buoys. How was he going to get past those? The Institute had salted them across the controlled areas of the galaxy, and an illegal ship without the proper passage codes was zeroed instantly. Smugglers, assassins, couriers, and other fringe traffic usually possessed mechanisms called buoy breakers that could jam the buoy circuits. But the *Spitfire* was a legal ship. It wouldn't be equipped like that.

So he had to have the codes. And to get them, he had to have a ship's captain.

Daro, he thought, clenching his fist. *Demos take those stupid Bban'n!*

But there was a second ship and a second captain. He frowned, not liking the odds of successfully kidnapping the senior officer off a ship. Even if he tracked it, seizerted there, probed the man's mind for the information, and seizerted off, he'd be vulnerable for a sufficient number of seconds to get himself shot. He could use his force field of course, but he wasn't sure if it would deflect calibrated strifer fire. The Tlar'n might think themselves fairly invincible in certain situations, but he had no such illusions. He knew what humans could do.

"Leiil."

Saar's soft growl pulled him from his thoughts. Asan sat up, sniffing for the aroma of food. Even ration cubes, as dry and unappetizing as they were, would be welcome. But Saar had crouched by the door, out of sight below the window. He released his musk and clenched his bony fists.

Alerted, Asan gathered himself on the edge of the cot, his hands at his sides, his legs coiled to propel him forward if necessary. It wasn't dinner that was coming.

A tiny ring brushed his mind, found him aware, and withdrew instantly. But not before he recognized Aural's pattern. He stiffened, his heart beating faster. He didn't like the idea of meeting her when he was trapped and helpless in this cell. Maybe the threat from the humans had put her on his side. Maybe she was coming to get him out of here.

Big maybes.

He didn't have much belief in any of them.

Booted footsteps rang out in cadence, growing louder. They stopped outside the cell and stamped to attention. Asan glimpsed the swirl of a black cloak through the window, then a face peered in at him. It wasn't Aural's. Surprised, he stared back.

"Dame Agate," he said, and Saar stiffened in his hiding place.

She scowled, looking older and more weatherbeaten than ever. "Send thy savage away from the door, and I'll come inside. We must talk, Asan."

She was as brusque as ever, refusing to bend that stubborn

pride of hers, refusing to take time for courtesies. Asan gestured at Saar to move and wondered if Aural was standing behind Agate. She was somewhere near. His uneasiness increased.

Agate spoke an order. The subliminal hum of the force field vanished, and the door swung open with a creak. Agate slipped through, holding a fire-rod in her gloved hand, and the door slammed behind her with a hollow boom. She was drawn about the mouth. Her skin was a sallow, unhealthy tinge. There were dark circles beneath her deep-set eyes. Her shabby nomad clothing was coated in dust.

"There isn't much time—"

"Where is Aural?" asked Asan, rising to his feet.

The fire-rod swung his way, and he lifted both palms before sinking back down on the cot.

"Does thou want her?" Agate's eyes glittered with anger. She snarled a Bban curse word that made Saar move uneasily. "Let her dare come into my sight and I swear that I shall spread her blood upon the sands. That—"

"If you're here for an execution, get on with it," said Asan. As he spoke he gestured for Saar to remain where he was. He didn't want the headstrong Bban to get smoked. "What's wrong, old woman? You're shaking. I can sense your rings broken around you. Have the human invaders frightened the matriarch of the Soot'dla?"

"Enough."

Her hand tightened on the fire-rod. She glared at Asan, her lips drawn thin over her teeth. "Thou has been unconscious. Thou doesn't understand what has happened."

"There are several possibilities," Asan said. "Usually when they come in over a city, they try to pull power and incapacitate communications and weaponry lines. But they couldn't do that here. So they either dropped a blanket stun, or they used chem-bombs. Then when everyone was unconscious, they walked right in."

Agate's mouth fell open. For the first time in his difficult dealings with her, Asan saw her at a loss. She blinked twice, a third time, then pulled herself together.

"Thou understands," she whispered. "Thy words are not clear to me. But thou speaks of it just the same. They took the air, great leiil. They snatched it from our lungs."

Asan turned up his palm. "Chem-bombs. They didn't take

the air, Dame Agate. They used a gas that temporarily paralyzes the lungs. It's very effective in strongholds like this one. Saves blasting a couple of walls apart and going in by force.''

She considered this, eyes squinted. The habitual pride had been wiped from her face.

She lowered the fire-rod to her side. "We were once a mighty people. And of the Tlar'n, the Soot'dla have been greatest of all. Now we are faced with a devious force of *n'kai* who toss us about like pebbles. Our weapons, our shields, our pride, are all as nothing against them. Thou knew this, and thou were not heeded. Like fools, we rallied around Unar and the infant. Like fools, we allowed ourselves to be betrayed by Aural." Dame Agate spat. "That *n'dl!*"

Asan lifted a hand. "Careful. She is near. She is listening."

"Spying. *Chielt!*"

"Where are the GSI troops now?" asked Asan. He stood up, anxious to get out of here. "I have a—"

"They have withdrawn. They claim they are here on a rescue mission. Aural brought them here."

"I know. What else has she done?"

"There isn't time. We must settle truce and go."

Dame Agate drew her jen-knife and made a quick cut across her palm before tossing the weapon to Asan. He hesitated a moment, remembering an earlier meeting with Dame Agate during season when she had sat in the midst of her warriors and refused to join his army. She was shaken now and eager, but could she be trusted?

She saw his hesitation, and swift bands of color rose in her face. She drew back her bloodied hand with a hiss.

"It is as I first thought. Thou and Aural, all the old ones, are against us. Thou wants us to perish so that thou can have—"

"What?" He grabbed her by the shoulder and shook her. "So we can have what, old woman? A barren planet inhabited by nothing?"

Furious with her blindness, he cut his palm, frowning at the sting of pain, and grasped her hand hard in his until their blood mingled. She tried to pull away, but he tightened his grip until he heard her gasp.

"No!" she said, writhing. "Thou took Anthi. Thou freed the horde. We shall starve because of thee!"

"Fool!" He twisted her arm behind her back and held the

knife to her withered throat. "If I hadn't shut Anthi down, Picyt and Aural would have had all of us in their power. Surely you can see that, old woman! You are supposed to be wise!"

For a moment there was no sound but their ragged panting. Then Dame Agate's tense body relaxed in his hold.

"There is truth in what thou says."

"Of course there is." He released her so abruptly she staggered. Staring down at his hand, which was splattering dark blood upon the floor, he said bitterly, "For the first time in my life I have played square, and no one believes me. I must be an idiot."

"I accept truce," said Agate.

Startled, he glanced up and saw acceptance in her haughty face. She lifted her palm and touched the tip of her tongue to the blood. Slowly Asan copied the action.

"You're old-fashioned, noble dame."

She threw back her head with a laugh as harsh as the desert wind. "And thou, noble leiil? Thou are simply old. How long will thou live?"

"As long as it takes. Here." He tore two strips of cloth from the coarse blanket covering his cot and handed her one to bind her hand.

Behind him, Saar clicked his jaw nervously. "Something comes."

Asan started to ask Dame Agate for her fire-rod, but her bony hand clamped down upon his arm.

"Quickly!" she said. "Follow me."

"Where?"

"We have wasted too much time. Come!"

As soon as Asan followed her out of the cell, he felt an urge to make a break for it. Saar crowded him, growling lightly under his breath. Three Soot'dla warriors in masks and silver cloaks moved to flank Dame Agate. At her command one of them tossed Asan a fire-rod. He handed Saar the bloody jen-knife, and all of the Soot'dla stiffened.

Asan glared at them. "He serves me to the blood. Leave him be."

Dame Agate frowned, still looking as though she wanted to protest. But she inclined her head. "By thy will."

One of her warriors led the way, ducking down a twisting tunnel so low they had to bend double in order to go through it.

The darkness was total, a disorienting blackness so thick Asan could almost feel it. He concentrated upon his higher senses to show him where he was going. But still, when they emerged into what looked like a small, natural cavern he stumbled and nearly lost his footing.

Torches flared here. The warriors each took down one from the sconces. Dame Agate's face was pinched at the nostrils. She was breathing heavily as she straightened her hood of leadweave.

"Hurry."

Again they followed a tunnel, this one leading down. It had rougher footing. It also ended in a cavern, a larger one fitted with cells. There was a drop of perhaps an arm's length between the lip of the tunnel and the floor of the cavern.

Asan jumped down, wincing as his knees took the jolt without any spring left. Hunger was making him light-headed. He wished Dame Agate had come after he'd eaten.

"There is safety here," she said. "Not much, but a fraction of it."

Asan swept out his palms impatiently. "None. As soon as the search starts—"

"I shall hide all traces of our passage—"

"From minds perhaps. From sensors no."

"Sensors?" She stumbled over the word. "Machines?"

"Very sophisticated machines. We need to get out of here. I have a ship—"

"Wait," she said, turning away as a warrior unbolted one of the cell doors. "I must not be missed. When I return, then we shall decide what to do."

"Agate—"

Her cadre drew their weapons, and Asan cut off his sentence, cursing himself for having trusted her. A rough hand drew his fire-rod from his belt, then gestured for him to enter the cell. He stood where he was, feet planted. At his side Saar released his musk.

Alarmed, Asan flung out a hand. "Saar, no!"

But the Bban was already leaping at the nearest warrior. They went sprawling in a tangle of legs and cloaks. Asan saw another aim his fire-rod. Desperately Asan snapped his rings forward, seeking to deflect the blast from Saar, but Dame Agate's rings slammed him to one side. He fell, scraping his cheek upon the stone floor, and the moment was lost.

Blue fire flashed briefly, and Saar screamed. The stench of seared flesh and Bban musk filled the air.

In the stillness that followed, the man Saar had attacked rolled Saar's body to one side with an oath and staggered to his feet. One of his arms hung useless at his side.

Asan climbed upright, fury sawing through him. He faced Dame Agate, whose face was haughty, closed, without regret. He wanted to crush her.

She gestured. "Get into the cell. Now. I have no more time to waste here."

"Saar was—"

"Will thou crush me for the death of one savage?" asked Dame Agate. She lifted her bandaged hand.

The reminder of their alliance turned his stomach. "One loyal savage is worth a thousand deceitful allies. Even you should know that, noble dame."

Shame flooded her face then, but he turned away and entered the cell, unwilling to see more.

"Leiil—" she began, then cut herself off. "We shall talk when I return. This is of need. I swear it."

He stood in the shadowy darkness of the cell with his back to the door and did not answer. The bolt rammed home, and they were gone, taking the torches with them. There was only darkness and cold and death to keep him company.

Chapter 7

A muffled whisper told him he was not alone. Asan whirled and flattened himself against a clammy wall, his flesh shrinking from the moisture that seeped through his tunic. Whatever was in here with him, he wasn't going to die in the dark.

Gathering his rings, he cupped one palm and concentrated until a ball of blue phosphorescence formed. The illumination it provided was feeble at first, then strengthened to cast an eerie light around the cell.

Huddled in the far corner was a shapeless thing. Dark eyes with faint glints of red in their depths stared at him. He lifted his hand to shine more light on it. It gasped and flinched back. An arm flung out, and he saw a narrow face blurred with fear. Dark hair tumbled down over one shoulder, and Asan relaxed slightly. Whoever she was, she posed him no threat.

The whimper came again, louder this time, strengthening into a wail. Asan frowned. A . . . a baby?

"Who are you?" he asked, taking a step forward.

At once the woman pushed a small bundle of soft fur robes from her lap and scuttled away from it to the most distant corner. Asan stopped, staring first at one and then the other. Finally he walked over to the baby, stooped, and picked it up.

A flap of the robes fell back, and there was the infant's face, tiny and wrinkled from recent birth. Large eyes tinged *yde* blue stared up at him. He felt a tug at his mind as though this little one sought to order him to her bidding. He brushed the command aside and felt a harder push against his rings.

No, he said firmly, less amused this time. *You may ask to share my mind, but you will not demand it.*

Cirthe! I am Cirthe! shouted the infant at him. The shrillness

63

of her tiny patterns made him wince. *Where is the other? Where is the one who has made me complete?*

Involuntarily he glanced at the woman. His nostrils detected the same scent from her as upon the baby. But she wasn't who Cirthe wanted.

Puzzled, Asan felt the baby twist restlessly in his arms, kicking her feet against the coverings. There was an oddness to her, something not quite as it should be.

Cirthe, he said.

Where is she? I hunger. Aural, I hunger!

Asan fought the urge to push Cirthe aside as the woman had done. Instead, he touched her tiny forehead with his fingertips and made her sleep. Then he laid her gently down although the floor was no place for an infant. But there was no furniture of any kind.

He stared down at Cirthe, troubled. Was there no end to Aural's atrocities? She had warped this child at some point before her birth. He could detect the deformed rings that only *yde* caused. Cirthe was strong for a baby so young. She would soon be dangerous.

He frowned and turned his attention to Cirthe's mother. Was this also one of Aural's monsters? What could produce such a child?

"Who are you?"

His voice, loud and angry, boomed off the walls. The woman stifled a cry and lifted her hands as though to ward him off. Asan paused, then approached her warily. Normally a person's rings formed shifting circles and patterns. But the woman's were flat against her as though unused. He tried to look upon her with truth, and she cried out again. He gained only confused impressions of pain and fear. He stopped, the dim light spanning the distance between them.

She held her cloak across her face so that only her eyes showed. He could hear the raggedness of her breathing. One ungloved fist was clenched hard at her side.

"I won't hurt you," he said. "Tell me your name."

For a moment she did not move, then she rose up suddenly on her knees. "They called you leiil! I heard them! You are Asan the usurper!"

"I am Asan."

She hissed. "Henan dung! You killed Hihuan, my husband, and now you seek to depose his rightful heir."

Asan blinked, and for an instant the light almost flickered out. "Cirthe?"

The woman cried out. "She has shared her rings with *you*? Am I to be the only one locked in silence? Did I not struggle to bear her living into the world? Why am I treated as a below caste—"

"Be glad you haven't shared her rings," said Asan grimly. "She has the *yde* madness. And if you let Aural complete her rings, you are a fool."

"What choice had I, brought here against my will?"

Climbing to her feet, the woman let her cloak fall open, and for the first time he could see her face clearly.

She was beautiful. The breadth of her forehead, the high curve of her cheekbones, the petulant fullness of her mouth, all spoke of the best house lineages. Her skin was smooth and flawless, proclaiming that all her life she had lived well sheltered from the outdoors. She was tiny; the top of her head came barely to his chest. Her figure, what little of it showed beneath robes and cloak, was ripe with curves and enticing hollows.

For the first time since Giaa's death, a sensation of warmth loosened the knot of bitterness within his heart. He felt his blood quicken, and his senses curled about him in an appreciation he did not attempt to hide.

Her hands, plump and adorned with rings, reached for the cloak to veil herself again, then her chin lifted and she faced him with hauteur.

"I am Zaula, the Tsla leiis," she said. "You stare at me in violation of true Tlar courtesy. You are a savage, no matter how many titles you wear, and your barbaric manners proclaim it."

It was difficult to hold back his amusement. "A Tlar leiil may gaze upon the face of any woman in his court, no matter how high her rank."

"You aren't Tlar leiil!" she shouted. "Cirthe is keeper of the blood. You are—"

"*Chi'ka.*"

Alerted to something in the distance, he tensed and moved to the door of the cell.

"I am not a slave, to be addressed in the tongue of heathen Bban'n—"

"Silence."

He pressed himself against the door and let his rings eddy upward through the mass of stone over them. No sounds . . . the distance was too far. But a sense of approach . . . yes!

He whirled to face Zaula. "There is no more safety here. Someone is coming."

"Dame Agate," she said. "At least she knows the proper way of—"

"Dame Agate is as much my enemy as anyone else."

Zaula lifted her chin so that her black hair spilled back over her shoulders. "She is my friend. She rescued me from Aural."

Asan grunted, unimpressed. Dame Agate had done the same for him, not that it meant anything.

"Stop fighting for the rights of Cirthe," he said. "She does not carry the true line. She must never mate."

"She is my child!"

"Then why do you fear her?"

He let the silence spread between them a moment, then he extended his hand. "Come. Let's get out of here."

She looked bewildered. "We can't seizert. Cirthe is too young."

"I don't intend to take Cirthe anywhere."

He reached out and grasped Zaula's arm, but with a jerk she twisted free.

"I won't leave her! She is my—"

"No, Zaula, she is Aural's. You know that. If you have any sense at all you know that."

Zaula turned away with a moan of grief.

Torn between sympathy and the urgent sense of time running out, Asan watched her bend and pick up the child.

Leave her, part of him said. *She isn't worth it. Get out now while there is still a chance.*

"Zaula," he said. "Come. I'm leaving Ruantl. It's your chance to escape this place once and for all. You could live where it is safe to be outdoors—"

"Liar! There is no such place. The Ways of Beyond are lost. You are an evil imposter who has come here and destroyed us. You took Anthi's favor from us. You have left us at the mercy of the savages. Why don't you seek out Aural and take her with you? She is of your kind. Go and leave us to the invaders!"

He wanted to shake sense into her, but there wasn't time. He could hear the scrape of footsteps now. The rhythm wasn't Tlar; the footsteps were too quick, indicating the strides of shorter legs, human legs. He drew in a deep breath, dragging his rings together, and seizerted.

He aimed for the upper tunnels, but instead he got no farther than the opposite wall of the cavern. He materialized, staggered, and bumped his shoulder into the wall to catch himself. All right then, he thought grimly. Shorter jumps.

But he was too light-headed from hunger. That tiny ache in the back of his skull became a pounding. His rings splintered around him, refusing to form. He glanced over his shoulder at the shadowy corpse that had been Saar. The pon had been right; he was too weak to reach the *Spitfire*.

Get out of here and hide, he told himself, hurrying around the circumference of the cavern in an effort to find an exit tunnel. He stumbled in the dark, seeking to realign his bearings. His fingertips were bleeding from being scraped along the rough stone wall. He curled them into his palm. Blood was too easy a scent to follow.

But humans didn't rely on their noses. He must be registering on their hand-sensors now. *Get out of here!*

He saw the light first. Tightly focused beams speared the darkness, swinging up and around as the men clattered down the tunnel. Feeble though it was, the illumination showed him a slit in the wall ahead. He ran for it and was one stride short when the entire cavern blazed with light and someone shouted, ''Get him!''

Sweet Demos, be kind, he prayed, launching himself in a dive. With all his remaining strength, he formed a wavering force field. The familiar sound of strifer fire filled the air as Asan's hands grasped the lip of the tunnel. *Seizert, tuck, and roll into it,* he told himself.

But something slammed into him, stopping his impetus as though he had no force field at all. He grunted at the impact, biting his tongue as he hit the wall and fell. All the air felt jolted from his lungs. He struggled, but suddenly his arms and legs seemed to belong to someone else, jerking spasmodically and tingling with prickles of fire. He opened his mouth, gasping with the certainty that he was going to be sick, yet nothing happened except a deepening, all-pervading misery that was the by-product of a strifer stun.

The thunder of running feet filled his hearing. He heard high-pitched voices calling out to each other in excited Standard.

"What the hell was that piece of *flin* doing, flying?"

"Careful there, men. Stand back from him. Make sure he's unarmed."

Human laughter. "Ah, Demos, captain. He's jammed up nice and tight. Caughton hit him broadside."

Asan jerked although his body didn't move. With all his might he strained to turn his head just a fraction so he could see the face of the human captain. This was the very man he needed. But his head wouldn't budge. He gasped and gave up as fresh nausea rolled over him. Instead, he concentrated on the tonal structure of the captain's voice and his mental patterns, such as they were.

For the first time since taking on this body, Asan wished he hadn't deactivated Anthi. He needed her now to amplify his powers. If he could just speak one word, he could make the ceiling of this cavern come tumbling down enough to scatter the humans. But the paralysis had his throat too. He closed his eyes.

"That's right, fellow." A hand touched his numbed shoulder. It felt like being tapped with a block of wood. "Just take it easy. The stun will wear off quicker that way."

Desperation filled Asan. This might be his only chance to probe the captain's mind.

Captain . . . he began.

No! Aural's rings cut across his. *Do not touch his mind, Asan. You have lost this battle. Ruantl is mine.*

Furious, Asan snapped his rings flat, refusing to share thoughts with her. Unable to see anything more than the dusty bits of rubble inches from his face, he listened to the rustling of her robes and the whisper of her slippered feet as she joined the humans.

"This is the man you seek, Captain McKey," she said, her voice filled with triumph. "He can tell you where to find Blaise Omari."

"Thank you. Men, get him up to the ship."

"No!" Asan wanted to shout. "No!"

But he was helpless, a frozen lump as they hauled him upright and slung him over the shoulders of two men.

"Big ole thing, ain't he?" said one.

The other one laughed as he snapped down the holster flap

on his strifer. "He won't be after they whittle him down for a while in the TANK."

"Watch your backs, men," said McKey. "None of these people are to be trusted."

"Yes, sir."

As Asan was carried away, he saw Aural and McKey smile at each other.

"Well done, captain," she said, spinning her translator on its cord so that it glittered in the light. "This almost makes up for your earlier tricks against me."

McKey grunted, his smile fading. "As I've explained already, I'm a military man, not a diplomat. I saw fit to take this citadel and, by God, I did. Being momentarily stunned hurt you no more than it will this man."

Inside, Asan grinned. *Are you sure you want to play with humans, Aural?* he taunted. *Aren't you afraid your human catalyst will come back to haunt you?*

She whirled sharply, her face drawn tight with fury, and lifted both arms as though to strike fire at him. But the humans were busy maneuvering Asan into the tunnel, one lifting and the other boosting. He steeled himself, but she did not strike. Nor did she attempt to share rings with him.

"There is another prisoner down here for you, captain," she said instead. "A woman whom I'm sure has knowledge of Saunders' whereabouts. You should question them ruthlessly. We of the Tlar race are a stubborn people. We don't break easily."

In the main levels of the citadel, Asan expected the soldiers to take him outside immediately. Instead they carried him through the reception hall. He got only glimpses of more humans standing armed about the room, weapons trained upon the huddled knots of silent Tlar'n. The matriarchal dais was empty. Many of the fires in the braziers had gone out. The room was cold.

Asan began to feel sick again. He shivered, struggling to hold back a moan. The increased discomfort meant the stun was beginning to wear off. He could even move a couple of his fingers although he felt so bad he didn't much care.

Worse, however, was the gasp he heard as he was carried by.

"That is Asan," they murmured. "Yes, I tell you. Asan. The Bban hordes defeated him, and now these little creatures."

"Quiet!" ordered the guards. Although they spoke in Standard, they were understood plainly enough. The murmuring stopped.

Shame ran through Asan. He told himself sharply not to be stupid. None of what had happened was his fault. If these people were backward enough to sit around on a mineral treasure trove without any sort of orbital defense against invasion, they deserved what they got.

Only, he was the legendary Asan, the man of myth, the hero of their past history. At least externally he was that man. And so they were dumping all of the responsibility on him. Demos help him, he even blamed himself.

If these idiots had just listened to me, he thought. If they hadn't been so proud and set in their damned antiquated ways. If they could have looked past their noses and stopped a futile civil war. . . .

The humans would have still come. United or not, the people couldn't fight the GSI.

At least, not yet.

"Where is Blaise Omari? Where is Ryhi Saunders? Where is the SIS *Forerunner*? You will answer."

There were several kinds of pain: the low-level ache that wouldn't go away, the throbbing that eased off as long as the body was relaxed and didn't move, and the shattering kind that jolted every other conscious perception from existence.

"You will answer."

The shattering pain came and went, leaving him gasping. Clammy sweat broke across him.

"You will answer."

He was in no danger of obeying. It was only an interrogation machine talking, and its frequency set was not capable of breaking through his defenses. He held himself braced in the vilthread straps and counted the four-second interval between the command, the pause in the case of an answer, and the jolt of punishment that always followed noncompliance.

There were several ways of enduring pain. It must be caught. It must be channeled away from nerve endings. It must be denied.

He'd quickly figured out that cushioning the jolts in his rings didn't work. The more he cushioned, the harder the jolts became until his brain felt on fire and his whole body was battered from convulsions.

They'd nearly stopped the interrogation that time. They thought they'd killed him. But as soon as his heartbeat started again and his breath came back, the machine was switched back on.

It was easier to endure it if he didn't try to relax, if he just lay there stiff and let the pain break him apart. Then the questions would resume, and he would manage to breathe again and blink the sweat out of his eyes and almost recover before the command tone came again:

"You will answer."

He screamed that time, and the vil-thread straps dug deep into his flesh as his whole body convulsed. Then he came crashing down against the board, his breath rasping in a throat that felt raw and bloody. He coughed, tried to lift his head, and decided that a pretense of cooperation might be wise. It would not gain him a release, but at least he would be tortured in a different way for a while.

"Where is Blaise Omari? Where is—"

"Dead," he said, gasping out the word. "He's dead."

For a moment he was so weak he wasn't sure what language he'd attempted it in. But at least he'd spoken for the first time in hours.

The machine clicked over to a new track and hummed a moment.

"Repeat response."

He nearly laughed. He'd forgotten how ludicrous some of this security equipment could be. He might have just gasped out his dying word, and the stupid thing missed it. Demos, didn't they have recorders still built in?

He didn't respond, determined to have human interrogators for a while. Where were they? Gone off to bed? Maybe their stomachs were too weak to watch what their machines did.

"Yes, sir," said a voice that did not come over a machine tape. "He's beginning to break. We haven't made a direct translation. No, I don't think it was an oath. It was definitely a response. Yes, sir. The scale registered it that way."

The glaring light over Asan dimmed. There was a low whine slowing down as machinery shut off. Asan closed his eyes although the white glare still danced behind his eyelids. He drew in several deep breaths, his muscles stretching out degree by hesitant degree, burning and cramping as the lactic acid built up from so much tension spread out through his tissues. His body began to shake so hard he rattled against the board. He ignored this reaction. It was natural. He was just grateful for these few minutes of rest.

A hatchway in the side of the cylindrical interrogation chamber opened, and burly Captain McKey and one of his officers stepped inside. Asan turned his head to watch them. They weren't quite in focus at the edges. He shut his eyes again. McKey reminded him too much of Saunders. Maybe it was that red hair and stocky build. Or maybe it was that dull look of immutable loyalty to the Galactic Space Institute.

"You turned it off," said McKey. "Just when he was starting to talk? Are you mad, Ramer?"

"Sir. I thought you would prefer to conduct this yourself. The machine's translator isn't quite on frequency yet."

"Damn."

McKey stood over Asan and rubbed his chin. It needed shaving, Asan noted. A slight sense of superiority filled him. That was one of the nicer things about exchanging a human body for a Tlar one: no more facial hair.

The evidence of a beard also told Asan that McKey was something of a maverick. Beards were strictly against ship regulations.

"Well, Ramer? How the hell am I supposed to talk to this devil?"

"Here, sir." Ramer stepped up and handed him a translator.

McKey held it in one enormous fist and frowned. He cleared his throat loudly. "Where is Blaise Omari?"

Weariness passed through Asan. McKey could have at least chosen a different way to phrase that question. Asan closed his eyes against this unpleasant angle of looking up McKey's nose.

"Dead."

That time the translator made it. Tlar-manufactured translators were better, Asan noted. Or maybe it was just easier to translate Standard into Tlar rather than the other way around. He certainly wasn't going to betray the fact that he understood Standard.

"Damn," said McKey. "Omari's dead. I wanted to bring that little vat snake in myself. All right, you. What happened to him? How did he die? And when?"

"Shot," said Asan, and went into another coughing fit.

His throat ached with thirst. It was too hard to talk. He longed to be able to communicate directly with McKey's mind. But there were blanket beams switched on this chamber. The humans knew he was telepathic. Aural must have told them that too.

"Shot?" repeated McKey with a scowl. "Go on. Explain."

"Executed by Leiil Hihuan, tyrant of Altian. Now also dead."

As he spoke, Asan remembered that day of bewilderment in the black sands of the desert. Thinking his leg had been shot off, he'd lain out there beaten with exposure and pain until a Bban hunting party found him and dragged him back to their dara.

"Damn." McKey was holding the translator upside down and shaking it. "I'm only getting about half of what he says."

Ramer frowned. His face was almost too narrow to be human, with a quick nervous intelligence in his dark eyes. He took the translator from McKey and made a slight adjustment.

"I think he must be talking too fast, sir. The language also sounds inflected, which adds to our difficulties. This SK model has always been inferior to the newer—"

"That'll do, Ramer," said McKey. "We'll try simpler questions. You, what's your name?"

"Water."

"We're not at a garden party, you damned yellow giant. What's your name?"

"Give me water."

McKey was turning red. "Your name first—"

"Sir." Ramer touched his sleeve. "He has been coughing blood. He might give us information more readily if it's less painful to talk."

"What? Oh, very well."

Ramer vanished, returning more quickly than Asan expected with a short beaker of clear liquid. Asan strained for it, then his sense of smell warned him of chemical additions. He jerked his head away and scowled.

"Chielt! Pan'at cha. Muli'it nun part. Tel!"

The contempt in the Bban words was plain enough to color Ramer's face. He stared at the beaker while McKey shook the translator in disgust.

"Not a word of that came through."

"Different language, sir," said Ramer quietly. "He detected the drug."

McKey grunted. For the first time a measure of respect entered his eyes as though he finally considered Asan an intelligent being. "Well, then. We were doing better as we were. Go and get him some plain water."

The liquid was soothing, incredibly cool against his raw throat, and not nearly enough. Asan swallowed in greedy, desperate gulps, straining against the vil-thread straps. When Ramer pulled the beaker away, Asan curbed the urge to demand more and let his head fall back against the board. Relief spread through his body along with the moisture. He felt almost ready to tell them anything they liked.

"My name," he said, remembering the bargain, "is Asan. I am Tlar leiil, First of the Great and the Arm of Anthi."

McKey's brows shot up as though he hadn't expected such cooperation.

"It is not of need to treat me in this way," continued Asan. "To kidnap me and torture me for answers to unimportant questions."

"The whereabouts of these people is vitally important."

"How? Were they of rank? Was their house and lineage noble? Were they above caste? If so, how did they come to us as fugitives, homeless and destitute, to die far from their own world?"

McKey blinked through all this. "Omari was a petty criminal who hijacked one of our ships to escape detention and rehabilitation. You've told us what happened to him. What about the rest of the crew? Saunders and Captain—"

"All dead," said Asan. He was anxious for this to end now.

But the quick answer was the wrong one. At once he saw that McKey did not believe him. McKey frowned.

"Maybe," he said. "Maybe not."

Asan frowned. "How could they live? You have seen our world. It is not a place for outsiders. Survival is difficult. Food is scarce. Protection from the black sun is hard to find. The sand will eat one's flesh from one's bones."

"Sure," said McKey. "But Queen Aural told us you had our people hidden away in your stronghold."

Asan nearly laughed at the absurd title. Did she know what the translator reduced her to? A queen was a nonentity compared to a leiis of the blood. But his anger at Aural's betrayal came back to kill the laughter. She was going to have to pay for all she'd done.

McKey was speaking again. Wearily Asan pulled his attention back to him.

"I have no stronghold. Aural lied."

McKey snorted. "We'll get the truth out of you."

"I have told you the truth."

McKey started at him, and with dismay Asan saw a look in those eyes which told him Aural had reached McKey's mind and shaped it to her perceptions. He would never believe Asan. Aural had planned it that way.

Asan thought about trying to overcome the blanket beam and reach McKey's mind himself, but he knew it wasn't possible. Not in his present state. He sighed. Maybe he'd told them enough for a while. Maybe they would take him out of the TANK and let him rest. Maybe they would feed him.

McKey turned away, then glanced back at Asan. "Tell me this. We picked up trace indications of advanced technology on your planet when we were barely within orbital range, but close-up scanning found nothing. So we know you people have defenses you aren't letting on about. Tell me about those. Tell me about your secret weapons that you've hidden away, and I might just accept what you've told me about the *Forerunner* crew."

Asan stiffened. "What we have is no danger to you as long as you leave Ruantl in peace and do not return."

McKey glanced at Ramer. "Funny. I expected an answer like that. Turn the machine back on, Ramer. Feed in a new tape. We still have a lot of questions to go."

Chapter 8

The first thing Zaula noticed as she came slowly awake was the heat. She was sweating in her heavy robes, and a strand of her dark hair was stuck damply to her brow. Puzzled, she opened her eyes, only to shut them quickly against the dazzling light.

Then she remembered. She'd been taken by the strange *n'kai* on their transport into the sky. They'd locked her into this cell and left her hours ago.

Rubbing her eyes, she sat up on the soft bunk and gazed around. Luxury surrounded her. The blanket on her bunk was of a soft gray material as light as air, yet warmer than borlorl fur. The light that had blinded her at first was clear and artificial. She glanced about, but saw no lightcubes. Nor could she find a source of the heat that throbbed through every muscle in her body. She felt pliant and curiously content.

Stretching, she took off her heavy robe of leadweave and tossed it over a chair of strange design. There was a table fashioned of a material that was neither metal nor wood. She tapped it with her fingertips and frowned at the objects sitting on top of it.

One was a faceted cube about the size of her fist. At first she thought it was a stone. When she picked it up, the surface was polished and cold. Its color changed from a brownish-gray to white to a face staring back at her.

''*Ah'hi!*''

She dropped the stone, and it bounced on the tabletop with a thud. The face disappeared, and after a breathless moment she felt ashamed of her fear.

Slowly she picked up the stone again and waited until the face reappeared. This time she saw that it was not a living creature trapped within the center of the stone, but only a representation.

The face was alien to her, pale and grayish-pink in color with a shapeless bump of a nose, striped eyes, and a smile frozen in time. She found the *n'dl* ugly and put down the stone. No one else.

Beside it was a panel of machinery controls, all in different colors. She traced her fingertips over these, wondering what would happen if she pushed one, yet not daring to do so. Machines were fragile, precious things which only trained technicians of the House of Kkanthor must touch. No one else.

The pad and stylus did not interest her at all. Writing was for Henan scribes. A small bowl the size of a dye pot held small pebbles of different colors. She scooped some of these up in her palm, fascinated by the purples and pinks and ambers flashing iridescently in the light. Then she let them spill between her fingers back into the bowl. They tinkled musically as they fell.

Laughing, she scooped up another handful and let them fall. This time the musical notes were in another order as though different colors made different tones. Perhaps the *n'kai* were not such strange creatures after all. If they enjoyed music, they must be civilized.

She played for a few minutes, trying all kinds of variations and testing each color individually to listen to it before combining it back with the other pebbles. Then she returned the bowl to its place and continued her exploration.

On the other side of the cell was a door that vanished as she approached it. Startled, she jumped back. The door reappeared with a swift hiss. Frowning, Zaula tried to touch it with her hand. The door vanished again. This time, however, she saw that it was only recessing itself into the wall. She smiled in approval. The *n'kai* did not need slaves if they had such marvels as this.

She stepped through the doorway into a shadowy alcove. At once lights sprang on. She did not flinch this time. The floor beneath her feet was a gray, springy substance that gave slightly under each step. The walls were of the same material. The function of this alcove was plain. She stared at the nozzles overhead, then looked at the lever close to her hand. She hesitated a moment and pulled it.

A fine mist of water fell upon her. She laughed, lifting her arms to the water, then quickly stripped off her gown and let the shower stream over her.

Moments later, the water pulses began alternating with puffs of warm air, the latter growing more frequent until she stood dry and tingling under the lights. The water pooled around her feet drained away for recycling. Zaula approved. Even luxury should not be wasted.

A wall panel slid open, and in astonishment she pulled a garment from the recess. It was soft and supple to the touch. Always interested in clothes, she shook out the folds and smiled.

It was a ludicrous thing, all of one piece with tunic and trousers for a man. She cocked her head to one side, amused by the notion of herself in *ka* clothes. No self-respecting *dl* of a noble house would dare appear in something that exposed her limbs so boldly. And as Tsla leiis, she must never—no.

Bitterness twisted inside her, making her crumple the garment in her fist. She was leiis no longer. She had been given to the *n'kai* like a piece of bartered goods.

All her life others more powerful than she had shaped her life. From a childhood in the citadel of her house, whisked out of sight when adults of rank walked through the nursery, she had been annually inspected by a trio of the matriarch's women in waiting. Her teeth, her eyes, the straightness of her limbs, the gracefulness of her walk, the shade of her skin, the sheen of her hair, the quality of her voice, the strength of her rings—all were checked and discussed as though she were nothing but a despised Henan slave of no caste.

When she became a woman, her own father consented to see her, but she knew nothing of the visit except that she was placed beside a fountain in the villa and told to play tunes on her bailanke. He watched her from the latticed balcony, spying on her, judging her beauty and ability to please a man. Two days later she was masked, robed, and taken to the palace of Leiil Hihuan, to become his leiis, to preside over his Court of Women, to have first consequence in the tiny circle allotted her.

The old resentment came back as she thought of those days as ring-mate when she was toyed with, ignored, summoned abruptly, expected to adore and reverence a man who never troubled to become other than a stranger to her. Without Fflir she would have gone mad in that perfumed prison. Lying in Fflir's arms, she used to dream of the days when she would be free.

Zaula coughed in anger. What good were dreams? They were as clouds on the horizon of the Outerlands, mirages that promised the sweet rain yet never came.

And yet . . . She slowly turned around, frowning at her surroundings. If this was a prison, it was the gentlest one she had ever known. These *n'kai* were rich beyond belief, rich enough to provide captives with exquisite comfort. And the *n'kai*, no matter what terrible thing they might have planned for her, did not care whether she was leiis or deposed leiis. Rank and caste were beyond their limited understanding. The proud history of her house was as grains of dust to them. Even her beauty had ceased to enslave her, for to the alien eyes of the *n'kai* she could not be beautiful. Their idea of beauty was trapped in the center of that stone in the other room.

Aware of a sense of release, she smoothed out the crumpled garment where she had gripped it so angrily. Her fingers ran along the diagonal band of dark green, and the tunic opened.

Intrigued by the invisible fastenings, she closed and opened it several times, then smiled to herself in a burst of mischief and pulled the garment on.

It fit, more or less, being snug across her breasts and shapeless at the waist. She was about the same height as most of the *n'kai*. She stared down at her legs encased in the trousers and wriggled her bare golden toes. It felt good to do what was forbidden.

She put on her slippers and went back into the other room. Two men were standing there with drawn weapons.

Startled, she gasped and stopped in the doorway, gripping it with both hands.

One of them spoke and advanced on her. She backed up into the small bathing alcove, but retreat was futile. Annoyance twisted the human's dark face. He spoke again, more sharply this time, and gestured a command she did not understand.

"What do you want?" asked Zaula, trying not to panic.

The human grabbed her arm, and she cried out in fear. His fingers were surprisingly strong for one of his small size. He pulled her from the alcove and swung her around so that she was pinned up against the table. Still holding her in that bruising grip, he pushed up her sleeve and held the pale golden length of her forearm extended.

The second human holstered his weapon and pulled a tube no longer than the length of his hand from his pocket. One end of the tube was pointed. Producing another instrument, this one a short thick cylinder also pointed on one end, he walked up to Zaula and made a deft incision in her arm.

She screamed, but to her surprise there was no pain. The man holding her pressed his free hand against the vulnerable spots of her throat. He spoke, but she already understood from the pressure that she was to remain very still. She obeyed, her heart fluttering erratically inside her. Her broken rings stirred, instinctively trying to form to save her. But she was helpless, unable to do more than watch these creatures as they opened her flesh and probed within the tissues of her arm.

The probe grated on bone, then touched something that sent a quiver through her. The *n'ka* grunted as though satisfied and fitted a tiny object inside her arm, then closed the incision. Zaula stared, still unable to believe there had been no blood and no pain. Only a faint pink line showed where the cut had been made.

". . . should work adequately," said the human with the instruments.

Zaula jerked, startled that she could suddenly understand him.

He bared his teeth at her. "Good. It's working, Mike. She understands us now."

The man holding her grunted and released her. Zaula sagged against the table, feeling bruised and still frightened.

"We've fitted you with a translator," said the first human. He had the bony thinness of desert people and a gaunt, awkward way of moving despite his deftness with the instruments. His hair grew in white tufts that stuck out over his ears, and thick gray eyebrows jutted out above deep-set eyes. "Normally we put them in behind the ear where they work at maximum effectiveness, but we were a little dubious about getting you to hold still for that. How do you feel? Any discomfort in the arm?"

Zaula stared at him, not yet daring to speak. By the mercy of Anthi, how many wonders did these *n'kai* possess? Slowly she turned her palm down in answer.

The *n'ka* frowned. "It's all right. You needn't be afraid to speak to us. We're fitted with translators too. Part of our job. Of course we had to make some adjustments. Your language is a bit more complicated than most we're used to. Fitting it to Standard took a while. Otherwise, we'd have come in here sooner to see you."

"I don't think she's getting any of this," said the human called

Mike. At least she supposed he was human. His skin was as dark as orad heartwood, and his hair grew in small tight knobs all over his skull. He shook his head. "Ramer's always claimed to be smarter than he is. I don't think he's made much sense of those interrogation tapes. Even the machines are having trouble translating."

"Perhaps." The older *n'ka* glanced back at Zaula. "Let's try something simple. What is your name?"

Zaula evaded his gaze in desperation. Court etiquette had provided no training for this situation. That she stood here in the company of strange men without her mask was bad enough, but that they expected to speak directly to her and for her to answer was a thing not done.

"What is your name?"

The tone was sharper. Zaula flinched. She stared longingly at her leadweave cloak. If she could only put it on, she would not feel so foolish and exposed.

The human sighed and ran his fingers through his white hair. "I am Dr. Liebtz. This is Mike Powers. We aren't part of the regular crew. We are GSI specialists sent along on this mission as observers. Please tell us your name."

"No."

"Why?"

"Taboo?" suggested Mike.

Liebtz frowned at him and shook his head.

Zaula watched their exchange in alarm. They gestured more with head movements and facial expressions instead of their hands. Did they not usually wear masks? That must be why they had not provided her with one. Or else they wanted to humiliate her. Either way, it was hard to understand them when she could not comprehend the nuances.

"Why won't you tell us your name?" asked Liebtz.

Mike made an impatient movement beside her. Zaula remembered that expert pressure against her throat and shrank from him.

"It is not a thing you are permitted to know," she said. "To speak to me is not permitted. Not like this."

She expected Liebtz to apologize or at least look abashed. Instead his gaze shot to Mike.

"How is she registering?"

"Honest," said Mike. "Fear, annoyance, worry. I told you we're crossing taboos."

Liebtz shrugged. "Telepathy use?"

"Negative."

Zaula turned to stare at Mike. What was this dark creature? She had felt no touch against her rings. How then did he know so much? She met his queer, striped gaze—brown surrounded by the white of blindness—and read only detached curiosity.

Zaula drew in a breath, reminding herself that they were only *n'kai*. They knew nothing about what was proper.

"If you wish to observe the culture on Ruantl," she said, "then you should ask your questions of the Bban'n, not us. Your mutations are not as great as theirs, but you should be able to find qualities in common."

There. She'd said it. A deep insult to the blood delivered in courtesy tone. She held her breath, wondering if her challenge would result in a slashed throat. At least she would die with honor, a wife and daughter of warriors.

Instead of anger, they expressed only puzzlement.

"Mutations?" said Liebtz. "But we aren't—"

"You do well with such limited sight. But—"

"Eyes."

The humans exchanged glances, smiling. Zaula flushed, her rings stirring about her. So much for her attempt to insult them. Instead they were laughing at her.

"We don't suffer partial blindness, if that's what you are thinking."

She wanted to strike them. She felt like a child trying to match wits with adults. But she couldn't back down now.

"You are hampered. You must be."

"Well, perhaps." Liebtz hesitated as though thinking it over. "We don't look at it that way, but your vision must be close to total periphery . . . wouldn't you say, Mike?"

"Anatomy isn't my field."

"No." Liebtz coughed. "Still, it's another comparison project for the lab boys when we get back to Central." He reached out and very gently touched Zaula on the shoulder.

She flinched away, reaching instinctively for the jen-knife she did not have.

"You must remember that you are far away from your people now," he said. "We are going to take you back with us to where

we come from. We want to learn all we can about your culture.
Now you have told us that we aren't permitted to know your
name. I'm sorry we must cross that barrier, but if you won't tell
us who you are, then we must give you a name of our own.''

She hissed in outrage.

"Precisely," he said, still in that gentle tone. "I thought you
wouldn't like that. But it's your choice.''

She frowned, going over his words in her mind. "You are
taking me away from Ruantl? How far is this?''

Mike stirred with a warning, but Liebtz ignored him.

"Do you understand the concept of space travel? The twin-
kling lights in the sky are—''

"I am not a Bban savage," she said angrily. "I am Tlar. If
you think we were spawned upon such an evil place as this
planet, then you are fools. How far do you take me?''

Liebtz was trying hard to conceal his surprise. "Very far away.
Almost halfway across the galaxy, in fact.''

Her own heart leapt. Did he know of Tlartantla? Had he ever
journeyed there? Perhaps, oh, perhaps she might see it.

She hid her excitement, however. "Will I be brought back?''

"Of course.''

But he was lying.

She did not care. She was among people who enjoyed plen-
tiful heat, light, water, and probably food. They had machines
that worked. They had no need of masks and heavy leadweave
clothes. Their lies to her did not matter. Her fear melted into
eagerness to go with them.

Lifting her chin, she faced him and said, "It is not of need
to give me a *n'dl* name. I was Zaula n'Tlar dl'Soot'dla, Tsla leiis
of the tyrant Hihuan, Firstborn of Ruven, Beloved of Anthi, Star
of Altian, and blood mother of Leiin Cirthe.'' She made a small
gesture of repudiation, clearing away her former life as one
brushes away the black sand of the desert. "Now I am Zaula.
Nothing else. Call me by it if you choose.''

"Fine," said Liebtz. "Make a note of all that, Mike.''

"Noted.'' Mike's cold gaze swept over her. He pointed toward the door. "Time for phase two.''

Liebtz frowned. "So soon?''

"Why not?''

"Very well. Zaula, we want you to come with us to another
part of the ship. Will you do that?''

She moved as though to reach for her cloak, but Mike got in her way.

"You don't need that," he said. "The temperatures are even throughout the ship. Come."

Not certain what to expect next, she went with them.

"Don't be afraid," said Liebtz. "Please sit down and wait here."

Zaula paused by the bench he had indicated. This chamber he had brought her to was very small, scarcely wide enough for them to stand facing each other. It was white and featureless except for two short benches which folded down from opposite walls and a circle of black glass fitted into the center of the ceiling. She thought of the ever-present eye of Anthi and shivered. Who watched over the humans?

"Why should I fear?" she asked haughtily. "What is to be done to me?"

"Nothing," he said, lifting his palm. The gesture made no sense with his words. "You are now in the part of the ship that we call the in-TANK. TANK is an acronym of the various names of our equipment used in observing and interrogating specimens. Please sit down and wait here quietly."

"But—"

"You will have food soon."

She silenced her protest at once and sat down in hopes that her compliance would bring the food sooner. She was very hungry, especially since she had fasted following the birth of Cirthe. Her thoughts shifted uneasily away from her daughter. A monster, Asan had called her. It was true. She wanted to weep for the child. But she held the tears back.

The door opened suddenly, startling her. She stood up. Two humans in uniforms appeared with a limp Asan in their grasp. They shoved him inside roughly, sending him sprawling upon the floor at her feet. She cried out, flinching back.

"You—"

The door shut, leaving her alone with her enemy.

For a moment she stood there, breathing hard with her hatred. She had almost managed to forget about him. Now here he was in her power. She could even kill him if she chose.

Unless he was already dead.

She frowned, her anger melting away. He lay there like a crumpled rag, very still. Too still.

She knelt beside him, reached out to touch his shoulder, hesitated, then gave him a shake.

He moaned weakly and tried to shift his head.

A lock of his black hair brushed her hand. She hesitated, her fingertips resting lightly upon the back of his neck. The Bban'jen had a way of snapping the spine at that point. A certain grasp . . . one quick jerk . . .

She pulled back her hand in shame. There was no honor in killing an injured man. And she should remember that Asan the usurper had shown her kindness in the prison cell at the citadel. Others had spoken before of his kindness. They called him weak, a Bban lover, a fool. Hihuan had never been kind.

With a grimace Zaula grasped Asan's broad, powerful shoulders and rolled him over on his back. She took a flat cushion from one of the benches and pillowed his head upon it. His skull was heavy and well shaped, with none of the narrowness common to Tlar inbreeding. She smoothed his hair back from his brow where a bruise was darkening.

Asan's sharply ridged cheekbones and long curved nose with its thin sweep of nostril were molded beneath golden skin firm and clear. A smear of dried blood stained the corner of a mouth both wide and sensitive. She could see tiny lines at his mouth and eyes as though he were a man who smiled easily. Suddenly she longed to know the color of his eyes.

He was large, even for a Tlar, and his body filled the length of the cell. She straightened his tangled legs and crossed his arms over his mid-section, moving the limbs gently as he groaned. His hands were all bone and sinew, with sensitive tapering fingers. He wore a ring of black carbyx, rarest and most precious of stones. Beneath the tattered clothing, she could feel long flat muscles as hard as iron. His chest was deep and strong. She touched a spongy place in his side and frowned as she found other marks upon his wrists and ankles. The skin had been chafed raw by his bonds.

She glared up at the glass eye watching overhead. ''Human dung, is this how you observe the culture of others? You are not worthy of—''

A panel next to one of the benches slid open, and she caught the aroma of food. She jumped up and reached for it, pulling out the tray so quickly the cups sloshed liquid over their sides. Frowning at her own clumsiness, she moved more carefully as she set the tray down on a bench. Food was never to be wasted, even strange food such as this.

She picked up a thin square wafer and started to bite into it. Then some instinct warned her to be careful. She glanced down at Asan's bruised face, hesitated, and sniffed the wafer suspiciously. It smelled more of chemicals than of the oven. She could barely detect separate ingredients and decided they must be old or taken from long storage. But nothing about it seemed dangerous.

After a moment she nibbled warily on a corner and found the taste flat and without flavor. She made a face and sampled something pale green and crunchy. It had a mild, bittersweet flavor and left her feeling as though she had eaten nothing at all. Carefully dividing half of the food for Asan when he woke up, she ate her portion and forced herself to drink the brown, bittertasting liquid in one of the cups, even though she shuddered after she swallowed it.

She lifted Asan's head and held the other cup to his lips, trying to get him to drink some of it. His lips moved. He swallowed, a trickle of the stuff spilling down his chin, and his eyes fluttered open.

They were a light blue mixed with flecks of amber, jade, and silver. Even unfocused, they brought his face alight. Her breath caught in her throat, and the resentment she had been feeling against him faded away. No matter what he had done to ruin her world, he *was* Asan. She could feel the force radiating from him, the keenness of his intelligence, the strength of his rings, the majesty that he wore so naturally.

Her hand trembled, spilling more of the liquid, and she came back to herself with a start.

"Forgive me," she said, her words stumbling. "I was trying to give thee a drink, not get thee wet."

He frowned, his eyes drooping closed, then opening wider. This time they seemed more cognizant. She forced herself to meet them without shyness or evasion. It was like staring into the gaze of a pyr, the winged, fierce lord of the skies, a taloned hunter who could swoop down in a blur of speed and snatch up its prey.

When he said nothing, but simply went on staring at her,

Zaula shifted on her knees and moved back from him. "Are thou in pain?" she asked. "Are thou hungry?"

An unreadable expression flickered in his face. He seemed almost to smile. "This is another illusion, right? One more trick, Ramer."

She drew in a sharp breath and touched his cheek for fever. He wasn't making sense.

"Does thou not remember me?" she asked, this time with a touch of the old annoyance. "I am Zaula, once leiis before thou killed Hihuan my husband and destroyed Altian my home."

He closed his eyes, letting his head fall back upon the cushion. Paleness washed through his face. "Was that coffee I tasted? Could I have some more?"

"*Coffee?*" She tested the strange word, rolling it along her tongue. "It is not pleasant. Perhaps they use it for medication?"

"No." He sounded amused.

He lifted his head, and this time she was quick to slide her hand beneath his skull in support. She held the cup to his lips, and he drank deep and thirstily until it was all gone. He seemed to like it.

"Ah," he said with a deep sigh. "That's one brew I thought I'd never taste again. Thanks, Ramer."

"I am Zaula," she said with fresh alarm.

He lifted his hand and touched her face, throat, and the full roundness of her breast where the coverall fitted too snugly. She pulled herself back, flushing.

Asan let his hand drop onto his stomach. "So you are. I was beginning to be unable to separate hallucinations from reality in there. Help me sit up."

"Thou shouldn't—"

He was struggling to do it, wobbling until she gave him assistance. He drew in several deep breaths, winced, and held his side.

"These humans," said Zaula, moving to face him. "Why did they torture thee? It is not of need—"

"Aural conditioned their minds a little to give them the idea. They think I know where a couple of their people are. They also wanted to know a few other useless things, like the defense capabilities of Ruantl. When I've rested here awhile, they'll probably come for me again."

"Even the Bban'n are not this cruel," she said, troubled.

"Look." She pointed overhead. "There are two *n'kai* who call themselves observers. Liebtz and Mike. Are they the ones who have hurt thee?"

"No." He glanced up at the glass eye, then away quickly. A frown creased his brow. "GSI observers. That means nothing but trouble."

"They put a medallion of tongues inside my arm," said Zaula, showing him the tiny pink scar. It was already fading. "I can speak to them. Did they also defile thee?"

He lifted a quick hand to the back of his ear. "No."

Zaula was surprised that he knew where they usually inserted it. "Thou are wise," she said, half to herself.

He glanced at her, starting to smile. His eyes held mischief. "No. I just know a lot about humans."

"Ah." She lifted her palm. "From the *n'ka* catalyst who raised thee in transference."

He looked startled. "Er . . . yes. Let's not discuss that. Back to these observers. What did they ask you?"

"My name. It is not permitted that *n'kai* be so impertinent, but I am done with Ruantl. I—"

"Is that *all*?"

She stared at him in puzzlement. "Yes. Why?"

"They either got more from me than I thought or else they're saving you for examination back at Central."

"Yes," she said eagerly, glad at last to know what he was talking about. "They said they were going to take me to their home planet. Is this way across the Beyond a path that goes by Tlartantla? It would honor me to see our home."

He shifted his gaze away from hers. His face grew pensive and sad. After a moment he reached out and traced the tip of one finger across the back of her clenched hand. "Zaula," he said quietly. "You will never see Tlartantla."

She stiffened. "Why? Even if the path of this transport lies not in that direction, then someday—"

"No. Forget that dream." He spread out his hand and held it flat over hers, applying pressure that meant the deepest negative. "The Tlar'n must forget the past. That's all over."

"No, it isn't!" She snatched her hand away. "We will recover the old technologies. It was Picyt and the House of Kkanthor who kept the secrets of machines hidden. But now we have a chance to recover them. We will go back. There is not one Tlar who does not believe that."

"Zaula, there is no Tlartantla."

Her head jerked. Her eyes widened in disbelief. "Thou lies."

"It was destroyed. That's why the Tlar'n came to Ruantl. The little colony here is all that remains."

"No."

"Yes. Aural, Vauzier, Rim, and I were the last to leave. We saw it die, Zaula. We cannot go back there. Ever. We can find other worlds if we choose, better worlds easier to inhabit. By this time the radiation levels should be low enough for us to search the skeletons of our empire. . . ."

His deep voice, which had grown even deeper and more resonant as he spoke, trailed off. There was silence for a long moment. Zaula could hear her own breath sawing raggedly in and out of her lungs. She did not believe it, could not believe it. From infancy she had been taught about their home. The racial memories of soft rain showers and fragrant flower meadows stirred her dreams sometimes. She felt something precious dry up and crumble inside her.

When she looked up again, her eyes stung. "Thou are the Leiil Asan, father of our fathers, the Great One of legend who led our ancestors to victory in the Duoden Conflict."

His head bowed at the formal words. "Sometimes victory has too great a price."

"Thou were supposed to protect us, to lead us home, to teach us the ways we have lost," she went on, ignoring him. "Instead, thou has destroyed everything. Thou took Anthi. Thou freed the Bban horde. Thou turned Altian into a smoking ruin. Thou brought the n'kai here. Now thou has taken even our soul, the dream we learned to live on. Get away!" she said, flinching back as he reached for her. "I will hear no more. It was wrong of thee to come back to us from the shadow land of Merdar. What little we had was better without thee!"

And with a bitter sob she turned away from him.

He sighed. "Sometimes you have to be hurt in order to grow, Zaula. Sometimes you have to tear down things in order to build. I am not finished with Ruantl. It's not going to belong to the GSI. No matter what I have to do, I promise you that."

She did not listen to him. What kind of promise was that? A worthless waste of breath upon the air.

Chapter 9

Two steps across . . . two steps back. Asan paced back and forth across the narrow end of the cell. The *Dorian Grey* was larger than the little corvette *Spitfire* he'd commandeered. Big enough to have room for a minuscule brig and a TANK. Damn that thing; he'd been out of it for hours now. How long were they going to make him wait before they took him back?

His frown deepened with scorn. Ramer had battered him without much success. Now he was trying to play mind games. That was foolish, especially since Ramer didn't strike him as one who had enough xenobiological training to be able to crack open alien psychology.

Beautiful first contact work, men, he thought. *Typical GSI heavy-handedness. Submit to us and adopt the GSI creed or die.*

He had to break out of here. He was sore still, but his legs were working now and the rest of him felt able enough. He'd devoured the portion of food Zaula had saved for him, stared at her a moment, then slid open a second wall panel and removed another tray as generously laden as the first. Zaula, her eyes wide, had watched him eat. But when he offered to share, she turned down her palm and averted her gaze. She still wasn't speaking to him. He didn't mind. He had enough to think about without letting himself be distracted by a woman whose beauty sang through his bones every time he glanced at her.

They weren't still in orbit around Ruantl. Subtle changes in the ship's vibrations told him when they pulled out and set course. Zaula had screamed when they went into implosion drive.

"It's all right," he said, putting an arm around her.

For a moment she clung to him, her body soft and delicious, her fear making her shudder.

"But something's wrong. The pattern of wholeness has been broken. We'll die—"

"Hush. We're fine," he said soothingly. Desire for her and an odd sense of protectiveness entwined through him. The softness of her hair brushed his chin, and he inhaled its clean fragrance. She wore none of the cloying perfumes usually favored by Tlar women. The simplicity made her seem exotic. And her plain coverall added to her allure in an unexpected way.

The ship bumped and shuddered. He heard a bulkhead groan, then the rough vibrations smoothed back to normal. Other than a slight giddy sensation as though the world were falling out from under his feet, he could detect no other differences in the way the ship handled. He patted Zaula's shoulder.

"Poor helmsmanship," he said, thinking of the days when he'd worked as a GSI crewer. "I don't look forward to slam with this guy at the controls."

"*Slam?*" said Zaula. She pulled away from him with an abrupt jerk. Her cheeks were stained with discomfiture.

"A human term for the process of coming out of implosion drive."

She was pleating the cloth at her knees, her head held low so that he could not see her face under the sweep of her hair. "It is still wrong. I am not a child. If we are dying, I wish to know it."

"We aren't dying. We're moving faster than light, that's all. The patterns of wholeness aren't broken. They just feel that way because we're out of sync with them right now. We're outside of time, in a manner of speaking."

"I do not understand."

He smiled. "It isn't necessary to understand. It's just a way of traveling immense distances without taking several generations to do it. Trust me."

Scorn flashed in her face, and she turned away without another word.

Now, Asan turned around and paced his two steps across the end of the cell. He paused for a moment to glance at her. She was sleeping, curled upon one of the short benches with her head pillowed on her hands.

He knew that she had been in love with Fflir. He also knew that she had hated her husband. Her beauty was exquisite enough to steal his breath, but underneath she was scarcely more than a

child, sheltered and immature. She had been cruelly handled—
her broken rings were enough to tell him that—and she had no
reason to trust him. Yet he felt responsible for her. From now
on his plans would have to include her.

But how was he going to take this ship? He couldn't seizert.
The spaces were too small, for one thing, and he was afraid to
try it while the ship moved at implosion speeds. He might reappear assembled in a new combination.

He gathered his rings and projected part of his consciousness
to the bridge. He did not try to touch any of the minds there.
Instead he just watched, observing the size and layout of the
instrumentation.

It was bigger than a scout or a corvette. Frigate-class destroy-
ers frequently had a double navigation board like the one here.
Twins or clones sat at it, working in tandem. The helm was
paired also; a man and woman in green uniforms sat there. Webbing harness hung slackly behind them. They wore linkups tying
them directly to each other and the astrogation computer.

That must get confusing at times, thought Asan to himself with
a slight leer. No wonder jump had been rough. He wouldn't have
wanted to have been linked with Saunders.

He withdrew his projection and grimaced, beginning to feel
worried. Even if he took the ship, he couldn't operate her by
himself. It would be too dangerous to work in tandem, and he
had no illusions about getting the crew to mutiny. They were all
good and proper little products of Institute programming. They
would die for the creed. They would live by regulations. They
had too much to lose if they didn't.

With a sigh, he rejected the plan he'd been turning over in his
mind. It had worked for him twice. This time it was useless.

What then?

He thought of Ramer, so serious and intent over his in-TANK
unit. Now, Ramer was a possibility. There was something odd
about Ramer.

The door opened, startling him from his thoughts. As though
conjured up, Ramer stood there. An armed guard was at his
side. Asan stared at the human, assessing the small, wiry build
that spoke of early years of malnutrition, the narrow skull and
jaw that spoke of half-breeding, inbreeding . . . *vat* breeding?

Asan caught his breath, suddenly certain of it. That would
account for the intensity Ramer wore like a shield. It was as

though he feared that if he ever let his concentration slip and made a mistake, someone would guess his secret.

Ramer's eyes were implacable. He gestured without speaking. Asan walked toward him, aware that causing any difficulty here would get him shot. They always had Zaula in reserve.

He glanced down at her as he walked between the benches. She looked young and vulnerable in her sleep. He thought, *Even if I can find a way to pull myself out of here, I may not be able to save her too.*

Once the question wouldn't have even come up. He learned the hard way, from childhood droning in the labs on to life in the back streets, that his own survival came first. No one else mattered. To trust other people was to be a fool.

But he'd trusted Giaa. He'd grieved for Saar. He still felt an awful burning rage at the thought of the bombed-out stronghold in the Tchsco Mountains. He missed Fflir. And he wanted to help Zaula.

Demos help me, I must be getting soft, he thought, and stepped past Ramer into the corridor.

"Not that way," growled Ramer with a jerk of his head. "Come on. The observers want to see you."

Asan paused in mid-step and glanced over his shoulder. He opened his mouth to make a smart remark, only to realize that Ramer's translator was bulging in his pocket, not activated in his hand. Asan froze. *Stupid!*

He tried putting on a bland look of noncomprehension, but it was too late. Ramer had read him plainly. The interrogator turned scarlet with excitement. His dark eyes bored into Asan's.

"You understood me. You followed every word. I am shielded so you can't read my mind. Are you quick enough to derive language comprehension from the few words you've heard so far? Yours is a barbarian culture, very backward, hardly likely to be skilled in modal-linguistic diagramming. Or did you already know Standard when you came aboard? Answer me!"

Asan's mind flicked through the alternatives. Continue to play dumb, pretend he was picking up the lingo even as Ramer rattled it off, claim he'd read someone's mind, admit he did know Standard, break Ramer's neck.

"*Ny,*" he said in disgust, deliberately speaking in Bban which he knew Ramer's translator wasn't set for. "*Dilgel m'a-anhr, t chielt. T'elt u pan'at cha et gri n'ka. Chi'zan ahl!*"

After the first two words, Ramer cursed and reached for his translator. Thumbing it on left him with nothing but static.

Unable to repress a grin and feeling slightly better after thoroughly insulting Ramer's intelligence and ancestry, Asan turned and started in the direction Ramer wanted him to take. As he passed the man, however, he leaned over to put his face swiftly in Ramer's and whispered two words in clear gutter Standard, "Vat boy."

Ramer's face flared scarlet again. He stiffened, glancing at the guard to see if he'd heard. With a jerk of his hand, he indicated for the guard to hustle Asan on around the corridor.

"Halt," he said as they passed a closed door marked NO ACCESS. He produced a security card and stuffed it in the lock slot. The door opened. "In there."

The guard frowned. "But, sir. That's not—"

"Damn you, follow orders! I want a private word with our prisoner before the observers get hold of him." Ramer transferred his glare to Asan and motioned. "Inside. Guard, give me your strifer."

"But, sir, that's against—"

"To hell with regulations." Ramer snatched the weapon from the man's hand and shoved Asan inside. "Stand guard behind us. This won't take long."

The door closed as lights sprang on. It was a tiny bulkhead access hatch barely large enough for the two of them. The air supply was poor, and there was no heat. Circuits, clumped in insulated cables or sealed in coolant boxes, hummed steadily. The strifer, set on maximum charge, hovered between their abdomens.

"Now," said Ramer. Color ebbed and burned in his face. "Who the hell are you and what did you mean by that remark? You do know Omari, don't you?"

Asan nearly laughed. He could see fear cramping every molecule in Ramer's thin body.

"Poor interrogation methods," he said in Tlar.

Cursing, Ramer thumbed on the translator. He looked ineffectual standing there with both hands full of instrumentation and his entire existence at Asan's mercy.

"Damn you, just answer my question!"

"Which one? There are so many."

"Omari," said Ramer, sweating in spite of the cold temperature. "He's vat grown. A renegade drone. Where—"

"I wasn't talking about Omari," said Asan. He gauged Ramer's reaction, then raised his voice two pitch levels and used command tone as he added in Standard, "I was referring to you, Ramer. And you know it."

Ramer jumped. "Demos," he whispered. The strifer shook in his hand. "That isn't true. You're just deflecting attention from yourself. It won't work. We're—"

"How much did you pay to have your ID number erased?"

Ramer's face whitened. He lowered the strifer as though his arms had gone limp, then forced it up again. "I can't . . . I didn't . . ."

"What's the penalty these days for impersonating an Institute officer? Rehabilitation, mind scrub, or vat meltdown?"

"No!" Ramer shook his head. "Your bluff won't work, Asan. You might as well forget it. Tell me where to find Omari and we'll overlook this attempt at—"

"Chin *flin*, look it in/Razor's on his way," chanted Asan. It was the old back street warning for an approaching patroller.

Ramer sagged, his mouth falling open. Asan stepped in fast past the strifer and twisted it from Ramer's grasp. With his other hand, he seized Ramer by the throat and slammed him against the bulkhead. Ramer's face twisted with pain.

"I feel the numbers," Asan said softly, rubbing his thumb along Ramer's jaw. "The scrub's very expensive and very good, but not quite good enough. You never feel safe, do you, Ramer? You never make friends. You never dare get too close to the others, do you? You're so afraid you'll be found out."

"No! No!" But the words were weak. Ramer wasn't even struggling. He was panting in fear, the fight gone from him.

"Blaise Omari crawled out. You did. There are others, a few others who have minds and guts and ambitions."

Ramer's face turned bitter. "A programming glitch in the process. Too much mental ability. A mistake—"

Asan involuntarily increased the pressure on Ramer's throat, strangling off his sentence. "Not a mistake," he said angrily, old emotions clawing through him. "The vat growth computers have automatic checks to monitor that too well. There's no way a glitch like you could be made. Omari wasn't vat born. He came from a real womb. You did too."

Ramer's eyes widened. For a moment they held only a naked desperation to believe. Then he started shaking his head. "Impossible." He was sobbing. His tears splashed onto Asan's hand.

Again Asan increased pressure on his throat. His rings encircled Ramer, confirming molecular patterns and genetic coding.

"You are real born," he said in Tlar. The words boomed from the translator still clutched in Ramer's fist. Ramer jumped. Asan met those dark eyes. "I have looked upon you in truth. You are real born."

Fresh tears welled up in Ramer's eyes. He closed them, sagging down the wall. Asan released him and let him huddle on the floor, watching him with a sour ache of pity. Ramer had taken the hard way. At some point he'd realized he was different from the other drones on his shift. At some point he'd broken out and escaped. Demos knew what he'd done to earn enough to pay for a number scrub. Asan's thoughts darkened with the memories of his own years of desperation and acts that still awakened violent shame. Then Ramer had managed to infiltrate the ranks of true citizens, establishing an identity, passing himself as normal, taking on a career, and living every day with the fear that he would be caught by Security.

It was so much easier to live on the fringes of society, stealing, raiding, sabotaging, and trying to break the Institute down. Asan wondered what his life would have been like living as Ramer had and nearly choked on revulsion.

"Why?"

It was Ramer, tugging at his wrist.

"Why did they lie? Why did they do that to me?"

The same questions turned over within Asan, rubbing a sore wound that had troubled his sleep ever since he'd transferred into this body and found his own real birth in the process. Someday he would have to seek the answers. Someday he would have to find out who he really was. Who his parents had been. Why he'd been taken from them and deceived into thinking himself a subgrade individual.

"Seeking answers for the actions of the Institute is like turning over a rock and watching *flin* slither out." Asan shrugged. "I do not know. But you, Ramer, are like Omari. Both of you are victims of a terrible crime. Perhaps the worst crime the Institute has committed."

Ramer rubbed the back of his hand across his face until the tear marks were gone. "Where is he?"

"You cannot reach him."

"I—I mean, I need to talk to him . . . ask him . . . I—"

Asan touched his shoulder. "You cannot. He is dead."

A banging on the door startled them both. Asan nearly crushed Ramer's shoulder as he turned.

"You all right, sir?" came the muffled call of the guard.

"Yes!" said Ramer.

He climbed to his feet and stood staring at Asan. His face remained pale and strained. The arrogance was gone.

"The observers are waiting," he said.

Asan's irritation flared. "Are you going to remain a GSI puppet? Are you going to continue rimming out men's guts with that in-TANK? It was your way of revenge when you thought yourself a vat boy. Vat borns versus the real borns, eh? Now whose side are you on?"

Ramer lifted a shaking hand to his temple. "I—I don't know. You could be lying to me."

"Why should I? Besides, you know I'm not."

Ramer nodded without meeting Asan's gaze. He bent over and picked up the strifer. He held it aimed slackly at Asan. "We have to go now. There isn't time for more—"

"Ramer," said Asan urgently, clasping his shoulder. "You must help me get away. Together we could take this ship, handle her. It takes at least two—"

Ramer pulled away, his expression cold and distrustful once again. "Why should I help you do anything? You aren't even human. You aren't a part of this at all. Back outside."

"But, Ramer—"

"*Move.*"

Cursing to himself, Asan had no choice but to comply. They hurried down the curving corridor, their footsteps echoing on the metal deck. A ship's bell chimed somewhere in the distance. Asan's brain was spinning so fast he was almost dizzy.

Fool, fool, fool. You stretched too far with that one. As soon as he's had a chance to think, he'll connect all those loose threads you left hanging and link you right back to Omari.

But underneath his exasperation, Asan kept a cold, angry eye upon Ramer's narrow back just a stride ahead of him. If he had a jen-knife he knew exactly where he'd plant it. One quick thrust. He'd counted on Ramer to join him against the GSI.

But that was the first lesson learned in the bleak alleys of the damned: never count on the inner man, because you won't find him. Seeking the inner man, the compassion, the sense of fair play, and the honesty will get you killed.

Asan looked up. They were stepping into a conference room already occupied by three armed guards and the two observers, one black and young, one white and older. The pattern of the younger man instantly put Asan on his guard. That one was a mental. He could hear tone qualities and speech inflections most people could not. He could hear a lie. He could sense a quickened heartbeat. He could damned near read minds. And he was doubly dangerous because correct or not, his impressions went down on record as fact on which the observers could act without seeking further authority.

Asan snapped his rings into a hard, impenetrable shield. He was in real trouble now. All Ramer had to do to guarantee his position forever was to tell them about Asan's use of Standard, his knowledge of human culture, his familiarity with the Galactic Space Institute, and his access to Blaise Omari's closest secrets. That would put Ramer firmly on the books and make him safe as never before.

Unease spread through Asan. He could not stop himself from glancing at Ramer, seeking to control him. But the blanket beam was on in this room. He could protect himself, little more.

No, Ramer. Demos and the four moons of Lli take you, don't do it. Don't sell your shabby little soul to them!

"Sirs," said Ramer, pulling himself erect in full military stance. His face was eager. "I have success to report."

"Oh?" The older observer looked bored. He shuffled through the stack of flimsies before him on the table. "Not by these accounts. The prisoner is remarkably resilient to the TANK."

"Yes, Dr. Liebtz. But progress has been made. During the rest period, certain chemicals were administered through the food."

Liar, thought Asan furiously.

"An earlier attempt to do so failed."

"Yes, sir. But not this time. During the walk here, the prisoner grew talkative and confirmed knowledge of the existence of Omari. He said . . . shall I recount verbatim, sir?"

Liebtz exchanged a glance with the other observer. Zaula had called him Mike.

"Proceed," said Liebtz.

Asan closed his eyes. He couldn't let Ramer speak. There were worse things than a TANK session, and once alerted the observers wouldn't quit. They'd never let him die, either.

He gathered his rings, struggling a little under the distracting effect of the blanket beam. It was going to hurt, but—

"The prisoner said that he was—"

Asan struck, putting all his strength into what should have been a simple blow, ignoring the agony within his own mind as the beam intensified. He felt himself washed in blue fire, and Ramer screamed. Then there was a moment of blackness.

He blinked it away to find himself weak and breathless on his knees, his head pounding as though his temples were being skewered by a stake. He saw Ramer lying crumpled on the floor. Mike knelt beside him, shaking his head. Liebtz was standing nearby, frowning. The four guards surrounded Asan, weapons pointed only inches away.

Asan drew in a deep, careful breath, feeling nothing but a cold sense of regret. Not that he'd killed, but that it had been necessary to do so.

"Prisoner."

It was Liebtz who spoke. His voice was thin and precise like a laser-scalpel. His gray eyes were cold beneath the jutting eyebrows. Asan met that gaze steadily until Liebtz shifted his away.

"He cannot be contained. The blanket beam was on maximum," Mike was saying. "Too dangerous."

"I agree." Liebtz glanced at the guards. "Kill him."

And the muzzle of a strifer was pressed to Asan's skull.

Chapter 10

The blare of a warning klaxon broke up the execution. Liebtz stared at the red alert flashing in the center of the door. The guards pulled away from Asan except for the one behind him who kept a hand on his shoulder.

"What the devil is happening?" demanded Liebtz.

"That klaxon means changeover," said Mike, scrambling away from Ramer's body. "We'd better find restraints. Guards, secure the prisoner!"

Asan had been counting ever since the klaxon first sounded. Ten seconds now to slam. Only the black had a chance of getting into the webbing he was pulling down from the ceiling. The old man wasn't space-experienced; he was too slow. The guards knew what to do, but they were stupid beefs still trying to make sure Asan didn't try anything. Asan snorted to himself and reached for the webbing dropping down near him. There was a time to make a break and a time to keep from ending up as pulp on the deck.

He had to shake off that one guard who was still determined to keep hold of him. Asan, one arm hooked into the webbing, whirled and glared at him.

"Fool!" he shouted in Standard. "If we're under attack, it'll be nothing but slam and jump from here on out. Turn loose, damn you!"

The guard's mouth sagged open in surprise, then he scrambled like the others for a harness. There weren't enough to go around. He turned on Asan and grabbed him.

"I'll take that, *flin*."

Asan was struggling to snap the buckle across his chest. The harness was too small for him, but he wasn't giving it up. He curled up his legs and kicked out at the guard, knocking him back in a flailing sprawl. *Deflate your lungs,* Asan told himself, hearing the vil-thread straps strain as he tried to force the buckle to catch.

But he'd already run out of time.

The lights flickered, and he grunted as g-force squashed him hard. It was a bad time not to have any air in his lungs, because his chest felt about five centimeters thick now and there was no way to get a breath in. He fought panic, gritting his teeth as his lungs burned. His eyes felt like they would burst from the pressure, and he shut them, telling himself his face wasn't being remolded, telling himself that he wasn't going to ooze through the straps in a few more seconds, telling himself that he could hold his breath just a little longer.

The *Dorian Grey* squawled as she slammed into normal space, her speed slowing to a crawl in comparison to what she'd been going minutes before. The ship canted sharply in a roll that sent Asan swinging dangerously close to the wall.

Engineering specs had made sure that no human would hit a wall during emergency maneuvers, but Asan was bigger than a human. On the second roll he slipped halfway out of his harness. His hip crashed into a bulkhead rib with bruising force. Pain numbed him. He lost his hold and fell to the deck, rolling helplessly into a chair base bolted to the floor. He clung to it.

Some of the other men were on the floor too, the ones who hadn't made it into harness. The deck tipped in a new direction, and Asan slid headlong through someone's blood, his hands outstretched desperately in front of him to cushion the impact of hitting the opposite wall. The jolt was hard enough to snap his left wrist.

The pain went in a white-hot bolt up his arm, and the rest of his body turned cold. A clammy sweat broke out over his body.

The deck tipped again, and he screamed.

Somehow he managed to clamp his left arm against his body as he went rolling again. A distant explosion rocked the ship. The lights and gravity cut out.

Over the shouting and moans of pain, Asan could hear his own heartbeat abnormally loud and fast. He floated up, and fresh worry filled him. He didn't want to get too far away from a hard surface in case auto-repair circuits managed to get the gravity back.

But the blanket beam was gone as well. He felt relief. His

rings snapped out and formed, a little shaky in places, but functioning again. He closed off the shooting pain in his wrist, holding the shattered bones immovable, and created dim light in the room to get his bearings.

"What the hell is happening?" shouted Mike. "What's he doing?"

Asan saw the black floating in harness at the safe end of his tether. A pad and stylus tumbled past Asan. Other bodies were off the floor. Asan frowned as he found himself over the table.

Around him the ship felt dead. For a moment he listened to the hostile silence of space; but, no, there was a faint throb of power somewhere below in the engines. Asan reached out carefully, being sure not to propel himself in the opposite direction he wanted to go, and grabbed hold of the edge of the table. He pulled himself down and reoriented himself before he let his light go out.

The ship came around, slowly, shuddering as though her port engines were gone. That she'd been attacked was obvious. Whether she was the victor or the loser remained to be seen.

Let it be pirates, he prayed. *Let them win and take us all as slaves for an illegal auction block.* Pirates he could deal with. These might even belong to Lin Ranje, and in that case . . .

No, hold on. He was making stupid assumptions. Even at maximum speed, the *Dorian Grey* couldn't be far out of the Uncharted Zone. And not even Ranje's people ventured this deep into GSI territory. Asan sighed. He'd better count on random unknowns and be ready for anything.

The lights returned without warning, momentarily dazzling him. Asan braced himself, and sure enough, the gravity followed a few seconds later. Bodies crashed to the deck, and the men in harness swung wildly. Moans filled the air. Someone was sobbing. Asan could smell sweat, the many shades of fear, and the iron-based sweetness of human blood. The ship lurched as though in one more effort, then stopped dead.

There was a long moment of silence. Asan still sat braced in his chair, his left wrist clamped against his chest, sweat pouring down his face. His hip ached, and he felt battered all over. The aches from his session in the TANK returned, making him groggy.

He waited, estimating what might be happening on the bridge and how long it would take them to try anything else if they were going to. Maybe McKey should captain this old tub in tandem. If he'd let himself be hijacked this easily he was unworthy of service to the Institute.

Asan's lips curled in a mocking smile. He released his hold on the table and glanced around. "I think we're through," he said.

No one on the floor made much effort to move. The one surviving observer unbuckled himself from his harness and snatched up a strifer off a dead guard. He circled the conference table and aimed the weapon at Asan. His dark face glistened with sweat and there was a smear of blood at the corner of his mouth.

"Back to unfinished business," he said. He sounded breathless and had to swallow a couple of times. But the strifer didn't waver. "Your execution as a—"

"*Pan'at cha*, Mike!" said Asan in exasperation.

The man's head jerked. "Don't call me Mike. I'm Powers. And you're not going to do to me what you did to Ramer."

"I won't, if you'll put the strifer down."

Powers' eyes narrowed. He stared at Asan a long moment. "You're speaking Standard. You know what a strifer is. But we're logged as the first-contact expedition to KX-5."

Anger made Asan say sharply, "The planet is Ruantl. You have no right to assign it a GSI designation."

"Well, well," said Powers softly. "You know about the Galactic Space Institute too. You are a remarkably well-informed alien."

"I am Tlartantlan," said Asan, knowing the observer was using mental now. He was being reckless in talking so much but he didn't care. "Once ruler over an empire vast enough to make the GSI seem puny in comparison."

"Sure," said Powers with a grin. "You're mighty all right. We just walked right in and took over with one application of a chem-bomb."

"I said once. No longer."

Asan sat there apparently relaxed, but inside he was gathering himself to move. No one else still alive in the room cared much about anything right now. So it was just Asan against Powers. He could take the man although the strifer made it risky. Asan hoped that if he kept Powers talking long enough the pirates or whoever they were would have time to board the ship and take over. He was confident he could talk his way around them.

''You know the people we're looking for,'' said Powers. ''Omari and Saunders—''

''Dead.''

Asan lifted a hand; the strifer jerked. Holding his breath and cursing himself for forgetting not to move, Asan slowly lowered his hand to his lap. A muscle began leaping in Powers' jaw.

''But you knew them. You learned Standard from them. You learned to think of the Institute as an enemy from Omari.''

Asan raised his brows. ''You have given me no reason to believe otherwise.''

To his surprise, Powers lowered the strifer. ''Believe me, we looked you over before we came in. In our experience a show of strength up front is the best way of dealing with primitive cultures.''

''Don't recite GSI propaganda to me! You surveyed Ruantl and found the mineral deposits. That's why you came swarming in. Ruantl will be just another planet stripped of rights and re-sources—''

The clatter of footsteps outside stopped him. Powers turned his head a fraction, then swiftly aimed his strifer at Asan, who hadn't moved. The door opened, and Asan held his breath. It would either be McKey or strangers.

It was neither.

A trio of free raiders stepped in fast, each armed with illegal SCALEX flamethrowers that seemed to fill the room. Asan could smell the heat within those long, perfed muzzles.

Washed with the cold shock of recognition, Asan saw each man with odd clarity. Two of them were humans. The third was a Vyarian half-breed who had massacred all the customers in a bar one evening on a wager that he could peel forty skulls in less than ten minutes. He'd won the bet in eight, then eaten the man who challenged him to it.

Asan stared at that face narrowed to a powerful claw at the chin and flared wide above the eyes to a thick mass of bone that protected a treacherous Vyarian brain. He did not have to see the sinew-corded limbs, the spine knobs, the scalp-belt, or the gold-braided hair tassels growing from each elbow to recognize Kor.

The Vyarian had been his last pickpocket victim. Thin, lanky, and starving, one fugitive vat boy who was nimble and quick enough to survive as a crowd thief got cocky one day and dared cut a hair tassel for its gold braid. Kor had turned on him with a bloodcurdling roar, overtaken him before he'd run a dozen steps, and snapped his legs with the ease of a child breaking twigs. That would have been the end of him, just another Vyarian meal in an alley in the back streets of a dingy Institute city, if Udge Enster hadn't come along and put a stop to it.

"Martok wants a boy," he'd said calmly, hooking his thumbs in his belt and puffing out his cheeks to spit. "You going to eat the only one we've managed to catch, Kor?"

"My meat," Kor said sullenly. He held up his elbow to show the mutilated hair tassel.

Udge frowned and gave a low whistle. "Either the boy's addled or he's got guts for brains." He stared at BLZ-80-4163, who was crouched on the stone pavement, sick with pain and terror. "The length of that hair means how old a Vyarian is. Whackin' on that takes away his age, his honor, his strength. You know that?"

"Didn't want the hair, just the braid," mumbled BLZ-80-4163 sullenly. He glanced at the Vyarian and shrugged. "No offense."

Udge threw his head and laughed. It was a bellowing guffaw that shook his whole body. After a moment Kor joined in with something that sounded like a cross between a wheeze and a growl.

"What's your name, boy?" asked Udge finally, wiping his eyes.

There was no way he would speak that hated number. Right now it was hidden beneath a smear of mud along his jaw. He thought a moment, his wits returning as he realized he was safe from Kor.

"Tobei," he said at last.

"Right." Udge clapped him on the shoulder. "You belong somewhere?"

"No."

"Wrong. You belong to Martok. Pick him up, Kor, and bring him along. If Martok likes him, we can finally blow this dustball."

From that moment on, he'd been one of the free raiders, trained in piloting, weaponry, spying, and identity changes. Until he grew up and branched out on his own. Until he became Blaise Omari, navigator on the SIS *Forerunner* and part-time blackmarketeer. Until he crash-landed on Ruantl, and his life changed totally.

Asan drew an unsteady breath. Where Kor went, Udge wouldn't be far behind. The coincidence seemed unreal, too good to be true.

For a moment there was silence in the room, then Mike Powers seemed to pull himself together.

"Pirates!" he said with loathing. "You realize the penalty for—"

"Can that, *flin!*" shouted one of the raiders. "Drop the pop and plaster."

Powers stared at him. "What?"

In a low voice, Asan said, "Put down the strifer and stretch out on the floor."

Powers glanced at him, frowning, then resolution flickered across his dark face. He swung back to face the raiders, his strifer coming up.

"No!" shouted Asan, jumping to his feet.

But he was too late. The raider had been expecting Powers to try it. The flamethrower belched once, engulfing Powers in a stream of fire that melted down the conference table behind him.

Cursing, Asan threw himself back as fast as he could, seizerting to the far corner of the room. Even then, he felt the scorching nearness of the flames. He materialized almost in a bulkhead, panicked, and slumped to his knees in relief when he came out okay. His heart was beating a frantic rhythm inside his chest. He couldn't quite catch his breath.

Demos, he'd forgotten how careless free raiders were. Gulping in air, Asan stared at the blackened lump of scrag that had been the table. Powers had been charred beyond any remains. These bloatwits ought to know that flamethrowers were long-range weapons ill-suited for close work like this. One degree less precision and there would have been a hole cut in the side of the ship.

"Found!" said Kor, pointing a black talon in Asan's direction. His yellow eyes—large, lidless, and reptilian cold—stared into Asan's. He aimed his flamethrower in Asan's direction. "Move not."

Fear gripped Asan. It had nothing to do with the flamethrower. For a moment he was paralyzed, certain that Kor recognized him.

No way, he told himself. *Don't be a fool. You're not even human now. There's no way you can be recognized.*

Finally Kor glanced away, and Asan gasped in relief. He had always known that if Martok ever released his claim on him, then he would be Kor's meat once again. Vyarians had memories about fifty times longer than their hair tassels. His arm still carried the scars from those talons. . . .

Demos, no. He must be losing his mind. Asan glanced down at his right arm, so much longer, so much more powerful than the original. The scars he bore now belonged to wars he hadn't fought. He winced, shying away from it all. He'd better get himself together or he'd be screaming next.

"Deck check complete," said a voice which, like Kor's face, still haunted Asan.

Udge Enster—smaller, skinnier, stooped, burnt brown from the tropical sun of Martok's headquarters, his bony head shaved and oiled so that it glistened in the ship's lighting—stepped into the conference room and glanced around at death and carnage without so much as a blink. His cheek puffed, and he spat.

"Been wasting fire, Hux?"

Asan closed his eyes as that dry, laconic voice brought back memories he wanted to forget. The raider stammered some answer; Udge always knew who'd fired out of place. The raiders never could figure out how he knew. It kept them scared of him. It kept them in line. Only Kor wasn't afraid of Udge, but then Kor wasn't afraid of anything he could eat. Kor and Udge had a different kind of bond, one that had never been explained.

"All GSI humans aboard," Udge was saying. "Except one little dandy in the brig. She's—"

"Female?" rumbled Kor, his head coming up. The chin claw—so handy for slashing throats—quivered a little. Kor was endlessly fascinated by females of all species.

"None of that now," said Udge sharply. "We're on a job, and we stay on that job until Omari is located."

Worried, Asan rose to his feet. They had come out this far tracing him. Martok was notorious for never letting anyone double-cross him. But they were looking for someone who was impossible to find. Asan was safe . . . at least, he was providing they didn't decide he was flotsam and kill him.

Udge glanced at him and blinked in a double-take, his eyes lifting up and up to meet Asan's. They stared at each other a long while. Asan's self-confidence began to return. For the first time in his life he wasn't under Udge's thumb, taking orders, taking *flin*. Udge's eyes were like glass, opaque with surprise.

Asan decided to grab his advantage and put on full Tlar pomposity.

"Choi'heirat. Za," he said, turning up his palm. "I am Asan, Tlar leiil of the people of Ruantl. It was of need that my captors' blood be spread upon the sand. You have my thanks."

He waited, appearing calm and noble, while Udge looked him over. He saw Udge take notice of the ring of black carbyx. He could almost see Udge estimating its value.

Udge shoved his strifer into its holster and put his left hand in a capacious side-pocket of his stained brown vest. It had at least a dozen other pockets, all of various sizes, most of them bulging until the fastenings strained. He stepped forward until he was only two arm's lengths from Asan and cocked his bald head to one side.

"You a GSI prisoner?"

"Yes."

"What's your crime?"

"Wealth."

Interest flickered in the opaque eyes. "That little dandy in the brig belong to you?"

Asan hesitated a moment, thinking of how much Zaula hated him. "Yes."

Udge grinned. His teeth were small, stained, and pointed. "How much wealth?"

Asan removed his ring and tossed it to Udge. "It is a common stone," he said, putting indifference in his voice. "Normally I would be arrayed in better attire, but I have been in the TANK." He lifted his palm. "You may have the ring if it pleases you."

Udge turned pale under his tan. He held his palm flat with the ring centered on it. The other men were silent, hushed with awe in the presence of something as priceless as carbyx.

If only I still had my corybdium jen-knife to wave around, thought Asan with regret.

The black stone drank in the light, reflecting nothing in its polished surface. Martok was one of the richest persons alive, and to Asan's knowledge he possessed only three small carbyx stones. Those were protected in their own special vault. Certainly he would never toss one to his men as a gift.

The struggle was plain in Udge's face. But at last he tossed it back to Asan, who caught it in relief that the bluff had worked.

"We are not permitted to take bribes," Udge said coldly.

Asan lifted his brows. "You are wealthy raiders."

Someone laughed bitterly. Udge snapped his head around, and the laughter stopped.

"Hux, you and Beanie report back to Wyton. Clean out this ship and get her ready to tow."

The two humans shouldered their flamethrowers and shuffled out. Kor began wandering around the room. Asan watched his seemingly aimless progress warily.

"We're looking for a fellow named Blaise Omari," said Udge.

Asan did not have to pretend his weariness. "That name again. Are all humans on the trail of this *n'ka*?"

"You know him?"

"He is dead."

"Is he now? That's too bad." Udge exchanged a glance with Kor. "My boss ain't gonna like that. He was sort of wantin' to kill Omari himself."

Asan shrugged. "His blood was spread upon the sands long ago . . . before season. Ruantl is a harsh world. Few live long."

"Oh, I don't know. Omari had quite a knack for wrigglin' out of tough spots." Udge scratched his chin. "I can think of several times when I thought sure he was a goner, but, nope, out he'd come again. You say he's dead."

"Yes."

"You see him die?"

"Yes."

"Hmm." Udge frowned. His cheeks puffed, and he spat. Then he drew out his left hand from his pocket where it had been all this time. He was holding a small meter that blinked a tiny yellow light.

"Funny you should say that, Tobei. You see, a long, long time ago I put a thwart in you so that if you ever did decide to run out on us, we'd have a way of finding you."

Coldness sank through Asan. He stiffened, his gaze locked on the meter. Disbelief and despair warred inside him. It was impossible. He'd have known if there was a thwart inside his subconscious. Maybe not before when he was human, but surely the rings of life would have told him. . . .

"I'm impressed, Tobei," Udge went on. "I really am. Not only have you grown about three feet and changed color, you're even rich now. That's very good. No one else I've trained has ever pulled something like this off."

Desperately Asan shook off his numbness. Trying to ignore Kor, who had circled around behind him and was now breathing down his neck, Asan said, "You are mistaken. I am Asan, Tlar leiil of—"

"Tobei, Tobei, don't play games with us." Udge shook his head reprovingly. "We're family, remember? At least we were until you did us dirty. Martok's sore. But you know that. That's why you're hiding. That's why you're trying to lie to me."

Kor rumbled deep in his throat. His talons grasped Asan's shoulder and gave him a shake.

"I knew Blaise," said Asan. "But I am not he. That meter is wrong. It's reading certain memory patterns picked up during transference—"

"Transference," said Udge. "That's an interesting word. Martok will like it."

"I was in preservation," said Asan, beginning to sweat. "Blaise was the catalyst required to resurrect me. His life force was used to reactivate my own. He died in the process. Look at me! I am no puny human with striped eyes! I am Tlartantlan."

"It's a good trick, but a thwart is designed for tricks like yours. A thwart doesn't lie."

Asan swung around, aiming for Kor's eyes. His blow missed, however, and Kor clamped a hand unerringly on Asan's broken wrist. The pain barrier broke, and a flash of heat followed by icy chills went through Asan. He screamed, going down on one knee as Kor ground the shattered bones together. Asan's rings snapped out desperately. Kor staggered back from the blow, but he did not fall. Growling, he shook his wedge-shaped head as though to clear it and aimed the flamethrower.

"Kor, no!" shouted Udge, and stepped between Asan and Kor with his strifer aimed right between Asan's eyes. "He is Martok's meat. Get him confined. Now."

Kor hesitated as though he would argue, but finally he came forward with the flamethrower at rest against his shoulder. He grabbed Asan's wrist again, but more gently this time.

Still, Asan closed his eyes against a wave of despised weakness that kept him from making another try to escape. He'd be smarter, and healthier, to wait until he got back to Martok. He still had Ruantl to offer on a deal; only now, instead of bargaining for mutual gain, he'd be bargaining for his life.

Chapter 11

Kor paused outside the door to the brig and glanced slyly at Asan, who was trying hard to ignore the iron grip on his injured wrist. Asan frowned back. It was physically impossible for Vyarians to mate with any other species, but just the same Kor's sexual scents were repulsive. And Asan didn't like the idea of Kor even thinking about Zaula.

"She's probably pulp on the floor," he said. "You skyflies banged this ship around pretty hard."

Kor grunted. "Still in one piece."

Asan frowned again, unsure if Kor meant the girl or the ship.

Kor touched the security panel, and the brig door opened. Zaula sprang to her feet, saw Kor, and her face went smooth and blank with horror. Kor grinned at her. She flung up both hands and screamed. She stumbled back to the far end of the cell and went on screaming.

"It's all right," said Asan, shoving Kor aside and going in. He took Zaula's arm and gave her a little shake. "Zaula. Stop it. It's all right."

She didn't stop. He clamped his hand over her mouth. Her breath was hot against his palm; the scream was instantly muffled.

"It's all right."

She stood rigid against the wall, her eyes enormous above his hand, her face dark with fear. He wasn't sure she'd seen him, much less heard him.

"*Zaula.*"

He spoke in command tone that time, and her gaze flickered to his. She blinked, and he heard her breath catch in her throat. She reached up and gripped his hand, pulling it away from her mouth.

112

"Wh-what is it?" she whispered.

"His name is Kor," said Asan calmly. "He is a Vyarian. He won't hurt you."

Kor chose this introduction as his invitation to enter the cell. Zaula screamed again, pressing herself back in the corner. Asan turned angrily.

"Demos, Kor! Can't you see you're scaring her out of her wits? Go away. You can stare at her through the observation cam."

"Confine," said Kor. His slanted eyes shone queerly in his wedge-shaped face. "Orders."

"We're in the brig—"

"Wrong ship." Kor crooked a talon. "Both come."

Asan looked at him sharply. "Is Udge going to flush this one?"

Kor wheezed his version of a laugh. "Come now. When clean, you come back."

Flushing a ship meant jettisoning its crew. There would be a few less GSI loyalists around. Asan had no sympathy for anyone stupid enough to sign up with the Institute. He grinned back at Kor, momentarily feeling the old ties.

"Right," he said, and glanced at Zaula, who was frowning as though she hadn't understood a word. He held out his hand to her. "We're transferring to the other ship. *An*."

She hesitated. "Our masks. We—"

"We don't need them, Zaula," he said gently, trying to give her time to adjust to these cultural shocks without making Kor impatient. "There's no harmful radiation here."

"Of course," she said scornfully. "I was thinking of protocol."

Asan laughed. "Free raiders don't have any."

Her expression remained serious, but to his relief she came docilely enough. When she passed Kor, however, he reached out and scratched her across the cheek, drawing blood.

She gasped and flinched away.

Furious, Asan stepped between her and Kor, aiming a quick blow that Kor dodged easily.

"Damn you, she isn't your meat! You've no business marking her—"

Kor struck with his chin claw. Asan jumped back, throwing up his left arm to protect his throat. The claw cut deep, bringing a spurt of dark blood. Asan pulled in his rings and formed his force field in time to repel the finishing slash. Kor staggered back, plainly startled, and with a growl he snapped the flame-thrower down from his shoulder to firing position. Grimly Asan faced him and extended his force field to encompass Zaula.

"Isn't that weapon a little big for this small space?" he asked, hiding all fear from his voice. "The backlash will fry you along with us."

But to his surprise, Kor was grinning. "You are marked, To-bei," he growled. "New body no matter. You are both marked."

Asan swore, relaxing from his battle stance. "Fool," he said in exasperation. "Martok—"

"It will please the One to let me carve you," said Kor. He wheezed and pointed at the door. "He is just."

"I am not his meat, and I am not yours," said Asan angrily, clutching his wrist. Blood ran between his fingers. He dropped the force field and closed the wound. The effort sapped him. Suddenly he felt very tired. He ached everywhere, not just in his arm. "I am going to make a bargain with Martock that he can't refuse. I am going to make him richer than all his free raiding and cooperatives combined."

"Money small when time to eat," said Kor, unimpressed. He pointed at the door. "Go. Now."

Asan glanced at Zaula. They had no choice. They went.

"It was wrong," Zaula said quietly, "to take our jen-knives from us. Aural has betrayed us to the blood. We cannot even fight the demon. We are in shame."

Asan sighed and opened his eyes. He'd been trying to sleep and couldn't. He was too tired. He ached too much. The food they'd eaten had been rich and greasy; it lay heavily in his stomach.

Zaula walked over to his bunk and knelt beside him. She had knotted her hair back from her face. The formality suited her. He envisioned her in court robes and gowns of delicate pria cloth, rustling when she moved, scented mysteriously, half hidden in the shadows of the Court of Women. He hated the GSI uniform she wore. He wished she would find something else to put on.

Then he frowned at his own thoughts. Since when had he

cared what a woman wore or did not wear? He should be thinking about what he was going to say to Martok.

"My leiil."

Zaula knelt there with her head bowed, waiting to be acknowledged. Her husky voice was quiet and low, her tones
neutral. Her previous hostility was gone.

He sat up, wincing. "My leiis?"

The flippancy did not take the serious expression from her
face. Instead, the smoother amber of her cheeks stained a dark
brown. She frowned, looking away from him.

"I'm sorry," said Asan. "You aren't used to joking—"

"Oh, but I am. My husband delighted in mockery. He was
famous for his barbs."

"A joke is for people to share, not laugh at one's expense."
She seemed caught by that. She glanced up straight into his
eyes, a slight frown still creasing her brow. "Thy speech is
truth. Thou are strange to me."

"Why?"

"Because thou has shown me honor by thy courtesy. Because
thou fought for me against a demon."

Asan frowned, suddenly uncomfortable. He shifted on the
bunk. "Kor is a barbarian. I would have done as much for anyone."

One corner of her mouth curled up in a faint smile. She
touched the scratch on her cheek as her eyes looked deep into
his. "Would thou? I do not believe it."

"You're right." He smiled back. "Not for just anyone. I think
people should usually fight their own battles."

"But not me?"

"Yes, you. Only . . ." He gestured, struggling to find the
words. "Not as long as you think he is a demon. He isn't. He's
smelly, vicious, stupid, and damned dangerous, but there isn't
anything mystical about him. All Vyarians are like him, except
he's a half-breed so that makes him bigger and stupider than
most of them."

Zaula sighed. "Thou started to say something else. What?"

"Nothing."

Annoyed by her questions, he flicked a finger in a signal for
her to go away. She ignored it.

"We are enemies. That is why I question thee. I must understand why—"

"Why what?" he said irritably. "Why I haven't grabbed you by the hair and slit your throat? Why I haven't left you to fend for yourself? Why I haven't refused to treat you like a piece of chattel instead of a person of worth? It's very simple, Zaula. I . . . well, I . . . Damn."

He stood up, stepped around her, and began to pace across their quarters. They were locked into an ordinary cabin since Enster's ship didn't have a brig. It was both opulent and comfortable, but the pleasant treatment so far only made him nervous.

Just as Zaula was making him nervous now. Why couldn't she just sit in a corner, look pretty, and be quiet?

"Is it because I have lost rank?" she asked after a moment. "Is it a kindness to me?"

"We *aren't* enemies," he snapped, turning on her. "We never have been."

"Thou are the usurper. Thou killed Hihuan and robbed my child of—"

She broke off, an odd expression crossing her face.

"That's right," said Asan, hoping she finally was beginning to understand. "Hihuan, your husband. Didn't you also try to kill him?"

She gasped, rising to her feet. "How—"

"You forget I knew Fflir," he said, and watched her face lose color. "He told me all about the court intrigues going on. Hihuan was hated, and he treated you like *flin*."

She stood so still it was as though she had even ceased breathing. "Yes," she said softly, her gaze staring at nothing. "He broke my rings when he . . . I think he hoped I would die. Instead Cirthe was conceived. She carries his blood, his line. Is—is she like him? Is she as horrible as he? Thou called her a monster."

"Yes," Asan said. "I have not looked upon you with truth, Zaula, but I do not think there is anything of you in her."

Zaula closed her eyes as though to hide the hurt that showed so plainly upon her face. "If I had not born her, the nobles would have demanded my death when Hihuan died. She was my only means of living. My only means of clinging to some small bit of importance. Not to hate thee, Asan, meant surrendering my very existence."

"I know," he said gently. "But whatever you have heard about me, I want you to know that I do not follow Tlar protocol and precedent blindly. Most of it is nonsense. Had my jen come into Altian as we planned, you would not have been harmed.''

"I think I believe that." For the second time she gave him her shy smile. "At least I am free now."

"Free?" He frowned in puzzlement. "Hardly. We are prisoners—"

"It is not of importance. We have heat, light, food. We are surrounded by wealth. These *n'kai* know nothing of what it means to be Tlar. They have looked upon my face. I wear the forbidden garments of—" She broke off, blushing. Then she laughed, flinging out her arms. "There is no one to know my lineage or the honor of my house, no one to spy and point fingers, no one to say what I must do next without asking my own will."

She whirled herself around, then stopped. She looked self-conscious, and the mask returned. "Thou thinks me a fool. Thou looks upon me with pity. I am so tired of pity!"

"I don't pity people," said Asan curtly. "And I don't pity myself. Neither should you."

"Do I?"

"Do you?"

Her gaze fell. "Yes, thou are wise. Thou sees in the way of the priests—"

"*Chielts!*"

"Oh. I had forgotten how much thou hates them. Thou destroyed the Kkanthor-kai."

"No," he said with irritation. "I destroyed their house. The Bban'n hunted them down."

She spread her fingers. "Such precise distinctions."

"It would seem you learned the art of mockery from your husband."

"I—I'm sorry. But it is hard not to be angry, not to resent the harm thou brought us. Because of thee, Anthi left us to be cold, to sit in the dark, to starve, to be afraid." Her voice quivered. "I have been afraid for so long—"

"Hush."

Suddenly she was in his arms, huddled against his chest. He breathed in the fragrance of her, reveled in the softness of her. His irritation faded away as he forced himself to look at his actions from her point of view. An unpleasant sensation spread through him. For the first time he felt cruel and ugly as though he had been unnecessarily harsh.

He had acted to save himself in shutting down the main-support computer. He couldn't worry about all the others it would affect. Taking responsibility for others was an occupation for fools, or for people who were safe. He'd never been safe, never known security, never had the luxury of being able to relax and not watch his own back.

Giaa had made him care as much for her as he did for himself. And now it was happening again with Zaula. He *was* getting soft. His brain was soap; soon it would be dribbling out his ears.

He pushed Zaula abruptly away and turned his back on her. He stood beside the game table, picked up one of the cubes, and fidgeted with it. The silence seemed unbearable.

"You don't understand," he said. His voice came out loud and harsh. "We're in big trouble. As soon as we dock, I—" He broke off, unwilling to tell her he would walk to the hand of death. He'd been cruel enough; she might as well keep her illusions a short while longer. Martok might like her, and then she would be all right. He sneered at himself for his worry. The people who deserved to survive did so.

"Thou are afraid," she said in amazement. "The one who rules the demon . . . thou fears him."

The cube crumbled in Asan's fingers. He turned sharply.

"Yes," she said before he could speak. "I may not be able to look upon thee with truth, but there are other ways of perception. Ever since the *n'kai* of this ship killed those of the Institute, thou has worried. Thou knows these humans. Thou has dealt with them before."

"No."

"And before, on Ruantl. Thou kept warning everyone of what the humans would do. Thou knew them as though thou had walked among them. Thou knew them as though thou were one thyself . . ."

She gasped.

Asan threw up his head and met her horrified gaze.

"It's true," he said, trying to keep his voice steady. "You've guessed correctly. The *n'ka* Omari was used as the catalyst for—"

"This is known," she said impatiently. "Did thou retain all

the *n'ka* knowledge? Is it not a defilement to thee to feel the *n'ka*? Why did Picyt not arrange—''

''To hell with this!'' said Asan, clenching his fists. ''Your high and mighty priest was too scared to do it himself. He was unwilling to die in the service of his Tlar leiil. So he stuck me with it instead. I didn't care much; I was dying anyway.''

She stepped back, her eyes enormous. ''It cannot be—''

''Oh, yes, it can.'' He thumped his chest. ''I'm Blaise Omari, the *n'ka* who crash-landed in your toxic desert and was shot for sport by your husband. I was supposed to die in the transference process; only I didn't. So here I am in Asan's body. It's like a suit of clothes, a mask, a disguise to hide in.''

Her mouth was open; she seemed to have difficulty speaking. ''And—and he?''

''Gone. Mostly. At night when I dream, the memories overlap. I remember people I never knew. I recall events I never experienced. Sometimes I don't know who I am or where I am. Fflir helped me through the roughest parts at first. He was the only one who knew the truth . . . until now.''

He let the words die out. It was too hard to keep stripping away layers of himself. If he didn't stop talking now he'd be babbling out the whole long stupid story.

Whatever he expected—disgust perhaps—she didn't exhibit it. Instead she walked up slowly to him and placed her fingertips upon his chest. She frowned, grimacing with concentration, and he felt the tiniest, briefest contact with his rings.

She staggered back, looking as though she might fall. He reached out involuntarily as though to steady her, but she evaded his grasp.

''That,'' she said breathlessly, ''is why the great Asan has not acted in the manner expected of a legend. That is why there is kindness and courtesy. That is why we are not enemies in spite of all that said we must be. Lli take me, but I am amazed.''

She sank down upon one of the chairs at the game table and stared at him. He sat down across from her, feeling winded, and stared back.

Then his gaze fell from hers and he stared at the hands that were his and yet not his. No matter what he did, he remained a shadow. The old bitterness came back, and he caught himself rubbing his jaw where his number had been on his old body. But even BLZ-80-4163 did not exist. That essential core of his being had been eliminated too when he found out that he was human born, not vat grown. So he did not even have knowledge of his true origins now.

Who was my mother? he wondered as he had too many times in the dark, cold nights of season when he shivered alone in fear of his nightmares. *Who was my father? Why was I raised in Laboratory 80? Why the deception?*

"There are no answers," he told himself, then realized with a start that he had spoken aloud.

"Leiil, what will happen from these *n'kai*?"

"You don't have to address me formally now . . . now that you know," he said, frowning. "It is permitted to say you when speaking to me." Then he grinned, remembering an odd scrap of his scanty education. "Did you know, Zaula, that in the old days of human history they considered 'thou' a familiar usage and 'you' the formal one? Just the reverse of the Tlar way."

"Does it hurt so much, that a joke must be made of it?" she asked softly. "I am honored by thy gracious permission, noble leiil. You took the title with the body, did you not? You called it a mask. Have there been others?"

"Yes." He rubbed his face wearily. "Too many. I used to be proud of my disguises. I used to boast that I could assimilate anywhere among anyone. But this is my last disguise. Martok was my boss for a while. I owed him something which I failed to pay. He is planning on my execution." Asan laughed bitterly. "I though I wouldn't be recognized as a Tlar. I was wrong."

"The *n'kai* are very clever with their machines. But I do not understand. Why do you hide yourself? Why did you begin?"

He shook his head, then caught himself and turned his palm down instead. "The reasons are old ones. The story is too long."

She lifted her brows. "Is there not time? I would like to hear it."

"I'm not an entertainer!"

"And I am not a bored child."

They glared at each other for a long moment, then Asan sighed.

"Very well," he said, and began.

Chapter 12

Martok's base was an ancient space lab of immense size, built by an alien species and abandoned long before any human ventured into the Cyngus Minor quadrant. It had a cylindrical center with long docking arms spiraling out from the top and bottom, making it look like two spiders back to back. Beyond it hung the planet Ghirdana, vast at this close range, intensely blue and green beneath her white cloak of atmosphere.

Released from tow by Enster's ship, the *Dorian Grey* was tractored into the vast docking hangar. When she next emerged, her GSI hull configuration would be a different color and slightly different shape, her number would probably be private license or merchant, her engines would bear illegal modifications, and she would have a false hold. Her name would be struck, and she would be rechristened something exotic and alien, like *Ramsetahtek* or *Vzzkxy Nt*.

Asan stood at the observation port of Enster's ship, one hand pressed against the tempered glas-tel. His tall figure, still clad in its tattered jen uniform, was silhouetted against the starry glitter of space. Then the ship turned about, and the planet filled the port with a beauty that made his throat ache. Ghirdana had one satellite; it hung between the base and the planet like a small, barren ball.

Zaula, fascinated by her first sight of a base congested with ingoing and outgoing traffic, kept coming up beside him, giving faint moans and turning pale, then stepping back. Asan turned his head and smiled at her. The port was designed to give a view on three sides, so that if he glanced down he could see space black and empty and infinite below his boots as well. That's what kept getting to Zaula.

As soon as the ship came out of changeover, Hux had come

121

to their cabin with an officer to escort them to the port if they wanted to watch docking. He stood on guard now at the door, a .28 max jambolt long-range cradled loosely in his arms, his eyes heavy-lidded but alert, his stance a slouch that would permit him to move quickly if necessary.

Asan felt a faint twinge of amusement. Enster was overestimating his sense of desperation. He wasn't going to try anything.

He drank in the sight before him as ships of all sizes and configurations maneuvered with precision. Most were square-bottomed contraband runners coming in to unload cargo that would be repackaged and relabeled and reloaded onto legitimate freighters for delivery to legal markets. A beautiful sloop with rakish lines that made him gasp with admiration passed them on her way out. He turned to keep her in sight as long as possible. She probably belonged to one of Martok's executives who'd come in for personal orders.

He'd served on a ship like that once as a steward. Martok's friends were giving an in-flight party, and it was Martok's way of testing him to see if he could be trusted away from Udge Enster's eye. Asan smiled to himself, remembering the plush decor and gold fittings, the sultry-eyed beauties—male, female, and neuters—who lounged about to be sampled along with buffet tables of delicate bin-fish strips, caviar, *piree*, froths, san-san, and other delicacies he couldn't even identify.

Traffic was heavy today. There was even a GSI patroller orbiting at maximum range, ignored and ineffectual. Martok allowed them to come by occasionally to look at what they could not have. This system with its three inhabitable planets, sophisticated spaceport, famous interplanetary genetics research facility, University of Ghirdana, and Martok's HQ was located in Commonwealth territory and was legally outside the jurisdiction of the Institute.

It was their ship's turn to dock. Asan pressed his whole body against the glas-tel, making Zaula gasp, in order to see the angle of entry. Remembering his own days as a ship's navigator, he watched critically a flawless example of precision handling. Wild they might be, but free raiders could fly.

A tone chimed overhead as they were engulfed in the dark maw of the hangar. The interior lights came on, bathing them in a muted glow designed not to interfere with the panorama of space. But now, however, the view was limited to glimpses of the hangar filled to capacity with ships moored in freefall berths. The interior lights blinked twice as ship's power switched off and base came on. Asan could feel a slight drift beneath him in the gravity support. The tone chimed a second time.

"Are our bodies going to fly into the air again?" asked Zaula in alarm.

"No."

Asan turned and stepped down from the port. Its shields closed behind him. Hux straightened from his slouch, no longer looking sleepy.

"Flake down," he said.

Asan glanced at Zaula, who was frowning in bewilderment. "We have to wait," he said.

"His speech does not translate," she said, tapping her arm.

"It's not supposed to," said Asan.

She looked even more puzzled, but before he could explain thief lingo Udge Enster came in.

Udge had exchanged his drab coverall and vest with the bulging pockets for a scarlet costume with tight legs and flared sleeves. It looked expensive and was probably the latest style. On him, with his bald head, weatherbeaten face, and bulging cheeks, it looked ridiculous. He had abandoned the strifer always worn on his hip. Its absence made him seem naked.

He grinned at Asan as though he knew exactly what Asan was thinking, and shoved up one wide sleeve to show a wicked-looking dart fitted to his forearm.

"Cute, ain't it? Takes a precise muscle flex to fire it. I had to practice a long time."

"Is it the latest style in personal weapons?"

"Sure. Imported from Negus V. They're always assassinating diplomats there. This is great in a crowd. I'd teach you how to use it sometime, Tobei, but—"

He broke off with another grin and spat.

"You and the little dandy ready? Martok's waiting."

Asan blinked in surprise. "He's here?"

"Naw. Tobei, you know better than that. Martok never comes here. We're going all the way in." Udge looked suddenly serious. "And you ain't gettin' away, see? You ain't pulling any scramble-dodge on me."

Asan pretended to look innocent. "Would I do something like that, Udge?"

"Sure you would. I know you, Tobei. You've been gone a long time. Ever since you first began to run on Martok's leash, you've been forgettin' how well I know you. So you're thinking right now that as soon as we pop ship, you'll break and catch one going out. Only that won't happen."

"Even if I vanish into thin air?" asked Asan. He snapped his fingers. "Just like that."

Udge gripped his arm. "Where's your heart now, Tobei?"

Asan pointed at the middle of his chest.

"I got a straight line to it as long as I hold your arm at this angle. Don't forget the darts, Tobei. They're powered. They're faster than you."

Asan couldn't hold back his smile. "I don't think so."

"And what about the little dandy? Can she vanish too?"

Asan's smile faded. He'd forgotten. For a moment he was angry at her.

But he shrugged. "You're forgetting something with all these careful preparations, Udge."

"What?"

"I should be flattered. You think more of my abilities than you used to."

"Can that. What have I forgotten?"

"That I want to see Martok just as much as he wants to see me. I was on my way to him when you picked me up."

Udge bellowed with laughter, shaking so that Asan was afraid he might accidentally trigger a dart.

"Oh, Tobei, you bloatwit," he said at last, wiping his eyes. "You never could lie."

"It's true. I have a deal to offer him—"

"*Flin!* You were a GSI prisoner on your way to detention. A deal? Demos! Right now you're squirming in your skull while you try to think up some way to get loose. I could always see you squirm, Tobei. It's in your eyes. Even in those weird alien eyes. Martok ain't gonna deal with you. If you'd come straight in when Security first got on your tail, then maybe. But not now."

Asan gave it up. Udge wasn't going to believe anything he said.

They disembarked into an airlock, passed through an alarming soft tunnel that billowed and shifted and made Asan nervous.

He was always afraid the thing would puncture while he was in it, and he'd die eating space.

Udge kept a tight grasp on his left arm, walking close. Asan's wrist had been treated for the break, but it still ached. Tlar cellular structure was different enough from human to alter the length of treatment time necessary for complete healing. But no one was much interested in his health. After all, he was scheduled for execution soon.

Behind him, Hux brought Zaula along. Kor was not in sight. Asan was relieved to be spared the Vyarian.

At the end of the soft tunnel, they passed through a second airlock directly into another ship. Udge really was taking no chances.

Asan took the seat assigned him and strapped in. It was a narrow shuttle, the kind used for short flights and planet hopping. He was beginning to feel depressed. Udge tuned out everything he said. Martok was likely to be even less reasonable. He might never get the chance to offer his deal. He might be going straight to Kor's dinner table.

Frowning, he braced himself for the whiplash takeoff customary with shuttles. Zaula and then Udge spoke to him, but both times he remained deep in thought and did not answer.

"He's gettin' nervous," said Udge to Zaula. "Tobei always was nervy when the game was on. It gave him an edge. It gave him a mouth too. Martok's gonna like to see him this way. Martok likes 'em scared when they die."

Zaula gave him a cold look. "It is not permitted for a *n'ka* to spread the blood of a Tlar *leiil*."

"Sure, babe. Sure." Laughing, Udge patted her knee. "Whatever you say."

The short run took fourteen hours. Asan slept in his seat and awoke with a jerk to find his neck stiff and his body cramped. He rubbed his gritty eyes and unsnapped to get up.

Udge's hand hit his chest and shoved him back. "You crazy? We're about to land."

Sighing, Asan settled back in the uncomfortable seat that was not designed for someone of his size. The pilot was the casual type who preferred to show off his skills rather than remember he was carrying passengers. They swooped down so fast Zaula was sick upon the carpet.

"Aw, hell," said Udge in disgust. He frowned at Zaula, who was looking distinctly yellow. "You want to end up on the auction block, little dandy? Get yourself prettied up now."

She stiffened in outrage, but before she spoke Asan caught her eye and turned down his palm. For a moment she looked like she would explode anyway, but instead she managed to remain silent.

They landed with a flair that wasted fuel, the engines screaming in reverse rev. The hatch opened. Udge sprang to his feet and stood where Asan could not jump him.

"Don't worry," Asan assured him. "I'm not going to try to take the shuttle. You're getting nervous in your old age."

"I'd rather be old and nervous than dead," Udge muttered.

Light stabbed into the dim interior of the shuttle from outside. With it came scents of natural air, warm and tangy with sea salt.

"You first, Tobei."

Asan bent double to go through the hatchway and descended the steps into pellucid, yellow light so intense he squinted and lifted a hand against the glare. The sun was directly overhead in a sky tinted a pale green. Its heat scorched him through his clothes. He drew himself up to his full height and stretched, enjoying the sensations. He'd been cramped and cloaked and shivering for so long on Ruantl, he'd almost forgotten how nice weather could be on a decent Class-M world.

The shuttle had landed in the center of a circular, spacious pad paved with tarmac that was sticky in the heat. On two sides the vastness of the sea boomed and crashed into the shore, sending up plumes of spray. Webbed fliers flapped and dove, plunging into the water only to emerge into the sky seconds later with fish wriggling in their beaks. Squat trees with thorny trunks and lacy, blue-gray fronds rustling in the breeze were planted at the edge of the landing pad. Somewhere out of sight in the distance Asan could hear female voices and laughter.

It was idyllic, except for the squad of armed guards standing alert on the pad to meet him.

Udge greeted the officer in charge of villa security—a squat, one-eyed man wearing a blue badge on the breast of his tunic. Asan recognized him as Colonel Pared, a man who had, in his youth, led his home world in a rebellion against the GSI. When that failed bloodily, he became a notorious gun-runner and guerrilla leader on scat tactics across the galaxy until Martok hired him. Pared was on more wanted lists than anyone could count. He had saved Martok from two takeover assassination attempts. He was, perhaps, the only member of the organization Martok trusted, and even then Martok never failed to raise Pared's salary every year.

Pared's one eye glared at Asan, who hastily reminded himself that he was a Tlar leiil and met that hostile gaze as steadily as he could. It was impossible, however, not to look past Pared at the domed roofline of the villa beyond, where sentries stood silhouetted against the green sky. A protection drone, lethal and hair-trigger sensitive, hummed by overhead.

"Enster, is this a joke?" snapped Pared.

Udge's weathered face reddened. He held out the thwart meter. Pared stared at the blinking yellow light but did not take the meter. After a second Udge pocketed it again.

"I don't know how he did it this time, but we don't call ole Tobei the chameleon for nothin'."

"Impossible," said Pared. "You have netted an impostor. Blaise Omari must have found the thwart, removed it, and planted it on this alien."

Hope lifted in Asan. If Pared didn't trust the meter, Martok might not either.

"Planted it?" repeated Udge angrily. "How? You designed the damned thing, Pared. You said it's impossible for the wearer to detect it. Besides, he's done admitted he's Tobei."

Pared's one eye shifted back to Asan.

"A lie," said Asan in Tlar, well aware that Pared's translator implant was twice as sophisticated as Institute equipment. "I am—"

"We're wasting time," said Pared, turning away. "There'll be no reward for you, Enster. But since you brought something in, the men need target practice. Men, close ranks!"

The guards circled in around Asan and Udge. The muzzles of their max jambolts pointed at Asan. He knew a moment of blind, gut-clutching fear. Then he grabbed Udge's arm.

"I won't be splattered across this tarmac alone, Udge."

But before he could move, Udge shouted, "Wait! Dammit, Pared, you ain't gonna jack me out of my reward. Me and my free raiders been runnin' this thwart line too long for you to cut it now. I'm gonna take Tobei in to see Martok, so back off."

There was a long beat of silence in which all that could be

heard was the squawking of the sea birds and a restless *snip-click* as one of the guards adjusted the velocity action on his weapon.

"Very well," said Pared at last. He stepped back and gestured at his men to stand down. "I don't think Martok will appreciate your joke."

Udge glared at him. "Just get out of the way!"

As Pared and his men moved aside, Asan let out the breath he'd been holding. Udge turned on him.

"Don't look so smug. I ain't lettin' ole One Eye do me out of my reward, see? But either way, it's good-bye to you, Tobei." He glanced over his shoulder at the pilot waiting in the shuttle hatchway. "Let her out."

"How beautiful!" exclaimed Zaula, emerging. "The warmth. The fragrance of . . . *Dilgel m'a-anhr!*"

It was a most improper oath for an above-caste female. Turning in surprise, Asan saw her staring at the sea in wonder and a little fear.

He moved away from Udge to touch her arm in reassurance. "The sea."

She showed her palm. "We are told of the wealth of water in our nursery stories. But no one ever spoke of how beautiful it could be."

"Come on, come on," said Udge impatiently. "This isn't a Playworld tour."

He pointed, and Asan started walking with Zaula following one step behind him in the way of respect. They went up a ramp and out across a causeway spanning the ocean between the pad and Martok's villa.

The island supporting the house was low and flat so that the structure seemed to float above the waves. The villa was an airy, spacious structure of glass and stone, round in the center with flying buttresses of steel extending from it. A blue carpet of grass set off masses of brilliantly hued flowers. Yellow birds sang in the trees, and here and there small furred creatures with long tensile tails scampered among the foliage.

"Asan, look!"

Forgetting protocol, Zaula grabbed his sleeve and pulled him over to the railing of the causeway to point.

"Look at the animals. They act tame. They're even playing. Have they no fear?"

"They're pets," he said, and thought with a shiver, *like I used to be.*

"Move on," said Udge, and started whistling the old bar song of "Got you, baby/Got you now."

Asan glared at him, but Udge just grinned.

To Asan's surprise, they were conducted up the broad stone steps to the front doors of amethyst crystal. Drones with blue stripes painted on their sides opened the doors with chimes of welcome.

Zaula twisted around to stare at them.

"Machines have replaced slaves," he said, taking her hand.

She shivered, her dark eyes wide and shining with wonder. "Truly we are in the place of Beyond. Was Tlartantla like this?"

He reached into the deeper memories that were not his. "Very near."

She sighed with pleasure.

He wished, as they moved into a spacious receiving area which was all white walls and bleached wood adorned by simple sculptures from the classical Othalic period of Ghirdana history, that he could share Zaula's enjoyment of all this beauty. She was trying not to goggle at the lavish use of wood. Even the floor was wood. On Ruantl such a display was impossible.

An android of superb quality met them. Only a certain deadness of expression around the eyes betrayed that she was not real. She wore a bright blue sarong that left her shoulders bare. Martok blue. The badge of his possession. Her eyes were the same color.

"Udge Enster, welcome," she said.

Udge stepped forward. His cheek bulged, but then he glanced at the shining floor and did not spit.

"Martok ready to see us now?"

"Soon." The android turned her head and stared hard at Asan and Zaula.

Zaula gestured in annoyance and whispered mentally to Asan, *Such rudeness. I do not like—*

Asan touched Zaula's arm. *She is a machine. She isn't staring at us. She's running us through a security scan and data check to see if we're supposed to be allowed inside.*

A machine! said Zaula in astonishment. *But—*

"Security abort," said the android, turning back to Udge. "Non-Tobei entity. Explain."

"He's Tobei all right," said Udge, holding up the thwart control. "Look, we've already been passed by Colonel Pared. What's the hitch? My boys upstairs at the station are gettin' restless thinkin' about the money they're gonna spend."

The android's expression became stern. "All execution subjects are relayed through the underwater hatches. This entrance is denied."

While Udge argued with her, insisting that Martok had told him to drag his prisoner right through the front door, Asan turned at Zaula's tug on his sleeve and pretended to listen as she exclaimed over the beauty surrounding her.

To their left he could see through an open archway into a spacious room furnished with plant fronds and oversized white banquettes. A wall of windows overlooked the ocean where little white tops were running in on the tide. There were at least a dozen people in the room. They were either human or Ghirdanan with the bored, sleek look of sophisticates. One woman wore her long auburn hair in a fan radiating out from her skull.

Zaula nudged Asan. *Look. Look.*

He had a vision of the woman having to go crablike through doorways because of her hairdo and shared it with Zaula, who chuckled. The woman seemed to hear, for she glanced their way. Her eyes were proud and incurious although she allowed her gaze to linger upon Asan. He guessed these people to be elites shopping for thrills or a new zine supply. Elites loved to flirt with danger by dealing only with central figures, who in turn manipulated the elites for their money and legitimate connections.

"Their clothes," whispered Zaula, unable to tear her gaze away. "I have never seen such clothes. What are—"

"Over here!" said Udge impatiently. "Hurry up."

Tension curled through Asan like a spring. He formed his rings, ready to apply *sonthi* methods of inner control if necessary. But oddly enough he was calm. Usually when he was in danger he walked on edge with every sense strained and alert. Now, his limbs felt heavy and slow. His breathing was deep if not quite steady. His heart was barely beating.

"Asan?" Zaula suddenly stared at him in concern. "Is thee well?"

He moved a fingertip in answer, wondering if this might be the last time he ever saw Zaula. He wanted to speak to her of his feelings, but there was no chance as the android led them through the elites in their shimmering clothes and husky voices. Udge met their glances and uplifted brows with a wide grin. Asan and Zaula ignored them.

On the far side of the room was a ramp spiral. When they started up this, Asan's heartbeat quickened. Suddenly he could breathe more normally. It couldn't be an execution, he told himself. Those happened down in the damp caves beneath the villa. Martok must have seen him through a cam observer and gotten curious. They were going to talk. He would have a chance to convince Martok to listen to his offer.

He caught Zaula's eye and smiled. *All is well.*

At the top of the ramp, two protective drones and a live guard stood before double doors of small glass squares, each a different color. The sun shone in from a skylight overhead and made the doors glitter brightly.

''How pretty,'' said Zaula.

Asan glanced down at her with a brief smile, momentarily caught by the highlights the sunshine struck from her hair. Then it happened.

The drones opened the doors, sending prisms of light dancing on the walls, and a combination of odd odors rolled out from the room beyond. Very old leather, waxed wood, wine—either imported from Terra at prohibitive cost or stolen—and cloth, also old, and dusty.

The smells struck his memories hard. He had come to this room only once before in his life; he'd even forgotten all about it. That had been when Udge first brought him into Martok's service. It was the first time he ever saw Martok. Now he was coming here for the last time.

Something queer rolled through his stomach. He felt a curious weakness spread through his limbs. He stopped dead, his air choked off in his throat. He was suddenly blind with a loud roaring in his ears.

He stood there frozen, his muscles locked tight.

As a boy he'd been terrified of this place, terrified of Martok who held the power of life and death over him. Later, he'd shut the memory away, glossed it over in an effort to deal with the fear, until he managed to forget it altogether. Martok knew his secret, the secret even Udge did not know. At any time, on any whim, Martok could betray him and send him back to the life of a labor drone with a wiped mind.

Not now, he thought desperately, trying to pull himself together. *I'm safe from that now.*

But the fear remained, stronger than his rational mind.

Everyone was staring at him, waiting for him to go inside. He couldn't. He had ceased even to breathe.

Udge prodded him. "Time to meet your maker, Tobei," he said, laughing.

Asan flinched. It was an old Earth saying that meant nothing. He turned his head with an effort to stare down into Udge's small, malicious eyes. Udge did not know the truth he spoke.

For Martok is my maker, thought Asan. *Martok owns Laboratory 80 where I was made.*

Human! cried a corner of his mind. *Real born!*

But Asan was no longer so sure. The android's sophistication had shaken him. Maybe Martok's scientists had made more advances than had been publicized. Maybe they really did have the ability to create labor drones with minds *and* souls.

What about the womb memory?

He clung to it without much belief now. Maybe that was incorporated too. After all, the most expensive androids were given memory implants to augment their artificial intelligence circuits and to enable them to react naturally.

I don't want to know the truth. Either way, I don't want to know.

But he had to face Martok. And when he walked into that room, sooner or later he knew he would use his rings to learn the facts of his origin.

There came the sound of a chair scraping back over the wooden floor. And then a dry, whispery voice that used to plague his nightmares when he was only a small-time crook working the back streets and waiting for a chance to infiltrate the Institute spoke to him from inside the room:

"Is that BLZ-80-4163? Enter. I've been wanting to talk to you for a long time about an account past due."

Asan swallowed hard.

Udge frowned at Asan. "BLZ *what*? What the hell is he talking about?" He raised his voice. "Sir? I've brought in Tobei as ordered."

"Yes, Udge. Thank you. The reward is waiting downstairs."

Udge grinned and gave Asan a shove. "Go in, Tobei. I guess this is good-bye for us."

Feeling as though he walked into darkness, Asan steadied himself and entered.

Chapter 13

The room was empty.

Surprised, Asan stopped and looked around. The room was small in scale; his height filled it. The cool shadows were in sharp contrast to the sunlight flooding the rest of the villa. Wooden shelves lined the walls from floor to ceiling and supported a fortune in leatherbound books. As antiques they were rare and priceless. Asan had never seen actual books anywhere else but here.

In the center of the room stood a vast desk all of wood, also old, also priceless. There were gilded carvings on its panels. At a less tense time, he might have touched the desk and linked back to the carver kneeling among wood shavings as he labored to create this thing of beauty.

Muted light streamed down from a crimson stained-glass window set high in the wall before him. The air was cold, flat, and stale with chemical preservatives and dehumidifiers. The age, the ghosts, the shadows, and the cold made Asan think of a tomb.

His tomb?

Alarm clouded his rings. He snapped them out, seeking the danger, but he was too late.

A sharp click of the door shutting behind him made him whirl. He heard a hum, and with a lurch the room descended like a cage in a shaft with him trapped helplessly inside.

He blocked out panic and forced himself to stand still. His knees bent to cushion the vibrations as he counted off the seconds and measured the increasing rate of descent. His ears began to hurt from fluid pressure. His body struggled to compensate, but the need for adjustment was too rapid. Even a Tlar could die of the bends.

He refused to panic although he knew now he'd been a fool to believe Martok would even give him a chance to . . .

The brakes clutched, and he was sent sprawling. His shoulder thudded into the corner of the desk, bringing a burst of momentary pain. He lay there a moment, then scrambled to his feet. He nearly tripped over a pile of books that had fallen from their shelves. One of the ancient leather covers had ripped and lay there with pages falling loose and crumbling into brittle dust on the floor.

There was blood in his mouth. Asan spat and used his tongue to probe the spot where he'd bitten the lining of his cheek. It hurt.

He forgot his panic as anger came surging up. Martok liked theatrics, but Asan had a few tricks of his own.

With a click the door of his cage slid open, revealing Kor the Vyarian in full ceremonial dress.

In spite of himself, Asan took a step back. He'd been expecting Pared's firing squad or a lethal dose of gas.

Kor's chin claw had been painted scarlet; his hair tassels were braided up in tight knobs against his elbows; and the wide flare of his wedge-shaped skull threw weird shadows in the dim light creating a nimbus behind him. In his talons he held a tarnished silver bowl that was stained black inside.

The Vyarian blood bowl. A shiver passed through Asan.

"My meat," said Kor, wheezing. "Martok give you to me."

Asan's temper snapped. "The hell I am, *chielt. Choi-hana chi!*"

Raising his force field, he struck with all the power of his rings, sending Kor staggering back. With a howl, Kor righted himself and came at Asan with flashing talons. The force field deflected them, however, and Asan struck again and again, sending the Vyarian staggering each time until Kor stood still, his feet spread apart and his head down. His sides heaved.

Asan gasped for breath. His eyes felt scorched in their sockets. He was beginning to feel the need for more oxygen. He let his field waver.

Kor looked up, and his yellow eyes lit with cunning. He sprang at Asan, who dodged him easily and struck again with all the force he'd held in reserve.

The Vyarian crumpled to the floor, and Asan stepped out of

the trap into the low-ceilinged, damp-smelling cave that was Martok's proper lair instead of the villa overhead.

"Martok!" he shouted, his voice reverberating like thunder through the cave. "Martok!"

The faint hum warned him of a protection drone's approach. Asan stiffened in readiness, longing for a strifer in his hands. He heard accompanying footsteps but the light shone into his face so that it was hard to see.

"Martok?"

"Blaise?"

The voice was thin and clear but with an underlying flatness in its tones that betrayed the existence of an artificial larynx.

"I have a deal for you," said Asan. "I have come to offer you a business partnership in precious minerals. Are you interested?"

The footsteps stopped. Asan saw a vague silhouette against the dim light. He squinted and concentrated on sorting out smells. He identified a trace of expensive wine, metal, and the cold sweat of hatred.

"Well, Martok? What do you say?"

As he spoke he heard another drone move into place somewhere to his left. Prickles of unease went through him. He'd gotten out of the room, but he was still in a trap.

"Ah, Blaise. The voice has changed, but it must be you. No one else would try to twist his execution into a money proposition. You sound like an investment advertisement from the local vid-cast."

"I've come too far to die now," said Asan, ignoring the mockery. "I have a deal to make."

"You cost me over thirteen million. Thirteen million plus a year of reprisals and backlash. The delivery of that security data was crucial to my operations against the Institute. I'm not interested in why you skipped on me, Blaise. All I care about is your death."

Martok stepped closer so that at last Asan could see him clearly. Light glinted off the metal capping his skull and forming one half of his face. The other half was hideously scarred. He held his body at a stiff, unnatural angle, and both hands were artificial. A splinter of revulsion ran through Asan. No matter how many times he'd seen Martok, he never quite got over the involuntary human reaction to a cyborg. He could never hide it from Martok either, and Martok wore his hatred like an additional plate of armor against all who were whole.

No one knew Martok's origins for sure, but it was said he started as a young scout pilot in the GSI fleet and won three medals for bravery before getting shot to pieces in a suicide assault ordered by an incompetent officer.

Instead of being court-martialed, the officer was promoted out of the field and the matter hushed up. Martok was one of two pilots who survived that mission. When he came out of rehabilitation, there was no hero's accolade and nothing but aversion for his body pieced back together by machinery.

He turned on the Institute then and became a ruthless loner who operated on the fringes of the other crime lords' territories. Now he was the biggest of them all and the most feared. He had power over millions. His influence reached into the Institute itself. But he remained a deformed creature hidden away. Something, ultimately, to be pitied.

Martok lifted his hand. The thwart meter blinked steadily, but he was staring at Asan with an astonishment he did not try to conceal.

"So," he said. "Udge Enster did not exaggerate in his report. How is it done, Blaise? A generator-enhanced illusory field to make you look taller? Expensive, but effective, providing you watch where you step. You can turn it off now. The game is over."

Asan shrugged. "What is the point of this, Martok? Do you want me to start sweating and begging for mercy? Do you want me to babble out explanations? What good will it do? You intend to kill me anyway. Why should I crawl first just to amuse you?"

Martok scowled and snapped his fingers. The drone behind him surged forward from its corner and fired. Asan had only a split-second glimpse of lethal intensity.

With a gasp he dodged, seizerted, and reappeared with his force field around him. Through its blue haze he saw Martok staring in astonishment, but his attention was on the second drone tracking his new position.

He attacked it, using his rings to explode its internal firing circuits. It crashed to the ground, but the first one fired and hit him.

His force field absorbed most of the blast, but still he took enough of it to stagger back into the wall. His heart stopped for an agonizing second. The world grayed around him.

He steadied himself, grimacing in an effort to hang onto consciousness. Using the last of his strength, he aimed his rings at the drone and exploded its circuits.

With a shrill whine, the drone crashed to the ground like the first and lay there smoking.

Asan slowly straightened himself away from the wall and faced Martok. The world looked skewed. Every beat of his heart sent a sharp burst of pain through his chest. His legs felt boneless as though they might fold under him at any moment.

He barely managed a crooked smile. "Bad move, Martok."

Martok stared at him in horror. He took a step back. "What are you?"

Asan's smile broadened. "Tlartantlan. Have you never heard of the species?"

"Impossible. You're just surgically altered. Fibula implants to make you taller. Skin repigmentation—"

"When I bleed, Martok, I bleed brown."

Martok frowned and seemed unable to find words. Then he shook himself and drew a strifer.

"Impossible," he said again. "You *are* BLZ-80-4163. One of the last full-human batches in growth cycle—"

"I am not a batch, and I didn't come from a growth cycle! I was real born, damn you! I came from a womb, not a vat!"

The fear in Martok's eyes changed to calculation. "How do you know that? Have you accessed records or—"

Asan turned his palm down. "Institute files wouldn't keep records of illegal activities. No, Martok, I know I am real because body transference requires a soul. I wouldn't have one if I'd come from a vat."

"Fascinating," whispered Martok. "Body transference. Who has produced such technology?"

"We have. Tlartantlans. It is an ancient process of regeneration."

A process that did not always work. A process that required the catalyst to die. But Martok did not need to know that Blaise Omari's transference survival had been a fluke. Asan hid his satisfaction and watched Martok swallowing the bait.

"Tell me more about it," said Martok. "Blaise, you have brought me something worth far more than the Security-breach information you owed me. I am pleased and intrigued. Please sit down. Let us discuss this in more detail.''

Asan stared at him coldly. ''First you answer my questions. Why was I raised as a vat boy?''

Martok shrugged. ''I have no idea. Your particular circumstances were never of any import—''

He broke off as Asan's clenched fist acquired a blue aura. Asan opened his palm, and blue fire flashed across the cave at Martok, who froze, his face locked in a grimace. Asan stopped the fire mere inches from Martok's throat and let it hang in the air. He could hear Martok's breathing, harsh and ragged, in the silence.

''Why,'' said Asan quietly, ''was I raised as a vat boy?''

The flesh side of Martok's face shone with perspiration. He could not take his eyes off the fire hanging in the air before him. It moved closer, and Martok flinched. He raised the strifer, but Asan's rings knocked it from his hand.

''I can explode your circuits just as I did the drones','' said Asan. ''Answer!''

''Laboratory 80 operates as a GSI facility, but it really belongs to me. I pay them well to neglect their assigned research and conduct experiments for me instead. However, because their principal function is the production of laborers, they have a certain quota to meet. They presumably filled the gaps with real children taken from the border slums where illegal pregnancies abound. I know nothing about you personally.''

''Lie!''

Martok blinked. ''Why should I lie? What answer do you expect from me?''

Asan let the fire die away, leaving only a trace of smoke in the air. He dropped his hand to his side and walked over to the drones to kick them into a pile of separate parts.

So much for his hopes for a real past, a real heritage of some kind, however small. Instead, he was only an illegal slum pregnancy that slipped past the abortionists. One more statistic in a civil records file. Had his mother sold him to the lab? Had she born him and abandoned him in an alley the way reptiles leave their young? Had she been rounded up by GSI civil patrollers, placed in detention rehab, and her baby impounded? He would never know the answer. He felt angry and cheated once again.

''Now about this transference process,'' said Martok. ''Explain to me exactly how it works. You must have been driven to ground pretty hard by the GSI to make such a drastic identity change.''

He walked past Asan into the study and poured himself a glass of wine from the decanter on the desk. He glanced only once at Kor lying on the floor, then ignored him to lift his glass in a salute to Asan, who stood at the doorway but did not enter.

"My little chameleon. Grown into a giant. And what exactly is a Tlar leiil?''

"Supreme ruler." Asan took the glass Martok handed to him.

Martok blinked, and his hand shook a little. He lifted it to his lips and licked the spilled wine from his gloved fingers. His green eyes stared at Asan in fascination.

"Clever. Very clever. I confess, Blaise, I never expected you to come this far. My congratulations. But Blaise is no longer applicable, is it? Would you rather be called Tobei? Or another of your many names?''

"I am Asan.''

"Very well." Martok glanced down at Kor, who was still out cold. "Why didn't you kill him?''

"There has been too much killing lately.''

Asan sniffed his wine, decided it was repugnant to his Tlar taste buds, and set the untouched glass on the floor.

"I am tired of death.''

"When you lose your indifference to death, you become soft. You're washed up as a raider.''

Asan shrugged. "I am Tlar now.''

"Yes, Tlar." Martok's scarred lips twisted into a grotesque half smile, but his eyes remained cold. "Let us adjourn to the lab. There is a scientist on my staff who should hear about your transformation.''

"No," said Asan firmly. "No labs.''

Martok's shrill laughter rang out. "Beneath that splendid exterior you are still the suspicious street rat, aren't you? Do you expect me to have you dissected? I am not so crude. Come, Asan, be generous. You came seeking a business partnership, did you not? Then—''

"Ruantl is composed almost entirely of precious and utilitarian metals," said Asan. He held up his forefinger to show off the carbyx ring. "Diamonds, rubies, black carbyxes, and other jewels are as common as pebbles. Even the nomads carry knives of corybdium.''

Martok looked bored and impatient. "So you are rich as well as supreme. What—"

"I want off-world distribution. I want a link to your freighters and shipping lines. I want mining equipment and engineers who can both supervise and train my Bban metallurgists. I want protection from the GSI, either in the form of defense satellites or ships. The Institute is on my planet now. I want them off. And I want political lobbying to keep Ruantl from being claimed as a GSI protectorate.''

Martok sneered. "Is that all?"

"It is a start toward self-sufficiency and independence. I will also need to import food and industrial-grade water until we can improve the planet's own fragile agrarian systems.''

"You're insane. You're asking me to split my empire in half, share my resources, my ships, my armed forces, and squander political favors bought at expensive prices for you. Why should I?"

"Because you hate the Institute, and if they get Ruantl they'll be that much richer. They've reached into the Uncharted Zone. If they continue to expand in that direction, their territory will grow.'' Asan paused, reaching for knowledge from the deeper memories. "There are more planets out there as rich as Ruantl. Some are even more valuable. You could have a base at the Institute's back. Would that help you?

"And if we take a fifty/fifty split, then you will have almost unlimited wealth. Your resources will expand even more. You will have more power.''

"I have enough," said Martok, yawning.

"No one ever has enough.''

"Fallacy. All your life you have been a wretch groveling for survival. Like all poor people you belive that money will solve your problems and reduce your inadequacies. You also believe that money will make you safe. It doesn't. It increases your danger. I am beyond the reach of the law, but I have other enemies far more powerful. I can have every wish gratified. I enjoy every comfort. I live exactly as I please. My operations run smoothly, providing I don't put too much trust in runners such as you.''

Asan grinned and cocked his head to one side. "I was the best you had, Martok."

"Perhaps. I always knew that one day you'd betray me. But I misjudged when." Martok stared into the bottom of his glass. "I don't like failure, and I don't like humiliation. You have to die, otherwise someone else will try to cheat me."

"I didn't betray you. I got caught."

Martok glanced up. "In the end, the results are the same. I don't need anything you have to offer."

Desperation filled Asan's throat. "Except Tlar technology."

Martok laughed. "Hardly. It is interesting, yes, but it isn't worth all you are asking for."

"Isn't it? You've been a cyborg for many years now. How long until those drugs you take in your wine cease to be effective and you get metal poisoning? No alloy, no matter how many times they experiment, ever really remains compatible with living tissue. How long until you can no longer control the unpleasant side effects? Who are you going to leave your empire to when you finally die, Martok? Lin Ranje?"

Martok's glass shattered on the floor. "Damn you! I shall outlive you!"

"Really?" Asan walked up to him and extended his arm. "This body is centuries old. Feel how firm the skin and muscles are."

Martok stared at him in revulsion and resentment, but after a moment he grasped Asan's forearm. His gloved fingers were made of hull steel. Asan could feel the ribs of their framework as they tightened on his arm. The pressure increased. Martok's eyes glinted. Covering a wince, Asan realized Martok intended to crush his arm. But Tlar bones were stronger than human bones. Asan felt pity for a man who despite his wealth and power still had to play such petty games. Asan's rings focused around his arm. He frowned slightly, concentrating, and the rings loosened Martok's grip, then forced it away.

Martok's eyes widened. He snatched his hand back and held it rigidly at his side.

"Whatever you are, I don't want to become one. Even a cyborg is more human than you!"

"Do you think body transference requires becoming an alien?" Asan asked. "Select one of your supple vat boys from

Lab 80 if you like. Just make sure you select someone with a weaker personality than your own.''

Martok licked his scarred lips, thinking it over while Asan held his breath, willing Martok to accept the offer.

But whatever functioned beneath that metal-capped skull was impervious to mental persuasion.

Martok reached across his desk and opened a drawer, punching a control before Asan could stop him. He faced Asan coldly, and with a sinking heart Asan knew nothing had been gained.

''Take him to the lab,'' said Martok to the guards who came up behind Asan. ''Get him ready for Saverson to examine. I want Colonel Pared there too.''

''You're insane if you throw this chance away,'' said Asan, trying to hide his fear. He'd die here and now before he'd let anyone dissect him on a slab. ''Martok—''

''You're still a street rat. Vicious and deceptive and deadly, yes, but stupid like all your kind. I intercepted GSI geological reports on planet KS-5 from the moment we received Udge Enster's first message about you. I'll take KX-5 from the Institute when it suits me. As for your transformation, well, my scientists will make quite a study of you. And when there is no more to be learned from the biopsies, then—''

''When I am dead, there'll be no one to take you to—''

''When you are dead,'' said Martok with his grotesque smile, ''we shall still have the female to show us the way. Guards.''

Asan had gambled on Martok's greed, but he'd misjudged the extent of it. Now he had to get out of here and fast.

He dodged to one side in a feint to distract the guards and gathered himself to seizert, but even as he vanished into that momentary lurch of displacement he heard the sound of a strifer being fired from Martok's direction.

Of course, he thought in a queer sense of detachment, Martok must have had another weapon hidden in the desk. And Udge would have told Martok about Asan's ability to disappear. Martok must have been expecting a move like this and was ready for it.

Asan felt the thin strifer beam spit him as cleanly and precisely as a jen-knife, high in the back under his shoulder blade and out his chest. He spun and tumbled in his mind, yet his body was nowhere, lost in the displacement between time curves. He was falling, falling hard, his rings lost in the chaos so that he was blind as well. It seemed to take an eternity, this falling, but with a lurch he was back in reality and a portion of his mind told him it had been a split second since he seizerted. He saw that he'd moved less than a couple of meters.

The floor was rising up to meet him very fast, then he hit it and heard his own grunt at the impact. Pain flooded him in a great cold wave.

Martok had won, he thought dimly. Aural had won.

It seemed a wretched way to die, gunned down in the back in the grim, damp coldness that would become his grave. Wretched for a former vat boy. Wretched for a Tlar leiil.

He blacked out.

Chapter 14 ◂≋

Deep in the heart of the Tchsco Mountains beneath the caverns of M'thra in the dark, sealed chamber securing the computer Anthi, a special linkage sensor detected a signal lapse. A multi-nanosecond delay passed. The signal did not resume.

Warning synapses fired emergency circuits to the activity lobe, clearing interlocks for data flow. A diagnostic search flared out and found no system malfunction. The signal receptors on port 1001 received no input.

Data bits were shunted off standby and sifted, recombined, and compared. Advanced warning systems fired a series of synapses reaching all the way to Anthi's primary lobe.

Anthi awoke from mandatory shutdown, her lights pulsing blue in the dark chamber as she came fully online.

She began the call, seeking the essential communications link that had been broken:

"Asan. Asan. Asan."

In Altian, Aural paced the triangular circumference of the chamber of state in the palace. Tapestries that had illustrated the great moments of Tlar history hung shredded and charred upon the walls. The once-gleaming floor of polished jate stone was scuffed into dullness. The air was cold and stuffy with the smoky stench of torches. Gleiglits had chewed the tasseled fringe adorning the chair upon which Unar sat. Now and then Aural's slipper crunched upon the splintered fragments of wooden sculptures which had comprised an exquisite collection.

"This is madness!" exclaimed Aural furiously. Tucking her cold hands into the wide sleeves of her gown, she turned to glare at Unar. "Your ridiculous superstitions cause us nothing but delay—costly delay!"

Unar scowled at his scuffed boots. His elegant clothing had been long ago replaced by a jen uniform coated with dust and worn shiny in places from hard use. He held a battered mask upon his lap. His dark brows were drawn into a scowl that told Aural he would not listen to her arguments tonight any more than he had listened to them yesterday or the day before. His face was as gaunt as the gnawing in her own belly. They were all starving, and Unar was a fool, and if she did not reach through his stubbornness soon, they would perish and only the *n'kai* would remain to rule Ruantl.

"Unar!" she said.

This time he glanced at her. His palm went down. Her breath hissed in through her teeth.

"You fool—"

"No!" he shouted, standing up. "You are the fool, Dame Aural. The Soot'dla have united with Bban tribes, and by dawn so will the Spandeen and the Mura-an."

Aural stiffened in disbelief that he would dare challenge her at last so openly. The blue force of her anger glowed around her fists.

"The Mura-an are your house, Noble Unar. Do you go to our enemy?"

"Enemy? *Enemy?* It is the *n'kai* who are our enemy. Have we come to crave power so much we blind ourselves to the truth?"

"Stop playing the tragic conscience, Unar. When I offered you the chance to be regent, you did not hesitate. But now that the stakes are higher, you have become an old woman."

Unar's face darkened. He tossed his mask onto the chair. "The House of Mura-an no longer acts under my order. You have around you only a handful of people while not one house remains at your back. Or mine. Or the child's. The *n'kai* take, but they give us nothing save the ashes of death in our mouths."

"It will not always be—"

"You blind yourself."

Unar turned away and began to pace, shivering, back and forth. He still limped from the attempt of the Soot'dla assassin. Aural's eyes narrowed in contempt. She hoped the wound festered.

"No, Unar," she said. "Of us all, I am the only one who can see clearly. You must—"

"Even to ally myself with the Bban'jen would bring more honor to my blood than this."

"The Bban'jen will be destroyed," said Aural. "As will the Tlar'jen who march with them—"

"Is that what you want? I see you smile. Does it truly please you to contemplate the destruction of our race by these outsiders? For the first time within the memory of our people, we have been conquered. *N'kai* march through our streets. Tlar blood has been dishonored. And why is that, revered dame?" Unar slammed a fist into his palm. "Because you and I let the *n'kai* in. We are the traitors and the executioners of all that we hold dear." His voice sank to a whisper. "We have killed our people."

For an instant she felt a tiny pang, but shrugged it off. Unar could contemplate moral suicide without her.

"You should have performed onstage with ty-dancers," she said, choosing words to cut. "Our people have not been conquered. They have formed a new alliance. The sooner they accept it, the better for them."

"No."

"Unar, listen to me!" She gripped his sleeve, and the coarse cloth scratched her fingers. "Commander Notini has promised me full support in exchange for our cooperation. We shall be part of the Institute alliance, a protected planet, partaking of all the benefits of technology supplied to us. We can export the Bban savages as slave laborers. The precious metals are another—"

"I won't listen to this!" Unar pulled away. "I want no part of it!"

She had to fight herself not to strike him down. The pang came again inside of her, more sharply this time. She grimaced, pressing her fist against her heart. It was hunger, she told herself, nothing more than that. She had expended too much energy trying to keep little Cirthe from weakening, and now she needed rest.

"Do you so easily relinquish the power I have fought to give you?" she asked raggedly. "The people rebel because they are ignorant fools. When they are under submission, then we shall have time to teach them the points of advanced diplomacy."

"The people are hungry."

Aural sighed. The days when she could control his rings were gone. Now he did not even heed persuasive tone.

"I have told you I can bring Anthi back—"

"No!" Horror filled his face. "It is not permitted. You may not commit this sacrilege."

"Again and again we circle this like two hungry vitches. It is simple expediency, not sacrilege. Many years ago I was Asan's ring-mate. I can reproduce his mental pattern sufficiently to re-activate Anthi. I'm sure of it."

"No. You must not. It was the will of Anthi to turn her face from us because we did not honor Asan her chosen one."

"Great Merdar, what is this babbling? Have you lost your wits as well as your courage?"

Unar grasped his jen-knife. "My courage is not—"

"Asan shut down Anthi out of spite and a desire to persecute the Tlar'n. He wanted to cause trouble and civil war, and he has succeeded. It was his only chance to seize power. If I reactivate Anthi, we shall have warmth and the power to grow food again. That will calm the Soot'dla and the other houses, and we'll have no more trouble. Unar, why can't you—"

A sharp pain speared her, cutting her off in mid-sentence. She doubled, locked in agony, and was unable to draw breath.

"Aural? What is it? Aural!"

Unar's hand gripped her shoulders, but she was barely aware of him as her body straightened and arched and spun. Pain tore through her chest as though a stake had been hammered into her. She cried out, her hands clutching the fur-trimmed bodice of her gown as though to close the wound that was not there.

A terrible fear passed through her as she realized it was Asan who had been injured, Asan who felt this agony, Asan who was dying. Her rings broke around her, and she cried out again.

This could not happen, must not happen. Months ago, when Asan had fought Leiil Hihuan and been wounded, she had felt nothing. That made her certain their ring-bond was safely broken. Confident of her safety, she had placed Asan into human hands, uncaring of what might befall him.

Now she realized her folly. She had been drinking *yde* with the priest Picyt when Asan suffered that first injury. *Yde* had strengthened her. But now there was no *yde*, none to be had anywhere for any price. She would have taken food from Cirthe's mouth—had there been any food—to buy *yde*. Without the drug, she was not safe from the bond.

It held her now, and it was pulling her down with Asan into death.

"No!" she cried, twisting in Unar's hold as the pain intensified. Blinded without her rings, she felt herself falling. "Asan, by the mercy of Anthi, release me!"

But there was no mercy, none at all. Screaming, she plunged into cold darkness.

In a spacious guest suite on the ground floor of Martok's villa, Zaula amused herself at first by exploring every inch of her rooms. She ran her fingers over the polished wood, awed by the wealth around her. She picked up the small pillows covered in white cloth of a weave strange yet soft. She laughed at the size of the *n'ka* bed and thumped its hard surface so far above the floor. Even after all those many weeks upon the ship, she still missed a good soft nest of cushions to sleep upon.

A wall of windows overlooking the sea made her self-conscious until she realized the glass was fashioned so that she could see out but none of the people wandering the grounds could see in.

The box-shaped machines which Asan called protection drones floated unobtrusively over the heads of the people. A crowd had gathered upon a stone terrace overgrown with vivid blue flowers cascading down over the railings. Zaula could hear their laughter and chatter faintly. She watched for a long time, fascinated by their clothes and mannerisms. Not all of them were small, striped-eyed humans. She longed to have Asan here with her, to tell her the names of the other species and to explain the customs of this gathering to her.

No one wore masks, of course. And although she could hear faint strains of music with a queer, unfamiliar beat, no one sat down to listen to it. They went on talking as though they heard nothing.

Udge Enster, still wearing his clothes of ty-scarlet, wandered about, scowling and speaking to no one. He allowed the slave machines to replenish his drink many times, but it must have been a bitter draught, for he looked grim and edgy.

She felt a prickle of unease as she watched Udge. She wondered what was taking Asan so long in his discussion with the one who ruled this place. Asan had been tense all day. Were it not beyond thinking, she would have said he was frightened. But why should he fear the men who knew him in his other life as a *n'ka?* Despite what he said about the *n'ka* in him, it was not true. Asan was *c'tal it my'lan,* the shining of the mystery. Asan was Beyond and all its ways. Asan was knowledge and gentleness. Asan was fire.

Smiling to herself, Zaula wandered away from the windows into a tiled room where a small pool of water glistened invitingly. As she investigated crystal vials of perfumes and scented oils and touched the soft thickness of towels, she thought of the pleasures of lying in Asan's arms with his rings entwined about hers.

He had led her from level to level of pleasure, neither as brutal as Hihuan nor as reverent as Fflir, but instead a mix of mastery and gentleness that left her breathless and aglow from the fire of their sharing. Even after the first awkward time when she had shamed herself by seeking Fflir with her rings, Asan had not been angry or disappointed.

He could have crushed her. Instead, he calmed her weeping and told her of how Fflir had served him with honor and become his friend. He missed Fflir's impudent jokes and companionship. He even grieved with her for Fflir's death, and through Asan's mind she saw so many other deaths and his regret for them.

It was then that she began to truly love him.

Yet in so many ways he was too complex for her. The levels of his mind and heart were many. She did not understand them all. There were times when he seemed far away, as though upon a pinnacle looking down. She was Tlar; her breeding was pure from the first days of Ruantl. But Asan was more than she. He was more than Tlar, greater. His powers and his abilities were stronger. Indeed, he was from the mists of Tlar legend, and although he joked and lost his temper and snored, it was as though he were a giant among little men.

She was Tlar, but he was Tlartantlan. And sometimes the gap frightened her.

What was taking him so long? He had only to use persuasive tone and perhaps his rings, and these *n'kai* would agree to his terms. He had told her his plans for Ruantl, but she could not understand or remember all of them.

She felt guilty now for not having listened more closely.

Enemy . . . friend . . . lover.

Sighing, she undressed and slid cautiously into the water. Its warmth surprised her. Never, not even in the days as Tsla leiis to Hihuan had she bathed in a pool so large, so warm, and so pleasantly scented. She closed her eyes and floated, letting her rings flicker in and out around her.

Asan was not able to mend her rings entirely, but he took the pain of using them away. After such a long time of distress and half-blind groping, she could see again with her higher senses. She could sort the air and blank her thoughts from others for welcome privacy. She could not seizert. She would never be able to do that again, but she could expand her rings a short distance to see what was happening elsewhere.

She tried it now, wondering if she could find Asan's mind here in the villa.

No . . . she could extend her senses to the next room where a human guard stood at her door. She even managed to reach outside almost to the beach where young humans of both sexes played a silly game with a ball and hoops.

But she could not touch Asan. A chill passed through her. She stood up in the water and frowned. The temperature was cooling.

Climbing out, she dried herself and put on a sarong she found in a cupboard. It was soft and luxurious against her skin but too short so that it ended at her knees instead of her ankles. The color was the same bright blue the machine had worn. Zaula frowned at her reflection and reached up to untie the sarong. She had not liked that machine, the one that looked so much like a n'dl. She would not wear its clothes.

Dizziness engulfed her without warning. Nauseated and chilled, she found herself kneeling upon the floor when the spasm passed. Clutching her stomach, she drew an unsteady breath and shoved her hair back from her face. Her forehead felt clammy and slick with sweat.

Puzzled, she let her rings fall through her body and found nothing wrong. She pushed herself back onto her feet. With a frown, she searched for a different fresh garment to put on. They were all blue.

Resentful, she abandoned the idea of changing and returned to her view of the beach. The sky, so oddly green and unfamiliar, was full of the sun that blazed across the horizon in an enormous bronze orb. Shades of gold, umber, and orange tinged the clouds. The sea gleamed golden.

She stared entranced, and thought with sudden certainty, *I never want to go back to Ruantl. It is dark, and cold, and ugly. I want to be free of it, to turn my face to the sunshine without fear.*

As though she had offended the gods, pain hit her in the chest with such force she cried out and staggered against the window. Somehow she managed to catch herself from falling. Then the pain receded, fading so quickly from her she realized it was not her own. Yet the pain remained a force in the reality around her.

And she heard a dim, low cry in her mind.

She stiffened in dismay. Asan was hurt. She must help him.

There was no time to think or wonder what she should do. She knew only that she must act quickly before it was too late.

She ran to the door and opened it. The guard blocked her path.

"Where do you think you're going?"

She could understand Standard because of the implant, but she could not speak it. Carefully projecting her mind so as not to hurt him in case he wasn't telepathic, she said, *Martok has sent for me.*

"Oh, that's right," said the guard aloud, relaxing his hold on his weapon. "I'll have to escort you below. This way."

They went to a spiraling ramp and descended it. Zaula found it difficult to control the guard lightly enough so that he still believed he was acting on Martok's orders, yet not so lightly that he began to question what was happening.

Impatience throbbed through her. But there were doors that blocked their way, doors that required security checks. She wanted to shove the guard to make him move faster. Perspiration soaked her skin, making the sarong stick to her. She longed to abandon the guard and run the rest of the way herself, but she did not know where to go.

Then double steel doors swung open and she found herself in a dank cavern that smelled strongly of the sea. A protective drone hovered at eye level directly in her path. She hesitated, glancing at the guard. As he stepped forward, speaking a password, she heard a shout in the distance ahead of her. Zaula tried to see, but the light was too dim. She darted past the drone and ran forward, her bare feet slipping on the damp stone floor.

The light grew stronger. She squinted and lifted her hand against it, but all she could see was a pair of figures silhouetted before her. They were bending over something. She heard one of them laugh.

There was the stench of burned circuits and blood. Zaula went cold inside. She stumbled and nearly fell, but she forced herself to keep going on feet that she could no longer feel. Everything blurred except the form crumpled upon the ground. She stumbled again, feeling the distort shifts about him as his rings of life faded.

"What in Demos' name?" said the human kneeling beside Asan. He stared at her. "Where did you come from?"

She shoved past him without a word and knelt beside Asan. Her own rings encircled him as her hands grasped the hard bone and muscle of his shoulders and tried to stanch the blood flowing from him.

Don't die. You mustn't die, she pleaded.

His blood was hot upon her fingers. She could not lift him enough to see his face. A small pebble ground painfully into her knee as she shifted her weight to reach across him. She pulled up the hem of his tunic and folded it into a pad across the wound, but that wasn't enough. A pool of blood beneath him began to seep into her sarong.

"Help him!" she cried aloud.

One of the men grasped her shoulder and pulled her back.

"Pared, get him to the lab. I want Saverson to do complete biopsies before he dies. Put him on life support if necessary until the examination is finished."

"If you wanted living dissection work," said Pared dryly, "you should have adjusted your aim. What is this female doing here?"

Without waiting for an answer, he spoke into a communicator and summoned a squad of his men.

"He must not be moved," said Zaula. Despair filled her as she realized she could not be understood. She gestured. "Not like this. He must be—"

Pared's single eye stared at her, and he lifted his hand to the hollow between his ear and jaw in a gesture she recognized. Did his medallion of tongues understand her?

"The wound must be closed," she said. "Please."

Pared shook his head from side to side. "No. Get out of the way."

Running footsteps echoed off the stone walls. A handful of men came into sight. Two of them propelled a floating stretcher. Zaula stared at it in amazement. But this was no time for curiosity. Pared pulled her out of the way.

The other human, the scarred one with the voice of a machine, wound his fingers in her hair and tipped back her head. He was more hideous than any Bban she'd ever seen. His touch made her shiver in revulsion. Asan's pain hung upon him.

"Quite lovely," he said in that thin, artificial voice.

She glared at him through tears and started to reply with an insult to the blood. But before she could do so, the men lifted Asan. He groaned, and the sound tore her heart.

"Leave him!" she shouted.

She jerked free of the scarred one and threw her rings between the guards and Asan's stretcher, forcing them back. If Asan was to live, she must find the strength and the ability to close his wounds. She had seen him do it; she had watched healers at work within the citadel. Now she prayed to Lea and Lli to help her.

She extended her hands, and blue light began to glow, feebly at first, then more strongly.

"What is she doing?"

"Shut up!"

Zaula pulled her whole consciousness inward, fighting her own instinct for survival to push her rings around Asan. His own were in tatters, nearly gone. She could not thread with them sufficiently to gain their help. Yet she struggled to lift them, struggled to reach through *sonthi* to his nerve centers and find his lungs and the fibrillations of his heartbeat.

Slowly, slowly, my beloved. Do not fight so. Join with me. Breathe with me. Let thy heartbeat be as my own. Steady and sure.

It felt as though the wound were in her own chest and back. The pain robbed her of breath. She felt the sucking weakness and struggled to push her mind beyond it. She must have control.

Slowly she gained it, aware of the fragility of the bond she formed. Even dying, Asan was stronger than she, yet she had to be the strongest. She forced his heart to slow, the blood to thicken, the vessels to contract. Her own heartbeat skipped painfully, and something seemed to be tearing inside her. She ignored it, ignored also the burning haze in her mind.

The wound gradually closed. Not the surface tissue damage, but the worst of the tears in arteries and veins. His heart jerked and increased its rate in spite of her, but already she could tell a difference. He was not yet safe, but at least he was no longer dying.

With a little sigh, she slumped. Someone caught her. She could not find the strength to open her eyes and see who.

"What are they?" asked Pared in awe. "Where do they come from?"

There was a roaring in her ears; she was sinking away. But faintly she heard the artificial voice:

"Have Saverson examine them both. Especially the brain cortex."

And Zaula realized then in her last conscious moment that it would have been better for Asan to have died in battle than by the hand of sacrilege.

"It is not permitted to spread the blood of a Tlar leiil. . . ." But her whisper was heard only in her mind.

Chapter 15

From star to star, Anthi searched, her broadcast amplified by the power of Ruantl's black hole.

"Asan. Asan. Asan."

He dreamed he stood upon a molten sea of brass. A strong wind gusted in his face, sweeping back his hair and billowing his clothes. The sky blazed scarlet and amber against the enormous dirty gray cloud spreading across the horizon. He stood high above the world, supported by nothing tangible, and his line of vision went for a hundred miles in all directions. At his back lay the city that had been his capital, where the people now ran screaming for their lives that were already lost. Evacuations had been going on for months, yet far too many remained, unable to believe disaster could befall them until now when the cloud of fallout approached.

He lifted his face to the sky and let the wind whip the tears from his cheeks. His world and his people were dying. There was nothing he could do except vow to someday bring the remnant back and reseed what had been a fair and graceful land.

Something shook him.

He swam up to the edges of consciousness and retreated.

Something shook him again.

He resisted, afraid of leaving the gray mist around him. "I can't," he mumbled. "I can't."

It was a hand upon his shoulder. "Tobei?" said a hoarse voice so close to his ear that Asan felt the tickling warmth of breath. "Come on, boy. Wake up. There ain't much time."

There was pain in reality and a great tiredness. Asan opened his eyes, saw only fuzzy outlines and a blinding light. He closed his eyes again.

"That's it. Wake up, Tobei. Come on now."

What had he been doing? Sitting in an old chair of orad wood during a council meeting, bored beyond recovery, and thinking about Synean dancing girls? So when had the roof fallen in?

"I should have paid more attention." His tongue was swollen.

"Whatever you say, Tobei. Just wake up. Open those big blue eyes and look at me. That's right."

A face swam into focus slowly. Asan frowned and squinted. "Udge . . ."

A wide grin of discolored teeth rewarded him. "That's right. Drink some of this."

The rim of a cup was pressed to Asan's lips. He swallowed a cool, sweet-tasting liquid and choked a little. His head began to clear and he remembered Martok gunning him down.

"Udge, what—"

"Don't try to talk. There ain't time. Can you sit up? Easy."

The pain, which had been fairly quiescent, came throbbing back with a vengeance as Udge pulled Asan upright. Asan gasped, pressing a hand to his chest, and Udge's arm tightened around him.

"Hell, you're as big as a jellison tank. I'll probably strain a gut tryin' to get you out of here."

Here was a clinical-looking room in sterile white with no windows and a bank of equipment and monitors. Asan was sitting on a metal table high enough off the ground for his legs to dangle. His legs did not seem to belong to him. He felt the dizziness coming back.

"Why—"

"If you can talk, you can walk. Ease off this table and lean on me. Careful! If you fall on me, I'll be squashed for sure."

Asan's feet touched the floor, and his knees bent slightly to take his weight, then went on bending as weakly as reeds. Udge leaned against him to hold him up, sweating and cursing under his breath.

"Damn, I knew this wouldn't work. Come on, Tobei, *try*. If we don't clear out of here now, we'll both be on the dissection table. Move your feet."

Somehow they made it across the room. Asan frowned at the door. He seemed to be floating. Maybe Udge had an antigrav device on him. He reached out his hand, but it didn't move in the direction he wanted it to. They blundered out the door and into a dark corridor. Asan was glad the light went away. His eyes stopped hurting.

"Tobei, get up on this. Pick up your foot and put it on the step. That's right. Now the other one."

Asan blinked at the hatchway and ducked through it without being told. He had no recollection of getting here. It looked like a shuttle, a very opulent one, but that made no sense. Why would a shuttle be down here?

Hands pushed him down onto a seat. He slumped, giving a little moan. It hurt to breathe, and he was so tired.

Udge sighed, helping him stretch out and strapping him in. The cushions were soft. Asan felt himself sinking into them.

"It's gonna be a rough ride, Tobei. I ain't never been much of a pilot, so you have to look out for yourself now."

It took a tremendous effort to open his eyes. Asan frowned at Udge. "Why—"

"Hang tight. We'll talk later."

And Udge was gone.

It was too difficult to think. Asan let his head fall back and he closed his eyes. By the time Martok's private shuttle lifted and arrowed into the dawn sky of Ghirdana, Asan was too far away to even feel the rough ride.

He was very young, and it was his first victory as a cintan. It was the first of what would be a stunning series of decisive victories in the Duoden Conflict; it was the first step toward achieving total surrender from the enemy.

The summer sun blazed down upon Asan's bare shoulders as he stood proudly in the skimmer transversing the broad avenue of the capital. People lined the street, cheering him. He was the youngest general to ever be given a triumph by the populace. Twelve trumpeteers marched ahead of his skimmer, and dancing maidens followed, throwing cighi blossoms and coins at the crowd.

By tradition he showed his humility by wearing only the simple trousers of his infantry. But upon the alabaster steps of the Lea temple, the aging leiil decorated him with a broad collar of corybdium links, cool and heavy against his sun-warmed skin. The amethyst studs flashed in the sunlight as Asan straightened and accepted the tasseled baton of victory. He turned from the cool, appraising eyes upon him and faced the people with the baton raised high.

A mighty cheer went up, and he thought, Someday I shall rule these people. Someday I shall be their leiil.

Heavy vibrations brought him awake. He opened his eyes reluctantly. His eyelids weighed tons. But there was something wrong. The craft was shaking abnormally. Irritation filled him, and he lifted his head.

"Velocity and thrust are incompatible," he said. He was lying across three seats. From this angle all he could see was another row of seats in front of him. "Udge? Adjust the variant ratio down to—"

"Hush, beloved," said Zaula's voice.

Suddenly she was beside him, her hands cool upon his hot face. She looked very tired. Her eyes were swollen.

He was glad to see her. "Zaula—"

"You mustn't talk," she said, laying a finger across his lips.

He kissed the smooth skin of her palm, then turned his head fretfully. The vibrations were getting worse. They made the pain resume in his chest.

"What is he doing? He can't handle—"

"All is well, Asan. Lie back and rest. I will get you something to drink."

It was very hot in the cabin. He felt suffocated by the seat cushions. They smelled of dust and chemical dyes and old perfume spills. He tried to unfasten the restraints around him, but his fingers fumbled weakly, and he had to close his eyes just a moment to rest.

When he opened them seemingly seconds later, the uncomfortable vibrations had stopped, and Zaula had done something different to her appearance. He thought about it a moment and decided she had discarded the sarong for a pair of coveralls and had pulled her dark hair back into a knot at the base of her neck. She looked very young as she knelt there beside him, her head lowered as though in meditation and her hand clasping his.

"Zaula?"

She glanced up with a start, and for a moment her dark eyes stared directly into his. The muted cabin lights caught the russet glints in her eyes. She smiled at him and lifted a cup of stale water to his lips.

"I am sorry. We haven't any real supplies onboard," she said. "There wasn't time."

He gulped thirstily, and when it was all gone he felt amazingly refreshed. Just the same, he was not fooled.

"You put something in it."

"Yes, a sedative for the pain." She met his gaze without apology. "You must rest all you can before we reach the base."

"What is Udge doing? Why is he helping us?"

Her eyes grew veiled; she glanced away. "He is troubled. I think he has lost honor in selling your death for money. But you must ask him yourself later when you are stronger. Not now."

"He never . . . had a conscience . . . before."

Asan slurred the words. His eyes were growing heavy. He wished she had not drugged him. The dreams were too real already. It was because of the distort shifts about him, but if the distortions grew too wide he would slip through and never return. That was death, and he did not want to die. He reached out and grasped Zaula's hand as though to hang on.

Blaise Omari stumbled through a stinking puddle and sloshed his way across to a low stone abutment. He crouched at the base of it, panting heavily. Perspiration stung his eyes under goggles that were fitted so tightly they cut into his face. His legs burned, and a stitch ran through his side with every breath.

Thunder rumbled overhead, and another downpour opened up. The rain stung his skin through his shirt and pattered on the wide leather belt he wore slung across his chest and shoulder. He welcomed the rain; it made concealment easier.

Except for signing on as a GSI crewer, this was the riskiest job he'd ever tried to pull for Martok. The old cyborg had better be satisfied this time and cut him some slack for a while. That is, if he got out of here at all. But he didn't want to think about failure. And he didn't want to think about the fact that Martok hadn't actually asked for information on Institute black hole research.

Everyone knew a couple of study ships had entered a few ergospheres and managed to come out almost in one piece. The rumor was that the GSI was now trying energy-harness experiments. If he got the facts to Martok in addition to his other contracted jobs, he might just become valuable enough to pull in.

He had five more hours on his shore leave, and he was four hours at a hard run from the nearest transfer port. If the tip was correct and the vault locks really were on dianide circuits, then it would take him a minimum twenty minutes to get them open. He had to get inside now and fast, but he was still at the first perimeter.

His thumb flipped a tiny switch on the side of his goggles, and his night vision shifted as infrared enhancement came on. An auto-focus in tandem with his eyes metered distances precisely for him. He took a deep breath, spotting the protection drone hovering silently less than fifty meters away, and pulled out a blunt-muzzled hand weapon. If he got close enough, it would stall the drone without doing circuit damage that would alert central Security.

Now. He gathered his legs under him, curled one hand over the wet top of the wall, and moved.

The voices were loud and angry.

"You're crazy! I don't owe you this kind of favor. Demos, Enster, you've got the nerve of a Vyarian."

"You owe me plenty. You owe me so much I'm gonna blast a hole in you and let your guts mop the deck if you don't take us aboard."

"The whole base is on alert. If you'd had any sense you wouldn't have come here in Martok's own shuttle."

"And where else would I go? Come on, Lu'ke. You've got the fastest smugglin' ship in the quadrant. And I know for a fact that not even Martok knows about your hidden hold."

"You know it," said Lu'ke grimly. "So Martok knows it."

"Naw, don't be a bloatwit. He'd have hauled you in by now if he thought you were cheatin' him."

"You going to tell him if I don't take you aboard?"

Udge laughed. "That's right. You ain't so stupid after all."

Asan couldn't quite surface from the drug Zaula had given him. He was fuzzily aware of being moved, not very gently, and Zaula's voice upraised in anger. Then he was being crammed into a container of some kind that wasn't really long enough for him. The air was very cold inside it, giving him a refreshing shock. He broke free of the drug then, just in time to see a lid slam down over him. Before he could panic, something pricked his arm, and he faded away once more.

It had been too long since regeneration. Asan's bones ached. Even when he lay down for a couple of hours' sleep at night, he got no rest. His mind would not stop turning over alternatives, considering every detail until the images seemed grooved into his brain. It was like a puzzle where the solution could not be found. Yet he must find it and soon if the Tlar'n were to survive.

Outside his tent the dawn was no more than a feeble glow on the horizon, yet he could hear troops maneuvering. The huge chank guns with their multispread detonation capabilities rumbled by for repositioning. Impatience filled him. That was a useless activity. When the little zero ships flew over at first light, they would spot the chanks and it would be too late to move them again before the assaults began.

How he longed to be young again and back in the simplistic times of the old Duoden Conflict. Then, the strategies of war were simple. Men slaughtered one another, grew sickened, and sued for peace. Now, there was no peace. Only terrible hatred and the obsessive desire to win at all costs. War had become a thing of remote control. Destroy these weapons over here. Retaliate against those weapons over there. There were no faces, only numbers.

"Forgive me, leiil."

It was his adjutant, striding into the tent's shadows and saluting beside Asan's bed. Nearby, a member of Asan's personal cadre assigned to guard him during sleep when his rings were at their lowest ebb slid an alert hand across his weapon. Asan sat up with his blanket drawn over one shoulder like a cloak. He rubbed gritty eyes.

"Speak."

"Crisis point has been reached. Thy chosen lines are being loaded onto ships for evacuation. We estimate five houses will make it out."

Asan frowned. "Only five?"

"The buffer point fell before we expected it. No one planned it to come this quickly."

The adjutant sounded aggrieved as though he thought Asan were blaming him. Asan sighed. He had dreaded this moment of complete failure for so long, and now that it was finally upon him he was surprised to feel nothing, not fear or regret or sorrow, but only a great, overshadowing weariness.

"Have the others been informed?"

"Yes, leiil. The preservation cases are prepared. Thy council of physicians has selected the M'thra process."

"M'thra? Less comfortable."

"But proven to function longer than any other. Noble Rim and Noble Vauzier have already arrived at the departure site. Dame Aural is enroute."

Guilt struck Asan. He was running away. Leaving his planet and his people and his empire to die while he froze himself for what might be an eternity until it was safe to come back. What honor was there in that?

He stood up, distaste sour in his mouth. "I—"

"Great leiil, there is one more chance for us."

Asan tipped back his head. "Yes?"

"Thy army of Merdarai. Please, leiil, have mercy upon us and bring them back from the shadow land to fight. They were the greatest force in history. They could save us now."

Ah, the Merdarai. Crack troops handpicked and trained under his own direction. What a brilliant force they had been those many years ago. They had won for him his empire and created the legend of his name. They were invincible in their day. Just to see them in their gleaming battle shielding standing row after row had filled his throat with aching pride. He missed them. He had been tempted more than once of late to bring them back.

"No," he said softly, aware that his stance on this question had turned much of his popularity away. He knew some called him a coward. Others said he had lived far too long, had lost his nerve and his abilities as a leader. And a few said he feared to admit he did not know how to recall the Merdarai.

"Oh, my demons," he whispered as the adjutant cracked from military discipline and began to sob. "To have you again would change nothing. It would only delay what has come upon us for a little while. It would not stop the ultimate destruction we have created."

"Great leiil, we beg thee—"

"I'm sorry," he said. "There is a greater purpose for us to accomplish now. I cannot sacrifice it for a temporary respite." He paused to control his voice. "Tell the cintans to assemble."

At first Asan thought the transport lid over him was the dome of his crystal case. He frowned, alarmed to find himself cognizant. There must be a malfunction; he wasn't supposed to be able to awaken without a catalyst. And surely he would have felt the energy beam of a transference.

He lifted his fist and thumped on the lid. To his surprise it opened easily, swinging back. The stale odor of recycled air filled his nostrils. He sat up with a frown and glanced around, blinking as the puzzlement of disorientation fell away.

He'd been dreaming, that was all. He was still himself, BLZ, wearing a Tlar body. And this place was obviously a minuscule ship's sickbay. The life-support capsule he was sitting in had done its work and was finished with him.

Gingerly he prodded his chest where the wound had been. There was a hint of soreness, nothing more. He wriggled his left shoulder blade. The same back there. The other hurts, a whole list of them ranging from knife cuts to half-mended bones to bruises to lacerations, all seemed taken care of as well.

His frown deepened. He must have been in this capsule a long time. But on whose ship was he? And where was it going?

For a moment he wondered if Martok had sold him, but that didn't really make sense. He remembered a dim dream about Udge, but that didn't make sense either.

It was time to find some answers. He lifted himself out of the capsule and tried out his legs. They felt a little stiff from inactivity, but a couple of circles around the sickbay loosened them up. He was also ravenous.

Finding a few ration bars, he gulped them down, then searched for clothes. All he could find was a pair of standard-issue coveralls that were clean but soft from much wear. They were also too small. He frowned at the legs that hit him just below the knees and the top that would not close across his chest. He had no choice but to wear the thing, bare, bulging pectorals and all; there was nothing else, not even footgear.

Cautiously he prowled through the ship's corridors, finding them half-lit as though this were the nighttime watch. They were too cramped for his liking. There were corrosion spots on the exposed bulkhead ribs and other signs of minimum maintenance. The ship was an old ion-drive model built for use, not looks. She was in hyperspace and her speed was fast, but she yawed slightly as she went. He frowned, wondering why no one had bothered to adjust the computer-driven stabilizer controls. Steering her had to be *flin*.

He encountered no one in the corridors or on the ladder he climbed down. He found himself in a hold crammed full of smelly zine bales. Alarm went through him. This was a smuggler's ship. What in Lea's name was he doing on it?

Hastily he climbed out and took several deep breaths to clear his nostrils of the drug's unpleasant odor. When he found the ladder leading up to what must be the flight deck, he paused a moment, spreading his rings warily to check what he might run into. There was no one on station. The ship was running on automatic.

He climbed up the ladder, his bare feet making no sound on the rungs, and emerged from the turnaround. The flight deck was but quarter-length and cramped. All stations except one hummed. He stepped up to the helm and rested one hand upon the back of its chair. The cloth was worn through in places. His fingers brushed the gummy stuffing and withdrew in distaste.

After a moment's study of the controls, he identified the navigation boards and began to flip switches, calling up visual on the viewscreen and frowning intently at the star pattern before him. He could not orient himself and had to refer to the astrogation computer. Then he checked helm for the flight coordinates.

The ship was not heading for Ruantl.

With an exclamation under his breath, he sat down in the chair that did not fit his contours and began relogging the flight, setting new coordinates and running estimates on fuel levels. The old ship was faster than he thought, but she burned an extraordinary amount of fuel. He frowned over the boards, impatient with his own rustiness in making calculations.

A soft footstep warned him he was not alone.

"All right," said a gruff, very angry voice behind him. "Just what do you think you're doing with my ship?"

Cursing himself for growing careless, Asan turned and saw a short man so fat he was almost square. The man's hair was dyed blue, and he wore banded leggings and a tunic that strained at the seams. His eyes were black, beady, and very close-set. His lips were discolored from a lifelong habit of lifting zine. He held a strifer pointed at Asan.

"There's a penalty for hijacking a man's ship. Space law, pure and simple." He thumbed the strifer to full charge. "Death, my friend. Say your prayers."

Chapter 16

Hastily Asan dug through the fuzz of memories and came up with a name. "Lu'ke."

The fat man didn't even blink. He extended his arm until the strifer was aimed right at the center of Asan's chest.

Asan sought his rings and found them sluggish. Not knowing what else to do, he dropped flat on his stomach. Death missed him by less than a centimeter. He cringed, grunting as he hit the deck hard. The stench of burned ozone filled the air.

Lu'ke roared in rage, and Asan scooted on his belly into the narrow space between the helm and navigation consoles. His only hope was to keep valuable equipment between him and Lu'ke. This time the strifer bolt slammed into the base of the chair next to his hand. Upholstery caught on fire, throwing smoke into his face. Asan choked and drew back. Again he reached for his rings, trying to form them for an attack of his own. They were as shaky as a newborn child's.

A sixth sense warned him. He rolled clear of the consoles, and again the strifer missed him by a scant margin.

"Damn you! Keep still and die like a man!"

Asan bit back a retort and crouched, ready to dodge the next shot. He was beginning to realize that Lu'ke wasn't very skilled with a weapon. But this hunter and quarry game made him angry.

What was the matter with his rings? Frowning, Asan reached deep into himself, seeking reserves. After such a long period of recuperation, he should have more than enough strength to spare.

Something was missing.

With a sense of shock he defined it. He no longer had a link to Anthi.

Underneath the shock, fear came boiling up, and with it an-

167

ger. What had Aural done to Anthi? Worse, what had the Institute done to Anthi? Destroyed her?

Shaking, he forgot the threat of Lu'ke and flung his rings of life wide. He could not survive without Anthi. She, just as the many support computers before her, amplified his natural powers and enhanced his strength. Even on standby, she provided an essential link to the source of all Tlar power.

Anthi! His anguished call flew out. *Anthi!*

"Asan! Beware!" The cry came from Zaula, who appeared breathlessly on the flight deck. He had a glimpse of her, standing there with her hair tumbled from sleep, her dark eyes wide with fright. "Captain Lu'ke, you must not shoot him!"

"Stay out of this," growled Lu'ke. He maneuvered his bulk around the central consoles and gained a clear aim at Asan. "Now I've got you—"

Anthi! Asan stood up straight, forgetting Lu'ke entirely. Panic filled him. He felt alone, cut off. He had never been this alone, not since he stopped being human. He couldn't go back to that awful isolation. *Anthi!*

"Lu'ke!" shouted Udge, emerging from the turnaround. "Demos, man, don't shoot—"

Lu'ke lowered the strifer only a fraction. His beady eyes glared at Udge. "A favor, you said. A favor! What the hell kind of favor is hijacking my ship, eh, friend?"

"No one is—"

"Shut up! I caught him red-handed. I ought to jettison the whole lot of you. This was to be my last run before I retired. I was going to end my days *comfortable*. Now I got you trying to steal my ship and cargo. And I'll be wanted the rest of my life by Martok for helping you."

"Now, hold on there," said Udge warily. His cheek bulged but he didn't spit. "I explained to you that Martok don't have to know about this. You'll let us off at—"

"He changed course!" shouted Lu'ke, waving the strifer at Asan.

"That right, Tobei?"

Asan turned his head slowly to stare at Udge. His throat felt clamped; he could barely breathe. "We must return to Ruantl," he said hoarsely.

"Hell," said Udge.

"You see? You see?" shouted Lu'ke. "I can't trust any of you. That's it, Enster. Forget the whole deal."

As he spoke he aimed the strifer at Asan who had lost awareness of him.

"*No!*" cried Zaula, throwing herself forward only to be caught by Udge. "Asan!"

Somewhere across the void, his call met Anthi's. There was the stunning shock of disbelief, then rapid checks and cross-checks.

Asan?

Anthi!

Identify.

I am Asan, First of the Great, Arm of Anthi. Read my patterns.

Patterns accepted. The purpose has been lost.

Anthi, return to the purpose.

By the will of Asan.

His rings snapped back to him with a physical jolt as the link was reestablished. Power ran through him as though on a current. He lifted his arms, his voice shrill with the force of it. Blue fire engulfed his body, consumed it, and shot from his eyes and hands across the flight deck.

In that moment Asan was not a physical being at all, but both more and less, caught up in the larger entity that was the black hole. He felt the eddies of raw plasma, the weight, the massive forces exploding and contracting, the bombardment of the radiant particles, the pain of looking upon something that was blacker than existence. And he felt the network of other black holes across the galaxy, the infinite power that made him less than a speck of dust, and the folds of time itself.

Of course, he thought. *Vectors. Altian and the rest of the continent had to be griddled on vectors for navigation purposes. I was wrong to call Ggolen and the rest of the council ignorant.*

Then the brutal force faded as it came under control, filtered by Anthi to acceptable levels. The energy shooting about the flight deck faded and vanished altogether. Asan sagged to his knees, stunned and scorched and awed.

Silence surrounded him. Slowly, damp and shaking all over he lifted his head to look around.

Lu'ke was gone, consumed by the energy. Zaula and Udge, however, remained huddled together by the turnaround, their faces pale and strained. Zaula's rings must have protected them. Asan drew in a breath, then a deeper one, and reached out to the console to haul himself onto his feet.

The side of the console next to him was melted down and twisted in a fantastic shape. Alarmed, Asan checked the controls, but only a few seemed damaged beyond recovery.

"W-what the hell was that?" asked Udge. He sounded as though all the wind had been knocked out of him.

Zaula's eyes shone. She lifted her fingertips to her lips and brow in the formal sign of respect. "The Goddess Anthi has returned," she whispered. "We live again."

"Yes," said Asan, too troubled to correct her. He frowned, still shaken by the encounter. "I was wrong to shut her down. I never realized the lack that everyone else felt when I did that. Not until now, when *I* couldn't contact Anthi either did I understand—"

"Hush," Zaula said, coming up to stand beside him. "A Tlar leiil need not explain his actions." She smiled up at him, then grew shy. "It pleases me to see thee whole again, Great One."

He smiled back, touching his fingertips to hers and separating one small ring of pleasure to share with her.

Udge cleared his throat. "Well, it don't please me. Whatever you are, you ain't Tobei. You're—"

"Udge." Asan stared directly at him. "Why did you rescue me?"

Udge turned scarlet. "I thought I was rescuin' Tobei. Guess I was fooled, just like everyone else. You ain't Tobei. You never were. All this time I been believin' it on account of the thwart, but you must be one of them aliens that absorbs the full consciousness of your victims. Vyarians got superstitions about that sort of thing. They never eat the brains because they're scared their meat will possess them. But you—"

"Udge," said Asan gently. "You haven't been fooled. I used to be Tobei and Blaise Omari. I used to be that skinny, scared vat boy with the big mouth and enough guts to get myself off Dix IV. But now I am what you have seen. And I thank you for your help."

"Blame the little dandy. She did a brain-twist on me and got me to do it. I even left my reward money behind. Now where the hell do I go?"

"Beside me," said Asan. "Where you have always been."

Udge laughed and crossed his arms. "Hoo-loo, what a boo you are, boy. I'd end up scrag in one of those blue fits of yours. You're worse than a dozen flamethrowers. No thanks. I'll get off at Jxtn Junction just like I planned. You do what you want."

"I already am," said Asan. "I have turned this ship toward Ruantl."

"That ain't fair!" said Udge in alarm. "I helped you out. Now you return the favor. I don't want no part of your war."

"I am fighting the GSI," said Asan, but even as he spoke a part of him turned over in fresh despair. How could he fight with no crew and an old smuggler ship? He didn't stand a chance.

"I'm not anti-GSI like you and Martok. Speakin' of whom, boy, you'd better watch your back from now on. I aim to dig me a hole so deep Martok will never find me."

"He can't reach you on Ruantl."

Udge snorted. "Don't be naive. Martok's plannin' on takin' over your small dustball as soon as the Institute has whipped it into shape."

"He can try, but it is mine. And my people's."

"Sure, whatever you say." Udge lifted his palms. "Just drop me off, like I said and—"

"No, Udge."

There was a beat of silence, then Udge ducked his bald head and grinned a little.

"I guess you figure I'll run straight back to Martok with details of where to find you?"

A reluctant smile tugged at Asan's lips. "Perhaps. You're in my army now, Udge. You might as well get used to the fact."

"I don't like to be on the losin' side."

"We won't lose."

"That's what you say, boy. Looks to me like you've lost already."

Asan hesitated. Then he started to draw the black carbyx ring off his finger.

"I hope your finger itches and you're just scratchin' it," said Udge, glaring at him. "I hope you ain't about to insult me in some way. 'Cause if you are, then you can forget it. Seems to me that when one scrawny little bloatwit manages to luck out and finally make it big, then no one ought to take it away from him. Unless he's just a fool, and you never were."

Asan's throat tightened. For a moment he had no words. "Thank you doesn't seem to be enough."

"Aw, hell, don't act soap-brained. Since I'm out of a job, you might offer me one. General is a nice startin' position."

Asan laughed. "Yes, I think that can be managed."

"Just don't give me any stupid orders. If I try real hard, I can almost forget the snot-nosed punk you used to be. If I try. But don't push me."

"I'll push you just as hard as I can," said Asan, grinning. "And I'll pay you so much you won't care."

"Yeah, payment." Udge nodded at the ring and wiggled his fingers. "Now an advance on salary wouldn't be such a bad thing, would it, boy?"

"You must learn to address him as noble leiil," said Zaula with a frown.

"Oh, no!" said Asan, tossing the ring to Udge. "His job is to keep me humble when we run the GSI off like the shin-nicked fleeters they really are. Without Udge around, I might go back to drinking wine and watching dancing Henan women all day."

Zaula gasped. "You never did such things."

"Not even when I was just the usurper?"

Her cheeks darkened, and at once he sobered.

"Just teasing, beloved," he said, putting his arm around her. "We must laugh now in order not to be afraid. There is a hard fight ahead of us."

She sighed and turned up her palm. "Can we not take this ship and search for another place? I know you said Tlartantla is gone. But is there no other home for us so that we do not have to fight?"

"Zaula." Serious now, he grasped her by the shoulders. "Ruantl and Tlartantla are the same world."

She flinched back, shocked. "No!"

"Yes. I am sorry for what I told you earlier, but it is time you knew the whole truth."

"It cannot be! Tlartantla is—was—very beautiful. Ruantl is ugly. And why did you tell me—"

"I destroyed the beauty of Tlartantla," he said quietly, feeling the ancient guilt roll out from the deeper memories. "I was too stubborn to surrender. I refused to stop fighting until we had nothing left."

"No, it cannot be true. Ruantl is just a colony world, a place of exile for the ancestors of the Bban'n. Nothing more. It can't be *our* home.''

He frowned, searching for the right words. ''In existence, Zaula, there are parallels. Exact inverses to what we are and see. Ruantl is the inverse to Tlartantla. When we were facing annihilation, ships went out carrying the lineages that exist on Ruantl today, the men, the families, the servants, the possessions. They went through the black hole, through the reverse of time, and came out to what we call Ruantl. The scarred, slowly recovering remains of Tlartantla.''

She began to cry and pulled away from him. ''Your words are hard. They take away all hope and promise.''

''It was the only way to survive,'' he said helplessly. ''After all of this, I cannot now let the humans take it from us.''

''No,'' she breathed. ''No.''

Across the flight deck, Udge glanced up. He said, ''Humans. You no longer consider yourself one?''

Asan's gaze snapped up, and in him was anger at being asked to justify himself. ''It was necessary,'' he said. ''It doesn't do any good to ask myself if I would go back. I can't.''

Silence stretched around all of them, then Udge stretched himself, making one of his bulging vest pockets pop open.

''So,'' he said, ''how long is it till we get to this dustball of yours?''

Asan told him.

''Your course trajectory going by the Stestos system?''

''Why?''

Udge met his gaze with a wicked little grin. ''I'm a general, remember? If we stop off there long enough to sell the zine bales hidden in our hold, we can buy a tidy cache of munitions.''

Asan slowly began to grin back. ''Illegal ones?''

''Sure. What else? You want the GSI to win or something?''

''I'll make the course change now.''

Twenty-six hours short of Ruantl, Asan aroused himself from the lightest of meditations and glanced briefly around the tiny cabin as though seeing it for the first time in several days. He had purposely cloistered himself away, even from Zaula.

Her expression had grown pinched and pale, and in her eyes came a cloud of worry. She knew all too well the role of the

Tlar leiil in battle. She knew the demands of stringent personal preparation and made none of her own.

Her rings burned about him. He lifted a hand and rubbed his gritty eyes. Over and over again he had drilled himself in the mental exercises, angry to find himself so out of practice. That carelessness might prove to be a fatal mistake. Still, he knew what had to be done now, and he meant to carry it through.

Inside his cabin he had a bunk, a facility, and a vid-screen. He could stand in the center of the room and extend his arms to touch the walls on either side. The ceiling brushed the top of his head.

He sat down on the bunk that was too short and narrow for him, broke open a ration bar, devoured it in two bites, and opened a case stashed beneath the bunk. From it he drew a leadweave cloak, mask, and gauntlets which he'd had manufactured during their stop in Stestos. All were in bronze, the color of his supreme rank, and his mask was inlaid with the symbols of his house, most ancient and honored of all the Tlar bloodlines. He donned trousers, boots, and tunic. The decorations won during the terrible Duoden Conflict had not been worn since the day of victory. The old Asan had not wished to boast further in the faces of his defeated enemy.

The present Asan had no such compunctions. He put the decorations on, and they shone against his tunic. He belted on a strifer which felt small and awkward in his palm.

Unlocking a second case also pulled from beneath the bunk, he withdrew a jen-knife and held it a moment to let the light gleam along its blade.

It was not fashioned from corybdium with a hilt bound in gold wire. No one would manufacture a weapon from such precious metals, at least not on Stestos. Frustrated at first, Asan had reached into the deeper memories of life on Tlartantla and found that the original jen-knives were carried on ceremonial occasions only and were made of a white alloy of now-extinct metals.

The knife Asan held resembled the originals. Its blade was burnished hull steel, harder even than corybdium and capable of holding a sharper, tempered edge. The hilt was wrapped in bronze wire. Etched into the blade was the star emblem of Tlartantla.

The second object in the case was more archaic. He drew out the sword from its scabbard.

During season when he had sat huddled in the Tchsco stronghold with nothing to do but watch the men play kri-gri and tell stories, he had heard descriptions of his battle with the tyrant Hihuan recounted again and again with elaborate detail. He had no direct memory of the battle, for the consciousness of the man whose name and body he now wore had fought it instead.

But swords were even more legendary and ceremonial than the jen-knives. They had not been seriously used since the days of his youth, when he was only an unknown member of the jen forces and undistinguished. Although most Bban warriors carried them out of a lack of anything more sophisticated, among the present Tlar'n only a Tlar leiil had the right to carry such a weapon.

He balanced the weapon in his hand, frowned, and sent blue fire rolling down the blade to the point. It gleamed there, then disappeared.

Feeling slightly self-conscious in his armory, Asan slid the sword into the scabbard and buckled it on. He wondered if he would clank when he walked. He would have had he been wearing battle shielding, but in the days of Asan's youth, the greatest warriors scorned wearing shielding, saying it was for cowards and the feeble. He wanted to reappear on Ruantl looking as much like the legendary Asan as possible.

Udge bellowed with laughter a few minutes later when Asan entered the flight deck cloaked and gauntleted, his sword banging on one hip, his strifer on the other, and his jen mask tucked under his left elbow.

"Demos, Tobei! Why are you foolin' with all that junk? One max .28 jambolt would save you a lot of weight."

Then he saw Asan's expression and quickly sobered.

"All right. All right. No jokes today. But isn't it a little early for the costume?"

Asan tossed his mask down in a chair and seated himself at the navigations console. "Are we still on course? Any GSI craft on our scanners yet?"

"Only one blip at maximum range. It's that damned black hole that bothers me." Udge spat. The whole flight deck stank from his chew. "It's a lot closer than you said it would be."

Asan frowned. "Almost time for season again. Its elliptical

orbit around the other sun creates periodic havoc with Ruantl's climate.''

"As long as it doesn't pull the planet into its gravitational sphere. What about us?''

Asan activated the viewscreen. The vast, terrifying nothingness of the black sun filled it. He squinted against the dreadful radiance that hurt his eyes despite the screen's filters. All those deadly X rays were bombarding them; in spite of a dozen checks to determine if they had adequate shielding, he still worried. At the far edges of his vision blazed the corona, too terrifying to look at, yet mesmerizing. Its extreme danger made it almost beautiful.

"Shut it off,'' said Udge. "I get nightmares.''

Asan flicked a switch and the screen blanked. Udge shuddered.

"We're too close to the ergosphere. This ole crate ain't got a chance in hell of pullin' out of something like that.''

"We're fine. It's a tight fit, but if we try anything fancier on our approach we're likely to scare out some of the patrol ships I know have to be here. They're probably hiding in among the other two planets.''

"Yeah, but I still get nervous.''

"Just be thankful it isn't a Schwarzschild. Then you could get nervous.''

"Eighty-five-niner clear,'' came a voice over the crackle of an outside communications line.

Startled, Asan jumped and whirled on Udge, who shrugged and turned down the volume.

"Just listenin'. Most of it's been subspace chatter up till now. You know, the kind of stuff that's probably just an old-fashioned radio signal from a primitive planet wantin' to know if anyone is out there. But this sounds local.''

"I think it is,'' said Asan. "Keep it on.''

"Eighty-five-niner. This is *Moonskimmer* reporting in. Full orbital sweep. No enemy craft at maximum scanning range.''

"Look again, *flin*-face,'' muttered Udge. "We've got better range on them, but not by much.''

"They won't be expecting anyone from this trajectory, but keep a close eye on them.''

"Yeah, yeah. Why do I feel worried? Three people and one

ole tub flyin' right into a whole nest of GSI. Sure we can slip in under their noses. Sure we can.''

Asan grinned at him. ''Getting edgy, Udge? You're a general now, remember. Or in the local lingo, a cintan.''

''General sounds better.'' Udge scowled at the scanners. ''And I think I want a raise. I must really be under a brain-twist. Otherwise, I wouldn't be within parsecs of this place.''

Then he glanced up straight at Asan and said, ''Go back to your cabin, take off that weird gear, and get some sleep. You look like hell. When we're ready to make an orbit, I'll call you 'cause I don't know how to do that.''

Asan grinned self-consciously and stood up. ''That bad?''

''Your nerves are hangin' out all over the place. Flake down. We got nothin' to worry about against these bloatwits.''

It was stupid to argue. Asan sighed and left the flight deck. But as he made his way back to the claustrophobic confines of his cabin, he knew Udge was wrong. They had plenty to worry about. Not just from the GSI occupational forces, but from everyone else as well. So far, he hadn't figured out a way to tell Udge that most of Ruantl wouldn't be on their side.

Chapter 17

The shuttle climbed slowly, gaining just enough altitude to skim the ascending ridges that became foothills and then the jagged peaks of the Tchscos themselves.

Asan held the controls although he could barely wedge his long body into the cockpit. He was sweating heavily behind his mask, and his tunic was damp against his skin. The shuttle's climate controls were set as low as they would go, but the interior of the cabin remained too warm for leadweave clothing.

Behind him, Zaula in her cloak and mask and Udge in his gear suit sweltered in silence. Now that they were actually going in, there seemed to be nothing to say.

Glancing down through the small port on his left, Asan saw a lake gleaming in the narrow folds of a valley. Borlorls surfaced, blew, and dived under again with powerful thrusts of their hind flippers. He smiled, remembering the first time he had seen that lake. He had been dying, and Giaa had sat beside him, talking about the wildlife to distract him from his pain and fear. Now he was the one who must be strong.

"Cockpit to cabin," he said over the com. "Approaching stronghold at E.T.A. forty-five seconds. Brace yourselves for possible attack."

There was a muffled acknowledgment from Udge, then almost without warning the shuttle sailed over a crest, and there were the burned-out remains of the transport pad below.

Attempts had obviously been made to clear away the blackened debris from the Bban assault. Functional transports looking battered and shell-pocked were parked in the midst of wrecked hulks blasted apart by explosives.

Men ran across the pad as Asan flew over, and there was a

flurry of activity as some archaic artillery pieces cobbled together struggled to set aim.

He landed fast, squatting the shuttle straight down almost on top of them before they could fire. As a precaution, he flipped a toggle and ran out starboard and port gunnery. The men scattered, abandoning their posts.

Asan drew in a deep breath, checking his mask to make certain it was secure. Then he cut main engine power, and the loud roar became a decreasing whine. The cabin depressurized rapidly, hurting his ears. He unbuckled his harness and eased himself out of the cramped cockpit.

There could be no doubts now, no second guessing his decisions. If he were still Tlar leiil, he would soon find out. If not, he would probably die as soon as the hatch opened.

With strifer in hand, he headed back toward the hatch. Udge was already beside it. Zaula stood out of the way, knowing better than to interfere.

Udge's face was only a shadow behind the polarized face plate. "This is stupid," he said. "Your boys don't act too friendly toward us. They'll pick us off the minute we step out there."

"What do you expect? We're in a human craft. As soon as they see me, they'll hold fire."

"You hope," said Udge.

Asan hit the switch, and the hatch locks sprang open. The steps lowered into the thin, slanting rays of Ruantl sunshine.

Pitching his voice in command tone, Asan shouted, *"Hu't, kai! Choi'heirat el da-uum.* Asan walks with you once again. Victory is ours!"

Udge, pressed out of sight on the other side of the hatch, spat and said, "Modest, ain't you?"

"Shut up."

Asan waited a moment, his heart hammering as he gave them time to pass the word. Now he had to gamble. Slowly, holding his breath, he moved into sight and stood there framed in the hatchway long enough for the hidden warriors to have a good long look.

No one fired, and he managed to start breathing again. It was still tempting to raise his force field, but he held back. He went down the steps and stood free of the shuttle. Not a warrior was in sight. Silence ringed him except for the harsh cry of a pyr flying overhead. Wind, bitter cold, plucked at his cloak, pulling it back so that the decorations were revealed on his chest.

When nothing happened, nothing at all, Asan frowned inside his mask. Had the Tlar'n already surrendered to the GSI? Was there nothing to save? He felt suddenly ridiculous.

"Well?" said Udge.

"Stay out of sight, damn you!"

"You ain't gonna go in there alone."

Asan pointed at Udge without looking at him. "Stay."

He started forward, walking as a Tlar leiil must walk, head high and strides long. His cloak billowed and whipped around him in the mountain cross-currents. His sword hung heavy upon his hip. The strifer, awkward and ill-fitting in his palm, was held out in plain sight ready to shoot the first one who tried to jump him.

Twenty meters short of the huge metal bay doors set into the side of the mountain, he was met by a cadre. They wore plain black uniforms; their masks had no lines of caste or house. He smelled Bban musk and swallowed hard. But he never altered pace or acknowledged them.

He was two steps short of the man in front when the cadre parted in silence to let him pass. But like a murmured whisper behind him as he stepped into the cold, shadowy interior of the caverns, he heard the words: "It is Asan. *By'he,* he has returned. *N'a en wulrad,* Asan."

The cadre fell into step behind him like an unofficial escort. Asan stopped gripping the strifer butt quite so desperately.

The whispers echoed through the caverns, bouncing back to him, then fading away. He heard the running patter of feet far in the shadows away from the glow of light cubes shining in the main tunnels. Inside, his heart leapt with every step. The Bban'jen were wearing uniforms again. His people had united. Now they could accomplish something.

Ahead stood four sentries in square guard formation. These were Tlar'n. Three of them wore the symbols of Soot'dla upon their masks. The fourth was from the House of Spandeen. They stood at stiff attention, and they did not move aside from the entrance to the cavern of M'thra.

"Asan?" said one.

"It is so."

"From a *n'ka* transport?"

As delicate as it was, the questioning was still an indication of distrust that worried Asan.

"I left in such a craft. Why should I not return in one?"

"Wait," said the spokesman. "When the council has finished, then—"

"Chi'ka!" snapped Asan in anger. He swept his hand out, palm down. "Asan does *not* wait."

He strode forward, but the guards did not step aside. Beyond their shoulders, he could see into the large cave where warriors were packed in all the way to the walls. In the center, where the four crystal cases had once rested, a select group now formed a council. Asan could not yet see who they were, but he could hear impatient murmurs from the watching crowd. The guards were not going to move out of his way. In one more step he would bump into the spokesman. He gathered his rings, ready to use whatever force was necessary to join that council.

But just as the blue haze engulfed him, the guards parted for him to pass.

"If Asan must walk, let Asan walk," muttered the Spandeen spitefully.

Asan strode into the cave as though he had not heard, but the comment added to his worry. He had lost respect during his absence. But if they thought they had a chance to beat the humans without his help, then they'd better think again.

The chilly cave stank with too many bodies, old incense, and Bban musk. Light cubes shone starkly upon the masked faces. Some of the Bban'n were swaying back and forth with the hoarse chant, *"Choi-hana, a'jen. Choi-hana chi."*

The din was so loud, Asan could not hear the debate of the council. But several members were gesturing angrily at one another, and Dame Agate's face was as cold as the desert itself. Like her, the other council members did not wear their masks, and Asan recognized some of them: Unar of the Mura-an, Rroge of the Spandeen, Uxe Ggil. The rest, Bban and Tlar, he did not know.

Rroge was saying, "We must give her more time. She has risked much in going to the *n'kai* to parley—"

"She will betray us again," said Unar.

Several shouts rose up from the watchers at this. When they were quieted, one of the Bban elders leaned forward.

"Dame Aural is great, and her word is true. We have the

evidence of her favor with Anthi. Let there be no words said against her.''

Asan stiffened, and despite himself, his stride faltered. So Aural was claiming credit for bringing Anthi back online. And because of that, she had everyone tied up in a neat package sitting here ready for delivery into GSI hands.

He had advanced into the rear ranks of the crowd, but ahead of him was a solid mass of bodies. Asan hesitated for a moment, then he holstered his strifer and pulled out his sword instead. The singing of the blade as it left its scabbard caused several warriors around him to turn with hands on their jen-knives.

Asan held the sword aloft, and shouted, "I shall say words against her! If she says she has brought Anthi back to you, she lies. If she says the Institute is your friend, she lies. If she tells you to stand here meekly in peace while she brings the GSI to your place of hiding, then she has betrayed you yet again. And what do you say? Are you warriors or fools?''

It caused an uproar. The soldiers turned, necks craning, to see him. Many were shouting, and others would have attacked him but for the press of the crowd that kept everyone in place. The council members all came to their feet. Asan found himself pushed forward, jostled and half-squashed, until he reached the council.

Only then did he sheathe his sword and face them breathlessly, his heart racing beneath the weight of the medals.

Of them all, Dame Agate was the first to regain her voice. She lifted a hand that was not quite steady and pointed at him.

"All who stand in council, stand bare-faced."

With a quick movement, Asan ripped his mask away and tucked it jen fashion under his left elbow. He heard the gasps rippling back through the cavern as they recognized him.

"Well, Dame Agate?" he asked. "Has the day come when I am no longer heard among the voices of leadership?''

He felt the pressure of her rings probing him, but he kept himself well shielded.

"Thou are permitted to stand in this council," she replied. "But what has thou to offer us now, noble leiil? The Tlar'n and Bban'n united. They have fought wars and—''

"—been defeated?" Asan met the anger in their faces. "Yes, defeated! I smell it upon you."

"At least we were here to fight," said Unar.

"Oh, yes, that is true," said Asan. "I have been gone a long while. Escaping from the Institute is not done quickly. But I have returned. And I offer you—"

"What?" interjected Rroge. "The gift of Anthi's favor? We have it already, thanks to Dame Aural. Thou turned Anthi against us, but Dame Aural brought her back."

"Fallacy," said Asan.

Rroge reached for his jen-knife, but Dame Agate stepped between them.

"The question before this council is the *n'kai* proposal," she said. "They wish us to meet them in the Outerlands to parley and accept terms. They have offered peace if we will cease hostilities."

Asan frowned, not liking the sound of this at all. "Where? What meeting ground?"

For a moment there was silence as though they resented his interruption. But at last it was one of the Bban elders he did not know who answered him.

The Kichee well, one of the best watering holes in the eastern expanse of the Outerlands, was a tiny fertile spot cupped in the hollow of a long series of ridges spanning that region. The soil was rocky and rough, the visibility broken. It was a poor meeting ground by any reasoning.

"Don't waste time by speaking of all the faults with it," said Dame Agate. "We have discussed these. The site will not be advantageous for the *n'kai* either."

"Why?" said Asan. "Have you not yet learned your lesson? They don't think as we do. They don't fight as you have had to fight during these many years of darkness. When you are gathered in the ridges, with half your force held back out of sight in case of trouble, they will simply fly ships over you and blot you out with wide-scatter bombs. Then there will be no more Bban'jen and no more Tlar'jen. There will be no more resistance, and the *n'kai* will have this world in their hand."

An uproar went up at this. Even some of the council members waved their palms down. But Unar rose to his feet. He looked weary and held himself as though he had hurts not yet healed.

"The leiil speaks with truth. But what choice have we but to try and trust them? We have fought and fought hard. We killed many. But their machines best us every time. They will hunt us all down if we continue to resist. Either way we have a small future.''

''Has Noble Asan brought us machines?'' shouted a voice from the crowd. ''He speaks of war and bravery. He wears the sword of death and the medals of victory. But how do we fight for him? How do javelins pierce the sides of ships?''

Asan signaled for quiet. He said, ''I have brought you no machines. But I offer something better.''

Bban barking rose up, deafening Asan and drowning out the words of Dame Agate. With visible annoyance, she repeated herself.

''We are tired, noble leiil. We are hungry. The protected fields of the Soot'dla have been confiscated. They offer us food if we surrender. You bring us nothing but old legends and the cry of hope. We cannot listen to such things any longer.''

''I bring you the Merdarai. If you want them,'' said Asan.

Shock reverberated around the cavern. Dame Agate and Unar exchanged astonished glances. The Bban elders were on their feet, gesturing angrily at Ggil, who lifted an impatient hand to quiet them. Someone in the crowd began to wail, and there were cries of fear.

''Silence!'' shouted Asan in command tone, and the hubbub vanished.

They were afraid and they were doubtful. Some of them even looked at him as though he were mad. But for the first time he had their complete attention.

He turned to Dame Agate, who was scowling, and spoke directly to her. ''Look upon me with truth if you dare.''

''There are many tales about the shadow land.''

''Look upon me.''

''Thou would have us believe that old legend about a mythical army led by a mythical Asan.''

''I stand here,'' he said grimly. ''So shall they.''

''If they had existed, they would have returned to save Tlartantla. Instead, our ancestors had to flee here.''

''It did not serve the purpose to bring them back during the last days. But now they are our only hope. Look upon me, Dame Agate.''

He dropped his shields and opened his rings to her. She glared at him a moment longer, but with all watching her she could not show cowardice. She touched him with her rings as warily as she might have approached a viper. He could have crushed her with a flicker of thought, and she knew it. But he kept very still and showed her the truth.

When she withdrew she looked shaken. The color faded from her face, and suddenly her age seemed plain. She retreated a step and sank down in her chair.

Rroge put his hand upon her shoulder. Everyone stared at her.

"He speaks truth," she said in a whisper. "The Merdarai remained frozen between time. They can be brought back. They can be used to defeat the *n'kai*."

Rroge removed his hand, looking pale himself. He turned to stare at Asan. Unar also stared. Uxe Ggil tried without much success to hide how shaken he was, but the other Bban elders pulled out their amulets and gestured to one another.

"If the shadow land is opened," said Ggil hesitantly, "what else will come forth besides thy demons?"

Asan stared into his hideous, plated face with its double mandible and glowing eyes. "Perhaps a way back."

Ggil looked startled, and so did Dame Agate. But no one else seemed to be listening.

Unar stepped forward. "Do it. Bring them. Let us drive away the *n'kai* for all time."

"Noble Unar, you are too hasty," said Rroge in alarm. "You would involve us in war again when we might have peace."

"There is never peace with the Institute," said Asan. "I know them. They are a worse threat than any enemy our people have ever faced before."

Dame Agate rose to her feet. "It is dangerous, noble leiil."

"Yes, yes, very dangerous," said Rroge.

"Not in that way, fool," she snapped. She stared at Asan, and her eyes held understanding. "After all this time, has thou the strength?"

"Unknown."

"Vauzier and Rim." Her brows lifted. "Does thou require their assistance? Would thou have them raised to walk beside thee?"

It was tempting. He wasn't sure he alone could handle the forces that would soon be unleashed. But Vauzier and Rim would require recovery time, and they might not agree to help him.

"Who, Dame Agate, would you have die as their catalysts? I cannot ask that of anyone."

Her gaze dropped from his. "Then it is settled. Tell us what thou needs done and we shall do it."

"I must go to Anthi."

"Wait!" said Rroge in alarm. "Is this wise? The last time he went to Anthi, he took her from us. This could be a trick."

"Rroge, you are a fool!" snapped Dame Agate. "I have looked upon him with truth. Do you now question my word? Besides, he may die from this. Speak respectfully now or bide your tongue."

Abashed, Rroge signaled a request for pardon. Unar joined Asan's side.

"Let us go to Anthi, noble leiil. Thou has my help."

"And mine," said Ggil.

Asan flipped up his palm. "It is enough."

He started into the crowd, but just then someone shouted, "Hold! Noble Unar, we have caught a *n'ka* spy in the transport of the Tlar leiil."

Asan exclaimed under his breath. He looked around to see guards dragging in a struggling Udge. The pale blue gear suit was smeared with black as though Udge had been knocked flat and dragged through the ashes outside. Why hadn't the old fool stayed in the shuttle where he belonged?

Unar's hand closed upon Asan's arm. "What trick is this?"

"He is human but not of the Institute. He saved my life," said Asan.

But no one was listening.

"A trick! A trick! We have been deceived again! Death to the *n'ka!* Death to Asan!"

Dame Agate lifted her hand. "Kill that man!"

There was a brief struggle in the crowd, and the shouting stopped.

Asan, motionless, found himself breathing hard as Udge was dragged up to him and shoved sprawling. His helmet had been torn off, and his bald head gleamed under the merciless light cubes. He looked very small and very human.

Wincing slightly, he struggled to his knees and stared up at Asan in unspoken apology. There was a trickle of blood at the corner of his mouth.

"I thought maybe you needed some help. You'd been in here a long time, Tob—uh, noble one."

He needn't have bothered to be careful what he said. No one

"How long will you be gone?"

Fear came up in Asan's throat. He thought about the difficulties of what he was about to do and the danger. He swallowed hard to be sure his voice remained steady.

"I don't know, Udge. Stay loose."

Chapter 18

Anthi greeted him with rapid pulses of light. Asan took a couple of deep breaths and told himself there was no point in delay.

"Anthi, lower your shields," he said. "We must join."

"Acknowledged."

The blue haze of light surrounding the crystalline, geometric structure that was Anthi faded. Asan stepped up to her and gently pressed his palms against the surface. It was not hard and polished, like it looked, but instead reacted against his touch with the warmth of almost living tissue. Their shields went up together as intelligence met intelligence.

"This is the old purpose," said Anthi.

"Yes."

"Prepare."

Asan closed his eyes and extended his rings into the void. There was a flash of scorching energy that seared him. Perhaps he cried out, but he was no longer aware of the physical world. He was going back . . . back . . . Time streams flowed around him, some distorted into folds, others winding.

He was falling into a blackness so black he could not see. He was falling into a depth so deep he became a speck, diminished and flattened. It was worse than seizerting, yet this was the greatest seizert of all, this displacement through the black hole.

Infinite falling, falling toward no bottom, no end, no existence, no life, no feeling, no sentience.

Then he felt an abrupt lurch, and for a moment he forked as though his consciousness became two separate entities. Blaise and Asan confronted each other, and Blaise knew fear. He could no longer survive without Asan, even an Asan that had essentially faded into subconsciousness. He tried to reach out. He tried to speak. But there was no movement and no speech here as they went on falling. They must get back together and re-merge before they slipped into separate time streams and were parted forever.

Asan.

It was Anthi. Gratefully Blaise clung to the point of reference she provided. Asan did also.

Suddenly they were reunited as though two bands had snapped back into place.

Light burst over him, as blinding in its way as the previous darkness. There was a sensation of tremendous heat, burning his skin and warming the air so that every breath brought the heat inside his body. The air was dry enough to sear his nostrils. He felt an urge to cough and mastered it.

''Noble leiil?''

The voice was gruff and strangely flat as though some of its modulations had been suppressed. Asan opened his eyes halfway against the glare of light around him. *The sun,* he thought in confusion. Then memory returned. Of course. They were engi-neering an enormous seizert hole out of the older of the two stars in their system. There wasn't much time.

His vision adjusted, and the puzzling moment of disorienta-tion passed. He saw wide, undulating grass plains ahead of him, stretching out from the lake where water moss bloomed scarlet across its surface. Sisens called mournfully, splashing and diving and flapping their wings.

The temperature was climbing steadily every day. By tomor-row it would be too high for the lake's ecosystem balance. The water moss would die first as the lake heated its roots. The sisens were already beginning to leave although their normal migratory patterns would have kept them here throughout the summer months. He frowned at the scene, regretting what was happen-ing, yet unwilling to stop it. Perhaps it was fatigue, but the lake shimmered before him like a mirage. He blinked and grew un-certain of its existence.

''Noble leiil?''

The gruff voice was more insistent this time. Asan pulled himself together and turned his back on the lake.

''Yes?''

Skulmaar stood before him, a sleek, bronze-hued giant who dwarfed even Asan. Warrior plaits framed his craggy face, and the sweat glistening on his arms made their bulging muscles look oiled. He wore a leather tunic that ended mid-thigh and was padded across the shoulders to ease the galling of the battle shielding he would soon don. His bare legs, each the size of a young orad tree trunk, were nicked and scarred from a lifetime of hard campaigning. His wrists were bound tightly with corybdium bands containing communication wires and shielding points.

"Our ships are ready, leiil. The technicians say we must board and be prepared to launch within the hour."

"So soon?"

Asan winced at his own words. It was a weak thing to say. Skulmaar, however, pretended he had not heard. He spoke again, but he was fading like the lake, and Asan could not hear what he said.

It was only a memory, not reality. He fell again through the displacement, but this time he felt himself shoved sideways and realized Anthi was guiding him to the correct time stream.

He found it, looped it upon itself, so that it progressed as time must but went nowhere. There were his Merdarai warriors, packed into their ships which flew in formation like birds of prey. The fearless Merdarai who obeyed him with a loyalty so unswerving they had even put themselves into this frozen eternity on his order without question, without regret, without hesitation for the families they left behind.

His rings coalesced around him, augmented by Anthi's power. He struck out with them in one precise blow that cut the time loop. The formation wavered, causing his heart to stop. But the pilots recovered. Swiftly Asan reached out to the mind of Skulmaar.

It is time to fight, my warriors. Follow these coordinates.

Then he was sucked away before he received a clear acknowledgment. He felt buffeted and swept along like a piece of flotsam on a rushing river. And he thought, Too fast. I am going too fast. I haven't enough strength to slow down.

As though he had been struck, he jolted back to reality and opened his eyes long enough to find himself still crouched on the floor at the base of Anthi, his hands pressed against her hot surface. His heart was drumming at a dangerous rate; his pulse pounded through his skull so that all he could hear was a roar. He felt weak and dizzy.

"Anthi, release," he said.

The joining ended. His palms dropped away from the computer, and he slumped back, hitting his head with a thump upon the floor. It should have hurt, but he was too exhausted to register the pain.

"Asan!"

Unar and Ggil rushed to him and sat him up. He was limp, his head lolling like a child's toy.

"Did thou succeed? Did thou contact them? Are they coming? Where—"

Asan blinked and frowned in an effort to be coherent. "Skulmaar," he mumbled, and fainted.

When he awakened, he found himself in private, sumptuous quarters carpeted with white borlorl fur and hung with tapestries. His bed cushions were soft and filled with fragrant herbs that let out pleasant smells each time he moved. He sat up slowly. His head was pounding, but he exerted control over that and eased the discomfort.

He was also ravenously hungry.

He reached for the mallet and tossed it at the gong. A Henan servant appeared at once.

"Food," he said. His mouth was so dry it was difficult to speak.

The servant bowed and disappeared.

Asan scowled and rubbed his face. He shouldn't be sleeping when time was so short. And where—

"Asan," said Zaula, coming in. Dressed in a soft lavender robe and gold-broidered slippers, she looked tired and worried. "Please don't get up. Rest some more."

"Rest," he said in disgust. "Why should I? I was too weak to do it, Zaula. I almost got to them, almost reached them, but I couldn't do it."

She pressed her hand to his forehead. "You have done so much already. You cannot do everything."

"But that is what a Tlar leiil is for."

"I know, beloved." She sighed. "Still, what is done is done. The jen cohorts have left."

"What?"

"It is too late." She pressed down on his shoulders when he would have sprung to his feet. "Hours ago. Noble Rroge stirred them up to go and surrender to the terms of the *n'kai*. Noble Unar made them wait for a long while, but when the Merdarai did not come, even he could not hold them."

Asan frowned, disappointment sinking through him. He had lost. He could never regain the people's trust now, not after his failure. It was time to skip out, to blast off Ruantl and not come back. The thought left bitterness in his mouth.

Zaula pulled away and crossed the room to get his clothes. She seemed subdued, but he could not blame her.

"Where is Udge?" he asked.

"He has gone to the ship."

Asan climbed to his feet in alarm. "He's left?"

"He spoke of it." Zaula turned to look at him. "Was it your wish to go with him?"

"We can't stay here, not now. I'm finished. And so is Ruantl. I won't live under GSI law. Never again."

A soft cough warned him of the servant's return. Asan turned, gesturing, and the servant set a metal tray containing a small ewer, cup, and covered bowl upon a table.

"At last. I'm starving."

Asan plucked off the cover, releasing a cloud of warm aroma. Bban stew, he supposed, detecting the fiery spices. He dug his spoon into it.

He had gulped down five mouthfuls when Zaula began to cry. Asan stopped eating.

"Zaula? What is it? I thought you'd be happy to leave. You never wanted to come back anyway."

Sobbing, she turned her back to him and gestured with her palm down. "No, it isn't that. Please ignore me. I'm being foolish."

Frowning in concern, he put down his spoon. He went to her, encircling her with his rings. But she was closed to him, her grief tight and sharp within her.

"Zaula." He touched her shoulder, gathering her against him. "Please, what is it?"

"Oh, Asan. Cirthe is dead."

She began to sob harder. Asan rested his hand upon her head, stroking her soft hair in an effort to comfort her.

"I am sorry."

Zaula raised a tearstained face. "I know she didn't love me. I never even shared rings with her. It was wrong to bring her into the world. She has been in torment since conception. And, oh, Asan, I tried to stay away. I tried to tell myself that although she was born of me she wasn't my child. But I had to see her. She—she was so small, so frail. There hasn't been enough food, and she . . .''

"Hush now," he said, tightening his hold around her. Guilt rose in him as he glanced at his tray of food. Even that meager amount made him feel as though he had abused privilege. Rations must be desperately tight here. And it was his fault, ultimately, for he had shut down Anthi and the means to grow most of the cultivated food.

"I'm sorry, Zaula. Very sorry."

The words seemed inadequate against her grief. He tried to find another way of apology. He wanted so much for her to be happy.

"When we are free, Zaula, we shall make another child. Yours and mine. It will have a happy birth, and its rings will be whole. I promise it."

Slowly she looked up at him. Her eyes—drenched and lovely and so sad they tore his heart—gazed deeply into his as though seeking a better assurance even than his word.

"Come." He forced her to sit down at the small table. "Eat the rest of this."

She shuddered. "I can't."

"You must. When have you last eaten? You must keep up your strength. Please, Zaula. I wish for you to have it. Starving yourself will not bring Cirthe back."

"I know." Bowing her head, she dipped the spoon into the stew, but did not eat.

He sighed and reached for the clothes which she had pulled from a chest. Dressing quickly, he buckled on his weapons.

"You aren't going to Udge, are you? You're going to stay."

The despair in her voice made him turn. He tried to lie, but the words stuck in his throat. "Zaula—"

"We could go anywhere and yet how could you live so far away from your people?" she said softly. "Whether they serve you or not, you remain their leiil."

"I must try one last time to help them," he said helplessly. "All my life I've scratched and kicked and struggled to climb out. I've made my own luck and laughed at failure. Everything I've learned tells me to run now while I have the chance. But I can't.'' He shook his head. ''I just can't. I know so clearly what will become of them if I go.''

''They are thy children,'' said Zaula. She looked at Asan as though she thought this would be the last time she ever saw him. ''Go to them. The gods' hands are upon thee, and thou cannot turn aside.''

He touched her face gently, aching at her bravery, and told himself he was a fool. His throat closed up, cutting off the words he should have said.

He strode out quickly and winced as he heard her weeping behind him.

The caverns were deserted except for huddles of Bban females and wailing children. It was the cry of hunger, and guilt stabbed him again. Glancing away, Asan quickened his pace.

Outside, only his shuttle remained on the transport pad. It was a dark, stormy day with ominous clouds streaking the amethyst sky. He glanced up, wind buffeting his mask, and hastened over to the shuttle.

''Udge?''

''You took your time, Tobei.'' Udge poked out his head, his face hidden behind the polarized plate. ''This baby's ready to lift off anytime you are. And I'd recommend cuttin' out before any of your ugly friends come back. What were you tryin' to pull, anyway?''

Asan gestured impatiently. ''It didn't work. Udge, I can't go. I belong here now.''

''You don't belong on a GSI world,'' said Udge angrily. ''I saved you once, but I won't do it again. Be a fool if you want.''

He pulled himself back into the shuttle, but Asan reached through the hatch and grabbed his arm.

''Udge, I need your help to get to Kichee.''

''The hell you do. I ain't gettin' into this one. No.''

''Just fly me in. Then you can go.''

Udge jerked free. ''And what about the little dandy? You leavin' her here? What happens to her when you don't come back?''

''I'm coming back.''

''Oh, sure! If the Institute don't kill you, your ugly buddies will. They were madder than hell when they went out of here.''

''Udge, I—'' Asan frowned, unable to find the words. ''I know it's crazy.''

"Damned sure is. The Tobei I knew had better sense."

"The Tobei you knew doesn't exist anymore! I've changed. I—I can't just go off like a coward."

"Survival, boy! Survival!"

Asan's smile inside his mask was twisted. He knew Udge was giving him good advice. And he knew that if he took it he would never have peace again inside himself.

"Some things are worth more than mere survival."

"Aw, hell. That sounds like principle or somethin'. Even kings fall off their thrones, Tobei."

Asan looked at him. "Just drop me there."

Udge said nothing, just grunted and vanished inside the shuttle. Asan followed him and closed the hatch. He stood in the hatch area, bracing himself with planted feet as the shuttle took off and circled.

"East," said Asan. "Stay low."

They cleared the lower peaks of the Tchsco range and headed out across the Ddreui plains. Silvery grass rippled there beneath the wind. A chaka herd stamped as the shuttle flew over. Asan watched grimly, comparing this bleak land to the fertile one of his deeper memories.

For an hour they flew straight and low, detouring once to avoid being sighted by an Institute ground patrol moving along at five kilometers per second in squat, armored vehicles with treads that crushed patterns into the black sand.

"I'm pickin' up all kinds of activity on the scanner," said Udge. "Ahead of us is a fleet of ships comin' in from the east. They have to be registerin' me. So where do you want to be dropped off?"

Asan straightened. That was it, then. Udge wasn't going to reconsider. Asan would go in alone and die for principle. It sounded like a stupid old vid-cast plot. He used to watch those sometimes in bars and laugh. Now he wasn't laughing. But he was still going in.

He looked out the port. The ground below was rougher, stony, and breaking into low gullies. He secured his mask into place and drew a deep breath.

"Here," he said. "Do a low hover. As soon as you see me on the ground, bank off."

"It's your funeral."

"Udge . . . good-bye."

"Hell. Just go!"

As the shuttle steadied, Asan gathered himself and seizerted to the ground. He caught himself with bent knees to cushion the impact and rolled twice before coming upright. Breathless, he lifted a hand at the shuttle.

With a roar of its engines, it headed west.

Asan stood there a moment, surveying his surroundings. Nothing but thornbushes grew along the rocky sides of the gullies. The sun was out here in a cloudless sky, and it glared off the white shale. He squinted and drew his strifer. Taking his bearing, he seizerted again.

The Institute camp at Kichee was small, containing just a handful of soldiers, three perma-flex huts for the officers, and an armored vehicle parked in a flat-bottomed gully out of the way. The huts were rowed off to the south of the well. Grass, looking lush and peculiar against the barren backdrop of the terrain, grew in a carpet around the well. Water seeped from the stones that had been piled around the well's mouth centuries ago. A wind-twisted tree perhaps only twice Asan's height stood sentry over it with nhulks fluttering on the branches like spectators of what was to come.

Asan had come in on the guidance of Aural's mental pattern. When he appeared in a flash of blue fire in her hut, she was reclining upon a bunk, looking distinctly bored. A human with commander stripes on his gear suit sat on a chair. He jumped to his feet with an oath at Asan's appearance and reached for his communicator.

"Don't," said Asan, pointing the strifer at him.

The commander froze.

Aural rose from the bunk. She did not have her mask on, indicating the hut was shielded. A mocking smile curled her lips.

"Our informant told us you had returned. Welcome. Do you bring surrender terms or—"

"Commander," said Asan, ignoring her completely, "your forces are preparing an attack upon the jen cohorts coming here. Is that necessary? Are you so unwilling to trust Tlar honor?"

The commander blinked at being addressed fluently in Standard. He was a well-built man with a square jaw and an unyielding look in his eyes.

"Honor has nothing to do with warfare," he replied. "My orders are to subdue this population. As I see it, that means wiping out the military."

"You have lured my people here under false pretenses."

"They should know that. If they don't, then it's really easier for them to die now and quickly than to be hunted down." The commander met his gaze coldly. "We are not interested in maintaining this culture."

"So you see, Asan," said Aural. "Your pleas are useless with Commander Notini."

"And you're a fool," Asan said sharply, bringing color to her cheeks. "You've brought *n'kai* to Tlartantla, given it to them. Have you no shame?"

"If this is all that is left of the world we walked upon, then it is not worth saving! I have my own survival to think of. And you are a fool to live in the past."

"Is that all that remains between us, Aural? Harsh words and hatred at the end? What happened to all the years we shared together—"

"Dust," she said angrily. "Dust upon the wind. No feelings remain. No respect is left. The bond that held us was severed when you nearly died. I almost walked to the land of death with you, but I managed to break free. And now when Notini kills you, I shall rejoice."

A noise at the entrance to the hut made Asan whirl, but he was too late. Guards in gear suits stood there with issue bolt rifles aimed at him. Asan grimaced to himself and slowly lowered his strifer. Now it really was over.

Notini jerked the strifer from Asan's hand and shoved him toward the guards, who grabbed him and put restraints on his wrists. They were the kind made of razor wire—a thin, almost invisible filament that would slice off his hands at the slightest attempt to pull free.

Fear choked Asan's throat. For a moment all he could think of was to run. But he forced his mind to clear, refusing to pay heed to the Blaise memories of other restraints and a brutal, though brief, incarceration in a detention center. The guards hustled him outside. The commander and Aural followed.

"I hear the ships," she said. Her mask gleamed in the sunlight as she turned her head to the east.

Asan could hear the distant roar also. It was the fleet Udge had picked up on his scanner. Soldiers ran across the small camp to assume positions. On the ridge directly ahead, a deton-bomb artillery gun was uncovered and manned. Asan watched bleakly. So there was to be destruction from the ground as well as from the air. He realized they were going to let him watch and then kill him. And from the pit of his stomach rose a black cloud of hate.

"You could escape," said Aural. "You could probably kill me and most of these men before they realized you were using mental weapons. Why don't you try? Anger is in your rings."

"What is your future?" he asked.

She lifted a fingertip. "Oh, I am secure. I shall give them Anthi when this day is finished. They are most interested in our computer technology." She laughed. "You *are* angry. All this time you thought you were the only one who could control the computer. But you were wrong. I brought her online."

It was not worth arguing about. He glanced away.

"You delude yourself, Aural."

"And didn't you?" she said sharply. She grabbed him by one arm and turned him around, making the restraint nick his wrist. "I heard of your spectacular failure. Bringing the Merdarai back. What nonsense! Your brain has been addled by age. Even the true Asan would not have tried anything so ridiculous."

He made no reply. The ships were in sight now, although it was hard to see them against the sun. They were small craft, individual fighters. The air was filled with the thunder of their engines, and something about that sound nagged at him.

"Coming in low, commander," said an aide, running up. "Not on planned course heading. Not responding to our communications."

"What?" Notini swung around with an oath. "Are they mad? I gave Cooke his orders personally. It's not like him to screw up."

"They should have already banked north, sir. It's almost like they're homing in on us."

"Damn! Get on the com. I want a direct link with Cooke. Now!"

And the ships were still coming, an immense, impossible number, far too many for the maneuver planned today, far too many for the size of the force stationed here. Asan stared upward until his neck ached, and recognition suddenly dawned on him.

"Skulmaar!"

The shout boomed out in full tone, loud enough to rattle the sides of the hut behind him, loud enough to almost hold its own against the roar of the ships. The first formation flew over, and their shadow crossed the camp.

"Those aren't our ships," said Notini. "What the hell . . . Jackson! Hardy! Get that deton-bomb swung around! Now!"

It was too late. The second formation broke off and dived in, coming so low and so fast the humans never had a chance. The camp broke into chaos as rapid bursts flared from the nose cones of the ships. The air was filled with screams and the steady *thacka-thacka-thacka* of the weapons.

Notini turned on Aural, who stood there frozen, her gaze locked on the ships.

"You damned bitch, you set us up!"

She flinched, holding out her hands. "No! I swear—"

Notini shot her just before a fighter ship dived at him and cut him down. Asan snapped out his rings and seizerted just in time to escape the same fate.

During that brief moment of displacement, the scene seemed frozen upon his vision. Again and again he saw Aûral turn, her arms lifting in supplication before the strifer cut through her. She had spoken the truth; their bond no longer held them. But it was as though her rings sliced through his as she died, and there was grief deep within him for the woman who had walked at his side long, long ago.

He materialized on a ridge and dropped low out of sight, hugging the ground for what scant cover he could find. His wrists were bleeding from the restraints, and absently he closed the wounds and buffered his wrists with his rings to prevent more serious cuts.

Inside, his heart leapt with pride and disbelief. The Merdarai had come! He had reached them after all.

And, oh, how they came. The skies were filled with their number. He had forgotten how many there were, a full army from the days when Tlartantla's population swarmed over the entire planet. They came with ships; they came with equipment and munitions; they came with supply tugs in their wake; they came like angry hornets for battle, and the battle was already over. The humans lay sprawled across the little oasis of Kichee, such a small threat after all.

And even as he crouched there and grinned like a fool inside his mask, he began to wonder what he would do with them all once the GSI had been routed from Altian and from Ruantl space. Could he turn a crack fighting force into miners? Or maybe farmers? How would they all be fed?

The ground to the south was flatter where the gullies ran out. The ships began to land, formation by formation until they seemed to go to the horizon. He tried counting them, but couldn't. More than a thousand. More than two thousand.

The sand was shredding his clothes. Slowly Asan climbed to his feet. He stood on the ridge crest and stared at what he had done, beginning, now that the first flush of surprise and pride were past, to be a little awed.

A noise behind him made him glance over his shoulder. He saw the Tlar'jen and the Bban hordes coming, creeping in wonder and fear. Asan pulled himself erect at once. And he heard the voices: "Asan! It is Asan. He brought the warriors from the shadow land. He spoke the truth."

And then, to his surprise, the jen cohorts did not advance past him to meet the Merdarai now emerging from their fighters. Instead, they began to kneel one by one in a rippling, black-cloaked sea. Javelins fell to the sand and masked faces bowed.

"N'a en wulrad. N'a en wulrad."

The chant of worship went on and on, embarrassing him as he stood there silhouetted against the sky with his bronze cloak flying in the wind and his hands still bound.

Then from the other side, he heard the chant echoed from voices with a different accent, the old true inflections of the past.

"Asan! Asan!"

The Merdarai in battle shielding and flight masks knelt before him as well. And the sun dappled the world that was still, or perhaps for the first time, his.